MW01116408

Echoes
and
Ashes

A Paranormal Mystery

Alexandra Frund Clinton

Copyright © 2020 All rights reserved. Neither this book nor any parts within it may be sold or reproduced in any form without permission.

Written by Alexandra Frund Clinton

ISBN: 978-1-7343988-8-5
Second Edition

DEDICATION

To my wonderful, loving husband, Sean, who consistently put up with my nonsense and encouraged me to finally finish what I started.

To my parents, Zane and Terri, who have supported my creative endeavors all my life, even while I was systematically ruining their house with my endless projects.

I love you all.

DEDICATION

TABLE OF CONTENTS

PROLOGUE

"So... I'm sorry, Eli, but that's it. Your network access has been terminated, and you have until the end of the day to clean out your desk before security escorts you from the premises. I... wish there was something I could do."

While Eli Gehring processed his boss's words, he didn't look at him. Instead, his eyes lingered a few feet to the left of his boss's head. An older gentleman in an outdated beige suit stood by idly staring out the window with one hand in his pocket and a cigar in the other. A foul-smelling smoke filled the room, but Eli's boss didn't notice, even as the smoke hung in the air like a cloud over their heads.

Seeing that Eli wasn't paying attention to him, his boss sighed and awkwardly glanced over his shoulder, trying to follow Eli's gaze, before looking back to Eli in confusion.

"It's not just you. It's everyone. You have to have heard the rumors. It's all going overseas—the whole department. I guess the bigwigs decided they wanted to cash in on the cheap labor offered in India."

Eli hated this room—the department manager's office. Of course, most people didn't look forward to getting called in for a closed-door conversation with their boss. His hatred was different, however. He hated the fact that the office was *old*. The solid wood

1

desk had been moved into the large space--a corner office with a view of downtown--some fifty years ago and had never moved more than a few feet since its placement. Nicotine-covered paintings of Wall Street depictions hadn't moved in nearly as long and had the sofas and cushioned chairs in the back alcove of the office not been so stained over time, the originals would likely *also* still be in their places. Most people wouldn't care about, much less even notice, such trivial details.

But Eli wasn't like most people. He thought of those things *constantly*.

He clenched his jaw and watched as the man behind his boss put the cigar in his mouth and put his hands on either side of the window sill. The man stood up slowly, climbing on top of the stone ledge one tentative step at a time until his entire body blocked the window. Two heartbeats later he stepped out and dropped towards the ground, fifteen stories below them.

His boss didn't flinch.

But of course, his boss couldn't see the man. Only Eli could. Eli had watched the same scene on his very first day with the company, on his very first visit to the department manager's office. It hadn't taken Eli more than two days to learn that the man was Arthur McElroy, the founder of the company. His picture still hung to the left of the grand staircase in the main lobby. He committed suicide in 1975.

Eli squeezed his eyes shut and willed his quickly beating heart to calm. Seeing such images never got easier, no matter how many years passed by. Sure, they were infrequent now, what with his anti-anxiety medication doing *something* to suppress whatever it was that triggered his *ability* to witness the horrible scenes. If he understood his benefits, however, that medication was about to become a whole lot harder to get his hands on. When he opened his eyes, blinking rapidly to try to focus on his boss once more, he found the man staring at him with a concerned frown.

"Are you going to be okay?"

Eli fought the urge to roll his eyes as he shrugged his shoulders. *Probably not,* Eli thought.

"As well as I can be, I guess," he replied and sat forward, hands clenching the worn wood of the office chair. "So, can I go?"

His boss's frown deepened but he nodded. He slid a folder towards Eli. Based on the logo it was from the firm leading the company's consolidation.

"Take this. It will explain the benefits you'll receive and how long they continue. If you have any questions you can call the number on the business card inside and they'll walk you through everything. Good luck."

Eli couldn't say he was surprised. He had heard the talk. No one had received bonuses in his department in two years, except for his supervisor. That was the first red flag for the IT department. Once his supervisor was made part of the back-office support team, well... the writing was on the wall, so to speak. A third-party company came in and wasted no time cutting people. For a while, Eli thought himself one of the lucky ones—one of the few they decided to keep on board due to his strong work ethic and need to support his family. But no, that wasn't the case.

They simply gave him until after the winter holidays. Then he and and his few remaining coworkers were all terminated. All he had, after almost a decade of dedication to the company, was the envelope of unemployment benefits and an outdated, unimpressive resume.

Eli took the folder and stood, exiting the office with a slam of the door.

Despite the loud noise, no one else on the floor glanced at him--not that there were many left to be bothered by him anyhow. They continued their work, typing away in their cubicles, oblivious to the surge of anxiety he—and likely the two other men sitting in chairs outside the office, tapping their heels nervously as they waited for their turn—felt. Eli doubted he was the first one to slam the door that day, and he probably wouldn't be the last.

CHAPTER 1

It took Eli a few moments to become aware of the voices around him—soft-spoken words and loving chuckles. At first, he thought it was part of his dream. A heartbeat later, however, Eli realized his wife hadn't spoken to him that kindly in months, not even in his dreams. He slowly started to stir and blinked his eyes open until he was able to mostly focus on the ceiling fan above him. Once he was sure he was fully awake, the fan was still a bit blurry—but that was likely due to the alcohol still in his system.

"Go upstairs and change honey," Eli heard his wife say, words gentle as ever, to their daughter.

The eight-year-old said "'kay," and went running up the stairs, the sound of her footsteps fading until her bedroom door shut them out entirely.

Eli sat upright on the faded couch, knocking over an empty glass with his foot and sending it rolling across the hardwood floor. He hissed as he stubbed his toe on the edge of the cluttered coffee table beside him. What time was it? Spotting the clock, the red, blinking digital display all but mocking him, he groaned. Where had the day gone? It couldn't have actually been four-thirty already, could it?

With their daughter was safely upstairs, Sophia came storming into the living room, snatching up the wayward glass as her lips curled in a snarl.

"Really?" she hissed at him, keeping her voice low so their daughter wouldn't hear another fight. "You're home all day and couldn't even manage to pick her up from school? We're lucky Lisa picked up Shelly today! She waited with Sarah until I could get there."

"I, uh, I just..."

The room was spinning. The bottle of cheap vodka was nearly empty. Had he truly drunk it all? He remembered getting up, dropping off a few job applications, and...

And the woman. That's right, it was the woman who kick-started his binge.

He'd been walking down Fifth Avenue to catch a bus when he heard a woman screaming in an alley, just as he passed. He had taken a few steps back to look down the alley, and that was when he saw her. Her clothes were torn and bloody, her arm outstretched towards him, begging him for help. He looked around but no one else seemed to notice her. Not a single person so much as glanced in her direction.

Eli had briefly thought about calling out to the group waiting at the bus stop but chose not to—which was ultimately for the better. Upon closer inspection, the woman looked... off. Her features were blurred, and he couldn't quite make eye contact with her. She continued to scream and scream, and her screams reverberated through his body, rooting him in place. He watched, helpless, as she was pulled away, down the alleyway by nothing at all. Despite her being pulled out of sight behind a dumpster, he could still hear her cries. It was then he realized that the people around him were not deliberately avoiding the woman. In fact, he was the only one who saw her. The only one who heard her agony.

Those sorts of screams never really went away, not ever. They were the cries of someone who knew they were going to die; someone putting every ounce of energy into getting someone's attention—every shred of hope they had that they would be saved.

Over and over again, he heard the woman begging him for help. He heard her pleas echoing in his mind. He heard them on the bus, he heard them down his street and into his apartment. Her screams haunted him, even once they had long since stopped ringing through the air. The truth was that the woman had died, likely years ago, and there had been some other passerby who had stopped, made eye contact with her, and did nothing. Eli had just happened to be re-enacting the moment.

That didn't make it any better, though.

He had intended to go home and nap until he had to pick his daughter up, but one quick drink had turned into three. Three turned into half the bottle. The alcohol diluted the traumatic scene as it diluted his bloodstream. That's what it took to help him forget the haunting sounds and images that refused to leave him even once his eyes were closed. It was the only thing that worked, albeit barely, without his medication.

Sophia snapped her fingers in front of his face, pulling him back to the present as she shook her head at him.

"I can't imagine any possible good excuse from you," she sighed, her disappointment and displeasure clear. "What the hell happened to you? Huh? I know you've never been the cheery type, and that's fine, but now... Eli, you didn't even like your job! I just don't understand why this is hitting you so hard. Just go do something that isn't sitting around the damn house all day!" She threw her hands up, before letting them fall and slap against her well-worn pencil-skirted thigh. "I'm taking Sarah to dance since you obviously aren't going to do it."

As Eli rubbed his eyes, trying to force the world around him to stop spinning, all he could think was that this was how it had to be. Sophia would never understand what he faced—she had never known him while he was off his anti-anxiety medication, which he found suppressed the Echoes he occasionally witnessed. That was what he called them—Echoes. Echoes of a traumatic end to someone's life. Despite them, his medication he was able to live a fairly normal, hallucination-free life, though some brands weren't as good as others. He'd vaguely mentioned his time under observation as a young teenager, but he never told her the truth. And if he did now, there was no way she'd believe him. It would only scare her, and that could lead to problems with Sarah as well.

The very last thing he wanted was for Sophia—or anyone for that matter—to think he was some sort of danger to his daughter. He loved her more than anything, even if he didn't seem to be an affectionate father.

Eli heard Sophia's heels click, snapping him from his thoughts again, on the master bathroom floor above him before they were kicked off into the closet and swapped out for her favorite flats.

He flopped back down on the couch, throwing an arm over his face to both block out the light and hide the shame rushing to his face. Eli felt terrible for not getting up in time to pick up Sarah from school. He felt worse for being in no condition to take Sarah to her dance class a few subway stops away. Shouldn't that have been the least he did to help out around the house? To provide something— anything—to their strained marriage?

Sophia had been working as much as she possibly could since Eli had lost his job. She had always worked part-time to supplement their income but primarily handled taking care of Sarah and her activities. It had never been much of a problem since Eli had worked odd hours, often getting called in to fix server errors or other technical problems outside of the business day.

But now Sophia's employers were making it a point to keep her under the full-time threshold. They weren't looking to take on another full-time underwriter, despite working her nearly thirty-six hours a week. They needed the money, but what they needed more were the benefits. They were still living on the care provided by Eli's former employer for the time being, but that would be running out before they were ready.

If only she could have been bumped up... Almost everything would have been better. He could have gotten the medication he needed to go a day without seeing something traumatic. Eli had lost access to the heavy-duty, name-brand prescription when he lost his top-tier healthcare when he was laid off, and if he could just take those pills again... He'd have been able to sit through a job interview without thinking about the body he had seen squirting blood on the front stoop of the building.

The generic brands didn't cut it anymore. They'd barely helped every time he tried to switch to them, hoping they would work and save him the non-coverage cost a month. Now they might as well have been sugar pills. He needed to get the good stuff.

Eli mentally sighed to himself. He sounded like an addict.

Things needed to get better. *He* needed to get better.

He heard Sarah upstairs, calling out to her mother from down the hallway. She was telling Sophia that they needed to hurry, or they would be late. If she missed warm-ups, she would have to do her warm-ups outside the classroom and join the group after their first break, and she didn't want to be left out of the group.

Eli must have dozed off at some point because he jolted awake again when the front door slammed shut. If Sophia or Sarah had said anything to him, he hadn't heard it. With a groan, he rolled off the couch, careful of the coffee table this time, and shuffled into the kitchen. He flipped on the overhead light as he entered. It was dark—he had lost the entire evening. The bread and peanut butter were left sitting out, so he assumed Sophia had quickly made sandwiches to eat on their way to dance class. He was about to reluctantly make himself one as well, since he hadn't eaten and had no intention of cooking for himself when he noticed there was one already sitting on the table.

There was a torn piece of paper sitting next to it with scribbles reading something like: 'For Dad feel better love Sarah.'

His heart clenched and he blinked rapidly, fighting back the sudden moisture that gathered. He hadn't thought he could possibly feel shittier, but apparently, he had further to sink after all. Eli glanced up at the clock to realize it already read six-thirteen.

Sarah would definitely be late to dance.

"I'm right outside—no, seriously, I'm walking through the gate now. I'll be there in five minutes."

Eli shoved his phone into his pocket and adjusted his tie as he hurried into the school building. It was parent-teacher night and Sophia had vowed to kick him out of the house if he missed it. And he would have missed the meeting... if his phone interview had gone better. At least Sophia would have forgiven him if that had been the case. He had no excuse, no good excuse, for missing it now.

As he entered the old building, he had to stop and read over the signs pointing down different hallways. He hadn't been in the building since they enrolled Sarah the prior year. His work schedule had often kept him busy when it came to Sarah's school activities. He had never made it to one school play, one open house, or even a single parent-teacher conference.

Eli had been wary about taking on the cost of the tuition, but he agreed with Sophia that it was better than the public school option in the area. Their combined income was enough that the academy didn't stretch them too thin, as long as they didn't want to take a vacation. Of course, now they were going to have to dip into their savings to make the next semester's payment if he didn't find a new job.

The school was an old, stone structure. It was well maintained, but still rather antiquated with many of the original fixtures still littering the hallways. He supposed he preferred the tuition costs went towards paying good teachers rather than modernizing the building if the students were comfortable despite the outdated amenities. Unfortunately, however, walking down the corridors that had changed so little over the years meant he could clearly see the history practically etched into the stone walls.

Inhaling deeply, Eli squared his shoulders and clenched his fists until his knuckles turned white. He had to be prepared to remain calm if something unwanted made an appearance.

The hallways were nearly empty, with only a few parents lingering around before or after their own meetings. The door to Sarah's classroom came into view and he frowned, seeing it was already shut. Glancing down at his watch, Eli muttered a curse. He was two minutes behind schedule. The damn room had been harder to find than the thought. Rushing down the hall he practically skid to a halt in front of the classroom... Taking another deep breath and exhaling, he quietly opened the door and stepped inside.

The two women stopped speaking and turned to look at him. They were sitting in the back of the room where the teacher's desk was diagonally opposite the windows and a set of bookshelves. The woman, who looked as though she may have been about ten years older than either Eli or Sophia, stood and beckoned him over. Eli approached and extended his hand.

"Mr. Gehring, I presume?"

He nodded, grasping her hand in a firm shake. "Yes. Please call me Eli. Mrs. Reid?"

"I am. Please take a seat." She swept her hand over the other chair and pulled up in front of her desk. Eli sat and gave a nod to Sophia, who, thankfully, didn't seem too upset with him for being a bit late.

"We'll start by going over Sarah's performance and grades, and then we will get into some other matters I would like to address," Mrs. Reid said, adjusting her navy blazer.

Eli did his best to sit quietly and listen to the woman, nodding every so often. As usual, Sophia handled most of the conversation: asking for details on missing assignments and upcoming field trips, a failed science project and beginner orchestra sign-ups. He didn't see the point in the meeting. Sarah usually did well in school, save for hiccups when things became particularly tense at home, and she had never had any problems with her classmates as far as he knew. Sure, the school scheduled these check-ins each semester, but were they necessary? Then again, what else did he have to do with his time? He had already scoured every online job site he could find, so he would have just sat at home watching reruns anyhow.

He inwardly sighed and tried not to look at his watch. Their backs were facing the clock, so he couldn't tell how much longer the appointment would go.

Just as he was starting to become restless, he caught a whiff of something in the air. Eli sat up straighter a bit and sniffed around, drawing the occasional look from the two ladies sitting with him. Finally, he leaned forward in alarm, sniffing again.

Smoke, he was smelling smoke.

Oh God, was this real? Or was this another Echo? Could he really afford to ignore it if they were in danger?

Eli stopped his shifting and looked between his wife and Mrs. Reid's faces, only to see them staring back at him in confusion. He sniffed again and noticed the smell of smoke was getting stronger. Eli twisted in his chair and looked around, trying to find the source of the smoke. He saw nothing.

"You... you don't smell that?" He asked slowly, trying to keep his voice calm and even as if there wasn't anything at all to worry about.

"Smell what?" Sophia asked, an edge to her tone as she looked around as well. When he didn't answer, she pressed her lips into a thin line, her head tilting as her eyes darkened. "Eli, please don't do this now..."

Mrs. Reid was looking at him with a raised brow. Eli couldn't help but feel that he was being rather judged.

With a shake of his head, he sat right once more and gave a quick, forced half smile. "Sorry, it's nothing. Go on."

"As I was saying, some of Sarah's behavior is starting to become concerning..."

Eli knew he should be listening to whatever it was the teacher was saying, but he simply found it hard to take her seriously. Sarah hadn't ever had any incidents at school and she seemed happy enough, which was all that mattered to him. Mrs. Reid went on to mention something about playing alone and questionable drawings, but Eli didn't take anything away beyond the fact that Sarah liked to do her own thing. She had always been that way, after all, and it was nothing new. This teacher should've known that as well with as much as they were paying the academy...

Eli continued to listen with one ear while he tried very hard, and failed equally hard, to ignore the smell of smoke overwhelming his senses.

As their meeting came to an end, Eli couldn't flee the room fast enough. He shook Mrs. Reid's hand once more, bidding her a good evening, and promptly turned on his heel to head for the door. There was noise in the hallway as other parents started to exit the surrounding classrooms. The time slots must have ended all at once. Eli quickly opened the door and turned into the hallway. He needed to get outside—he needed to get fresh air--he needed--

The shriek of terror and slew of cursing escaped his mouth before he had a chance to really think about his actions or the other parents around him. That was secondary as he found the source of the phantom smoke.

In front of Eli, lying right in front of Mrs. Reid's classroom, lay a blackened human form with sections of skin sloughing onto the floor, leaving bloody patches of red in its wake. The unfortunate creature was still breathing, choking, gasping for air that didn't seem to be there.

The smell of smoke was too much. Eli gasped for air, mimicking the unfortunate creature in front of him. His legs failed him, locking up as he tried to back away, and he nearly collapsed atop the thing. He barely pushed away from it in time as it put a hand out towards him—towards the window behind him--another patch of blackened skin flaking to the ground.

The arm dropped as the figure let out one final, pained breath. And then, it was gone. As if it had never been there to begin with.

But Eli kept crawling back from the spot it had been, eyes wide with fear. When he hit the base of the window, he grabbed the ledge and pulled himself upright, holding himself up with one arm and working to loosen his tie with the other, though he doubted it would help. He barely noticed all of the eyes staring at him from down the hallway but based on her wide eyes and slack-jawed expression, Sophia sure did.

By the time the scene disappeared, and Eli had caught his breath, the hallway had emptied. Parents moved on from the spectacle with a murmur of hushed words, leaving only a few teachers—including Mrs. Reid—to stare at him. Eli coughed a few times to clear his throat of the lingering taste of smoke and turned to face Sophia.

She was mortified.

It was a mix of anger, fear, and embarrassment on her face. It was as if, now that she saw he was alright, she wasn't sure if she wanted to punch him or go hide in a corner. She was shaking, hands tightened into fists at her sides.

Without a word, she marched down the hallway, leaving him behind.

CHAPTER 2

The words had all been said before. Eli stood, head hanging as he leaned on the kitchen table, and Sophia unleashed on him. She was in tears this time. She wasn't one to get emotional. Sophia had always been the picture of strength. She was the one holding their family together when things got tough. It shouldn't have always been on her to articulate their problems and find solutions to fix them, Eli knew that. A decade together had caused them to fall into a routine, caused him to become too comfortable. He had taken her and her unwavering strength for granted and it seemed he had finally pushed her past her breaking point. Screaming in terror at nothing at all in the school's hallway while their daughter's education was on the line was enough for her to want to call it quits. She couldn't do it anymore. Eli needed help, and if he wasn't going to get it, then he needed to leave until he would.

She even went so far as to suggest a divorce if he wasn't willing to help himself. She wasn't going to deal with him drinking all day and talking to things that weren't there—she wasn't going to raise Sarah around such disconcerting behavior.

Eli knew he should fight. He should fight for his marriage and for his daughter, but he just... couldn't.

He was so tired.

Not only was he exhausted from trying to suppress the gruesome things he had to see and hear, he was tired of holding it all in and keeping it to himself. If there was a chance that Sophia would believe him, that she would understand and accept him, and see why it wasn't as easy as 'just getting help'... but she wouldn't. He knew she wouldn't. She was far too practical for such things.

Then Sophia stopped. Maybe she sensed he was willing to walk away for a little while to deal with things on his own—or at least deal with them away from her. Or maybe she thought he wasn't even paying attention, thought his mind was elsewhere. She snapped her mouth shut, her teeth audibly clicking, and marched to the closet where she pulled down his old duffle bag.

"I need you to go," she whispered, looking into his eyes and wiping her tears away. He noticed that they stopped. She had made up her mind. Her well-deserved outburst was over and her ever-rational mind returned to her.

"I'll say goodbye to Sarah and—"

"No," Sophia snapped, thrusting her arm out to stop him in his tracks. "No, don't even go near her room. She'll start crying again and then you'll end up staying. I'll talk to her once you're gone. I'll take care of her—like I always do."

Eli very nearly chose to fight back, to demand to see his daughter. With one deep exhale, he let the thought leave him. It was better this way, or at least, better for him. At the moment, he couldn't help but feel a bit selfish. He had been dealing with so much for so long. It was time to take a break. Either he could get his mind together and return to his wife and child, or he couldn't.

If it came down to it and he couldn't find a way to live with his curse... well, Eli doubted he would last long on his own. At least he wouldn't be a burden on his family.

Without another word, Eli picked up the duffle bag from where Sophia had thrown it at his feet.

The only reason Eli continued to patronize the Burke Street Pub was because on the few occasions an unwanted Echo popped up, it was rather tame. Nothing bloody or brutal, nothing terrifying or traumatic. There was only one spirit who, as far as Eli could figure, had a heart attack in his booth and simply lay with his head on the tabletop until he disappeared.

Eli could handle that.

That night, there was nothing to worry about, not as far as his Echoes were concerned. The booth was occupied by a group of young men who didn't seem at all bothered by anything otherworldly. Eli hummed curiously and made a beeline for the bar, hopping up into a slightly uneven stool near the back door. It was surprisingly comfortable—familiar, even. Eli could hardly call himself a regular, and he hadn't been in almost a decade.

There was a time when he and his buddies would go out on a Friday or Saturday, drinking away their evening while playing pool or darts, but those days had long since passed. He kept in touch with very few of his school friends anymore. Sophia had never liked them, and though she hadn't explicitly told him not to associate with them, he knew better.

Eli didn't recognize the bartender, but the young man seemed pleasant enough. Young. Probably still in college. With his entire life ahead of him. Eli sighed, shoulders slumping.

"Hey man," a voice said from behind Eli as he felt a hand clapping him on his shoulder. Eli glanced up to see Eddy, one of his longtime friends, sitting down next to him. "Sorry to hear about you and Sophia."

Eli nodded and took a swig of his cheap beer. "Can't be helped. Things just haven't been going right lately."

Eddy shrugged and reached down the bar to grab a basket of peanuts, sliding it over to sit in front of him. "Well, the two of you did get married pretty young."

Eli fought back a look of annoyance as he glared at Eddy from the corner of his eye. Most of their friends and family had said the same thing when they chose to marry. Eli had recently dropped out of college and Sophia was struggling to finish. They probably should have waited but, hey, no use dwelling on it now. Their marriage falling apart had absolutely nothing to do with how old they were when they committed.

"Still no luck with the job hunt?" Eddy asked and waved at the bartender, who gave a nod and returned with an open beer bottle. Apparently, Eddy still frequented the establishment enough for the employees to know what he drank.

Eli shook his head with a wince. After all his efforts, he still hadn't received an interview, even after almost eight months.

"So, what are you going to do now?" Eddy asked, leaning to the side to pull over a bowl of peanuts.

"Not sure," Eli responded. "Find a place to stay and find a job to hold me over. Hard to do one without the other, though."

For now, Eli figured he would have to find a cheap motel until he could get on his feet again.

"If you aren't picky, I can probably help you out with both."

Eli looked at Eddy in surprise. Eddy had never been the... helpful sort. He never went out on a limb for anyone else. When Eli had called him to break the news, it had mostly been because Eddy was an entertaining drinking buddy and was still local, not because he hoped for help.

Eddy shrugged and said, "Hey, don't look at me like that. I'm not a terrible friend, you know. I mean, you might think so after I tell you the options I have, but somethin' is better than nothin', right?"

"I'm desperate for anything at the moment."

"You'd have to be," Eddy said with a smirk, "to accept either of these options."

As it turned out, Eddy knew a few people—questionable people. Eli started to wonder what his college friend had been up to in recent years but decided to ignore the red flags going off in the back of his head. Income meant medication, and medication meant saving his marriage. He couldn't afford to be picky at the moment.

"So, yeah, if you don't mind doing some tech repair work and getting paid under the table, this guy can help you out. Just don't ask where the stuff came from, and you're golden," Eddy explained. He slid his beer bottle to the side, and another was in front of him in moments. "This other guy—his son's studying abroad for the semester. They were going to sublet his shitty apartment, but the deal fell through. It's a college kid's apartment, so it's going to be terrible. Studio. Basically a bed, bath, and microwave. But it's fully furnished and on the bus line so it's convenient. It'll probably take most of your pay to keep up with rent, but you know how this city is."

Eli did know how the city was. The rent was god-awful and all the apartments were pretty crappy. The only reason he and Sophia were able to get such a great deal was because the landlord liked them and let them move into a nicer place once it opened up for only a slight rent increase. He would never be able to score a deal like that again.

"So, what do you think?" Eddy asked, gulping down another handful of peanuts. "Do you want to at least check the places out?"

Eli shrugged. "Yeah. I don't have any other options, I guess."

Eddy clapped Eli on the back with a grin. "Alright, good. C'mon, let's have a wild night. You're a free man again! You can crash at my place for a few days."

Eli wasn't sure exactly what he had expected. Honestly, when he thought about it, the storefront made sense. There were gates that could be pulled down during the off hours like many others in the area. The door was unlocked but a bell alerted everyone to his presence and a camera recorded his movement. One guy sat behind a counter, fiddling with an iPad. He glanced up at Eli and gave him a nod before pointing to a door towards the back before returning to his work.

The floor was covered in old, disgusting blue carpet, and the walls had been patched up repeatedly. An off smell of mildew and cleaning solution hung in the air. Eli internally huffed, thinking this was a very poor environment in which to do tech repair.

Eli walked through the back door as directed and found an older gentleman locking up a few filing cabinets. He supposed the man was the manager he was set to meet—though the man hardly appeared managerial. He had on well-worn jeans and an equally well-worn sweatshirt which may have once had a sports team emblem but had faded nearly to nothingness from years of wear.

"Gehring?" the man asked, raising a brow and taking a seat at the desk. The room was small, the desk was an old metal piece that had probably come from a school at some point, and his chair squeaked loudly as he sat in it. Just like the front, Eli felt it didn't suit a business supposedly running tech repair.

Eli nodded, "yes, sir, Eli Gehring. You're... Lou? Sorry, Eddy didn't tell me your last name."

"Mell. Take a seat. Eddy says you're in tech?"

"I started school for programming and coding... dropped out. Mostly did IT work over the past decade. Network and device repair," Eli replied, glancing around the office. He had a bad feeling about the place—and not just because it was clearly a front for illegal activity. He guessed Lou was going to tell him he had the job, but it was going to be jailbreaking and wiping stolen goods. Sure, that was horrible, but it was the feeling in the air. Something lurked in the shop. It simply hadn't shown itself yet.

"Great, great... Eddy says you're willing to do some work under the table. That's what I'm looking for—someone with your skill who will show up and... repair... the devices my guys bring in. You know. Off the books."

Eli sighed and thought, "Called it." Still, if it could provide him some temporary cash flow, it would give him the cushion he needed to find another job and still contribute to Sarah's tuition. And Sophia's rent. And now his rent...

He really needed a job.

"Do you, uh, have a lot of trouble? Is it a risky gig?" Eli asked, shrugging. He heard movement from his left, and he glanced over. There must have been another room behind the door he had initially thought was a closet. Two concurrent thuds rang out from behind the door—but Lou didn't move. Real, or not real? Real, or not real? He couldn't tell.

The older man rubbed his stubbled cheek, and hesitated. "What, you mean with the police? Nah, not really. They don't have much reason to come here. If you're good at what you do, then they won't have any reason to come in either, yeah?"

In Eli's opinion, he felt like Lou's words were a vague threat. Like he was telling Eli, "You better not be the one to draw attention to us or I'll throw you in that back room."

Seeing how the thumping in the back room had now turned into a cacophony of pained groaning, with still no reaction from Lou, Eli decided he did not want to test the unspoken threat.

"Yeah," Eli replied, his hands tightening on the arms of his chair.

"Great, now let's take you out front and see what you can do with an iPhone."

By the end of the night, Eli had a weekly schedule and a promise of a few hundred dollars, depending on how many of the 'pieces' he finished in a week.

CHAPTER 3

"You know where the University is?" Lou shouted from the back room, making Eli jump. He hadn't heard the man come in through the back door.

Eli was over a month into his stint at Lou's shop and it had been... a time. It was easy work, at least compared to the long hours he spent troubleshooting devices for inept coworkers in the corporate world, but it did not leave Eli feeling good about himself. How many people were like him, using their phones and tablets to apply for jobs? Living paycheck to paycheck without the ability to buy replacements? He tried not to think about where the goods came from and where they were going, but he wasn't the sort to be able to separate his work from his moral compass (however lax that might have been.)

But his rent wasn't going to pay itself and Sarah wasn't yet entertaining calls.

Eli groaned, dropping his tools back into their box and rolling his shoulders in an attempt to work out the knot forming at the base of his neck. "The campus on this side of town? Yeah, I know it." In fact, he had dropped out of it almost a decade ago.

"Good," the man said as he walked into the main room with a large, recycled cardboard box in his arms. "Take this up to their student center. Wait on the second floor by the balcony. Someone will come to and give you an envelope for the box. Bring it back here immediately."

Eli looked down at the half-finished, "refurbished" iPhone in his hands and set it down with a sigh. "What's in the box?"

Lou scowled at him as he let the box hit the display case with a *thunk*. "Don't worry about it. Just drop the box off and bring the envelope back. Got it?"

This was the part of the job Eli disliked the most. He could turn a blind eye to the items of questionable origin that made their way through the shop to get his job done. He could ignore the money changing hands in the back room and the envelopes picked up at odd hours. However, he didn't want to be involved in any of those aspects. Eli wanted to keep his head down, do a bit of repair, and get paid. He didn't want to become an illegal errand boy.

But it seemed he didn't have a choice. With each passing week, Lou took to pushing additional, unscrupulous tasks onto Eli. The job was quickly becoming unbearable. Though was surely aware of Eli's disdain for the delivery work, Lou stared down at him until he stood and reluctantly accepted the box.

"Just bring back the envelope?"

Lou nodded.

Eli slid the box over to his workstation and grabbed his jacket. The box was light, and its contents slid about inside, padded by little more than some wads of newspaper. Whether there was a phone or tablet, or something more interesting, Eli couldn't say. Whatever it was, it wasn't any of Eli's business.

As convenient as it would have been for Eli to hop on the subway and take it down two stops to the campus, Eli doubted his employer would be reimbursing him for the fare. Until Eli could afford a monthly pass, he had to save every dollar that he had. And so, Eli was stuck walking all six blocks to the campus with the box in hand.

At the very least, it was a lovely autumn day. The sun was out, and a comfortable breeze swept through the city, making him thankful for his jacket. It brought back memories of taking Sarah to the park when she was still stroller-bound. Sophia would pack lunches and they would spend hours and hours enjoying the sunshine and fresh air. Those days felt like distant memories from another life rather than only a few years back. Those days, like the current one, made him feel as if he didn't mind living in the city so much. Of course, he knew that at any moment something terrible might be right around the corner.

At a certain point, Eli could tell he had crossed onto the university's open campus. Not only were the buildings newer, cleaner, and more secure, but most of the people around Eli were in their early twenties and carrying backpacks or side bags. They almost all had earbuds in and cellphones out. Very few of them glanced up at Eli as he forced his way through the crowd and toward the student center.

He slipped into the line of students heading up the stairs to the second floor, feeling out of place amongst the young twenty-somethings. Eli had never felt particularly adult-like, despite being a father. Now that he thought about it, perhaps his immaturity was one of the issues plaguing his marriage... But now he felt so *old*. With a shake of his head, Eli let out an annoyed sigh as he raised the box Lou gave him to avoid a group of oncoming students. A short brunette would have plowed him right over had he not lifted it to make room for her.

Eli sidestepped the crowd and went to a small table at the top of the stairs overlooking the mass of people below. He hoped classes were in the middle of changing and that it would ease up if he waited it out for a few minutes.

While the student center did, indeed, empty, no one came up to him bearing an envelope.

After the first ten minutes, Eli couldn't help but become antsy. Would Lou think he had skipped off with the money that was likely in the envelope? Or that Eli was secretly meeting with police to rat out Lou? He was sure he was overreacting, but he *really* did not enjoy being a mule or whatever he was.

Eli browsed his own phone for a few minutes until he ran out of rejection letters to delete. He stood again, placing his hands on his head, and paced about before looking down from the balcony to see if anyone was waiting below. No one. He let out yet another annoyed sigh as he turned to lean against the railing. There was a wide bulletin board spanning the length of the wall across from him, and as he stood staring at it, one of the notices caught his eye.

It was a clean, professional advertisement printed on glossy paper, unlike the other photocopied pages tacked onto the board. It had a picture of a rather *distinguished* looking gentleman—a man with a full, white beard, small spectacles, and even a bow tie paired with a tweed jacket. Next to the photo were the words 'Doctor Lennard Deittman, PhD, Parapsychologist.'

Psychology Fall Semester Seminars Presents: Doctor Lennard Deittman, Ph.D. Tuesday, September 17th, at 5:30 pm. Are you curious about the science behind the paranormal? Doctor Deittman, renowned psychologist and pioneer of the parapsychology field, will be discussing a set of cases and presenting the research behind his findings in a series he calls, "A Trick of the Mind."

Eli stepped forward and read the sheet again. It wasn't exactly something he'd been expecting to come across. Was this guy for real? He actually studied the paranormal, unlike those fake investigators on television? It did appear he was a real doctor. A scientist. A man like him might even believe Eli—though Eli couldn't help but doubt that there was really anyone out there who might have had an explanation for the things he witnessed. Still, he was desperate.

So desperate that he was helping sell off stolen goods to pay his rent.

Licking his lips a bit, Eli raised his phone and took a picture of the flyer.

Behind him, there was movement. Eli turned on his heel to see a teenager looking into the cardboard box he was supposed to be dropping off. "Hey! Don't—"

The kid held up a thick envelope, barely glancing at Eli.

"Oh. Yeah, okay." Eli stepped forward and took the envelope before giving one more glance at the flyer. "Hey, are you a student here?"

The teenager looked up, a scowl on his face. "No, I just hang out in a student center for fun. What's it to you?"

Eli opened his mouth and then closed it again, rethinking snapping on his boss's 'client.' "Are these guest lectures open to anyone?"

"We pay thousands of dollars to go here—you think they're going to open their lectures to the public?"

With a roll of his eyes, Eli raised his hands and shook his head. It wasn't worth a fight. "Fine, whatever, it was just a question. Have a nice day." He started to take a few steps towards the stairs when the kid groaned.

"Yeah, those special lectures are open to the public, but the seats are first come first serve. They're pretty popular. You probably won't get in."

Eli gave the kid a nod and hummed to himself before quickly descending the stairs. Lou would be waiting for him.

The thought of the parapsychology seminar was enough to put a spring back into his step. Eli traveled the blocks back to the shop in long, brisk strides, his mind distracted by the possibility of speaking to an expert. It wasn't until he neared the shop's block that

Eli thumbed the envelope he had shoved in his pocket and started to worry once more about his time away from his desk. He had been gone for well over half an hour, and he knew Lou wouldn't be thrilled. Hopefully he could hand over the envelope and finish his work for the day, then he could—

Shit.

As Eli turned the corner of the shop's block, he saw the telltale-colored lights of a police car bouncing off the windows and walls of the surrounding buildings. He hoped beyond hope that it wasn't in front of Lou's but with a few more steps, his hopes were dashed. Two officers were walking through the entrance. Eli paused for a moment before continuing to walk, bypassing the store entirely. He would drop the envelope off on Lou's car windshield behind the building.

And then he was done.

Eli was stupid to take such a risk for quick cash, and if the police didn't come looking for him, he would count himself lucky. Maybe a pizza shop was hiring.

CHAPTER 4

It was by sheer force of will that Eli managed to arrive on time for the five-thirty lecture. He knew himself well enough to know that if he showed up after it started, he wouldn't go in. He would mill about outside the lecture hall, hands in his pockets, before changing his mind and heading right back to his crappy apartment or an equally crappy bar.

Inhaling deeply, Eli pulled open the door to the large classroom, a wave of nostalgia washing over him as he was transported back to the days of his younger self, and stepped inside. He was greeted with a cacophony of sound spilling from the room as people spoke in murmurs of intrigue, waiting impatiently for the presentation to begin. He was actually somewhat surprised to find the lecture hall was packed full, just as the teenager had warned. Many of the attendees appeared to be students, based not only on their age but on the backpacks and notebooks at their desks. As he glanced around the room, however, he spied many dolled-up professionals and uniformed workers also littering the space. Eli hadn't expected parapsychology to draw such interest beyond those campy television shows and web series.

Eli craned his neck, searching for any open seat between the students. No luck, however. He wasn't interested in climbing toward one of the rare vacant seats in the middle of the auditorium.

It would draw far too much attention to himself, and he was happier sticking to the sidelines rather than disrupting a dozen people for an inevitably uncomfortable chair. He resigned himself to standing at the back of the room near another young woman who appeared to be another observer like himself.

While some folks grumbled as they reluctantly took up a piece of wall for themselves, Eli didn't mind standing in the back. If he was so inclined, he would sit on the ground. The young woman in front of him was on one of the steps, leaning against the wall, and no one seemed to mind.

The lecture hall was stadium seating. The guest speaker was standing below while a young man helped connect a laptop to the projector. After a few moments, the screens in the front of the room came to life. Standing up top, in the far back, was actually preferable. To Eli, the screens were more or less at his eye level.

'Doctor Lennard Deittman, Ph.D.', read the displays, along with a brief bio and a photo that looked to be off of a book sleeve. It was a professional headshot, though the man in the picture was a bit younger than the man standing in front of the audience, with fewer creases along the face and salt-and-pepper hair, rather than the soft weight covering the man's head and beard now.

Deittman stepped over to the podium while the young man continued to fiddle with the laptop. Eli's eyes lingered on the young man setting about his work. He was very fair-skinned with pale, blond hair, and an wearing expensive gray suit that washed out his features. He certainly stood out against the dark colors of the lecture hall. Deittman himself was also dressed quite nicely, outfitted in a three-piece suit, complete with a pocket watch. The doctor had something of a European air, humming to himself as he imagined the man speaking like those faux-Sigmund Freud types who had prescribed him his medication.

And as soon as Deittman opened his mouth, Eli knew he was correct.

"Good evening everyone," said the older gentleman, his words coming out in what Eli believed was a German accent. "I am pleased to see so many faces before me today. Though this was primarily meant to be a lecture for psychology students here at the University, I do welcome those others of you who have chosen to join me."

The young man handed Deittman a small remote before leaving the center stage and taking a seat at the front of the room. Deittman nodded and pointed the device toward the laptop to move on to the next slide.

"Before we begin, I would like to provide you with one caveat: if you have come here in hopes of hearing ghost stories, you will be sorely disappointed," he said and paused for a few moments as there was a bit of shuffling. "We are not here to debate whether or not the paranormal exists, merely instances where my team and I have been called in to investigate something that was considered to be paranormal, and yet was not. We are discussing the psychology and physiology behind paranormal reports."

Again, Deittman paused. If Eli were to guess, he'd say Deittman had gone through this a few times before. A smattering of people who could easily slip out of their desks and sneak to the doors did just that. One of the ends next to Eli opened up and he claimed it for himself. Though other seats were now available, the young woman in front of him remained sitting on the steps, pulling her legs to herself to allow others to scurry past her.

After the shuffling ended, Deittman continued. "First and foremost, I am a psychologist. I received my doctorate from the Ludwig Maximilians University of Munich. I went on to further my studies at the University of Edinburgh, which has quite a reputable department of parapsychology, should you be interested. I taught at Edinburgh for a brief period before founding my own research firm. It may surprise you to know that there are many wealthy patrons who encourage the study of parapsychology and the paranormal, though, of course, their names shall remain confidential."

Deittman began his lecturing, covering a few famous legal cases relating to supposed paranormal influence—one trial involving the death of a girl during an exorcism and two civil suits relating to haunted property sales. Deittman went on to explain the outcome of each case and why each one had any supernatural element thrown out of court.

Eli hadn't been in a classroom in years. Even on the occasions he did take extra courses for different IT certifications, they had been online. Despite pushing himself to get to the lecture on time, he'd expected to be bored out of his mind as he waited for the speaker to finish in hopes of a meeting afterward. Instead, however, he found Deittman to be rather engaging. Eli shifted his weight a few times and furrowed his brows as he tried to follow along with some of the psychology terms with which he was unfamiliar, not that there were many he did know beyond his own diagnoses, but beyond that, the lecture was far more entertaining than he anticipated.

Deittman scrolled through slide after slide, showing off different locations or individuals with their faces blurred out for privacy. He would provide a bit of background on the reason he was called in on a case: *one was a subject who had recently lost her spouse and was convinced he was returning to communicate one last message.* He then went on to explain the root of the phenomenon: the widow had been prescribed a series of antidepressants that conflicted with her existing medication, and her recent disposition to vodka-tonics caused poor sleep with dream state hallucinations. Wishful thinking also played a part.

There was another case where a young boy was supposedly possessed. Deittman attended and met a priest sent by the Catholic church. Though the man was prepared to do an exorcism he was doubtful of the authenticity of the situation. He had Deittman perform an additional evaluation while he was present. Deittman determined it was not a case for the church, but child services—the boy was being abused and had created multiple personalities to deal with the abuse.

"Now, in all of these cases, there was an underlying cause—a cause that could be explained by science. Of course, this is a psychology lecture so those are what I am covering. However, I have to make clear one thing: there are things that science cannot explain. I have seen individuals who claim to communicate with spirits discover information they could not possibly know. I have witnessed exorcisms after I was unable to provide any professional benefit. I have watched as a woman located a missing child when the police failed, simply by touching his teddy bear. I do not have an explanation for these things... at least, not yet."

The crowd of students was on the edge of their seats, waiting to see if Deittman would reveal any other of his strange and magnificent stories. Eli glanced at the clock on the side of the room, and his shoulders slumped. The lecture time was almost up.

"Now, we'll move on to any questions," Deittman said with a small smile as moans of disappointment reverberated throughout the hall.

"I was wondering about something mentioned in the lecture summary," said a young man Deittman called upon. He had glasses and somewhat unkempt brown hair.

"Yes?"

"Well, it said you were looking to recruit members for your research team but that applicants needed extraordinary abilities. So, like, what does that mean?"

Eli had noticed the little blurb listed at the bottom of the lecture summary on the University website when he looked up additional lecture information. It offered compensation but applicants would only be considered if they had 'extraordinary abilities.' He wondered if his curse, his *Echoes*, would make him the sort of applicant Deittman wanted.

Lord knew he needed money.

"What do *you* think it means, dear boy?" Deittman asked, clasping his hands in front of himself.

The young man, likely a student, hemmed and hawed in embarrassment as if he regretted saying anything at all.

"I don't know... like... psychics and mediums? Telekinetics? ESP?" he said.

Deittman chuckled and shrugged.

"Yes, well, I suppose you are on the right track. I chose to use the phrase 'extraordinary abilities' because I *do* believe in what you might call 'extra senses'. Do I believe they are necessarily paranormal? No, not necessarily, though I have certainly seen some individuals do things that I simply cannot explain. What I have discovered in my research is that so-called paranormal activity is more likely to occur when someone who has these *extra senses* is about. We all emit energy, every one of us. I believe some individuals emit slightly *different* energy. Energy which is likely to draw out the things that consume or utilize such power. Are those people more likely to also be labeled as psychics? Perhaps. Regardless, this is all theory and I have not yet captured substantial proof to legitimize my theory."

So...ghost hunting. Eli raised a brow and crossed his arms, staring at the man.

Obviously, of all people, Eli was not one to outright say that ghosts did not exist. He had seen them, or something others would call ghosts. He didn't know if he was eager to admit that to another person, however, since if it got out, he would certainly be marked as a crazy person.

Plus, did he really want to go to a place known for attracting ghost hunters? He witnessed enough terrible things on a daily basis just walking down the street. What would a graveyard or haunted house have for him? On the other hand, maybe he could make his terrible curse work for him. Wouldn't *that be* a turn of events?

He snorted to himself. From the corner of his eye, he caught the woman on the floor turning to look at him. Eli stared back at her and she gave him a smirk and a shrug.

Now that he saw her fully, he definitely didn't believe she was a student. Whereas everyone else was dressed for hours spent in classrooms, she appeared ready to hit a dive bar. Her hair was messy and pulled back into a ponytail. She wore a black top under a leather jacket, tight, torn jeans, and black boots. The woman's features were sharp, and her eyes were dark—Eli found her attractive but in a dangerous sort of way; not like Sofia who he believed was beautiful.

At the thought of his wife, Eli shifted uncomfortably under the other woman's gaze. He forced himself to look away and ignore her.

"Any other questions?" Deittman asked, and hands went up in the air.

"Dr. Deittman," one young woman asked after Deittman pointed to her, "please don't think me rude. This is a serious question. Parapsychology is not a widely practiced field—at least, not reputably. Do people ever... well, think you're crazy? Or a fraud?" The young woman flushed red and looked as though she wanted to hide herself behind her mass of red curls.

Eli raised a brow and focused on Deittman once more. It was a valid question, and he'd been wondering too. Deittman simply smiled and shrugged.

"I am positive there are many people out there who find my work to be...*invalid.* However, if no one studied in this field, then no one could say for sure the paranormal doesn't exist. Perhaps it doesn't exist *now,* but that doesn't necessarily mean it may *never* exist. Perhaps it's all about evolution. If that is the case, if we give up now, then we will never know when it happens.

"Think of this: research has suggested humans did not always see the color blue. Early writings describe the color of the ocean as wine or blood, which suggests not that the ocean changed color but that we could not see the color to recognize it. Such a shift happened somewhere down the line, and we are now forced to use literature to determine when a possible step of evolution took place. Would it not have been easier if someone was studying colors? If someone was researching what people saw and how they saw it? Perhaps then we would be able to pinpoint a non-physical change in humankind. That," Deittman waved and dropped his hand back to his side, "that is what I am doing. I am studying a field which has the potential for evolutionary change. If a change should come in my lifetime, I can document it to the best of my ability."

That settled it for Eli. Deittman was the real deal. He knew what he was doing, and he knew what he was talking about. Nothing he had said made Eli believe Deittman was looking to convince anyone of the paranormal. He was merely discussing his research practices and potential theories.

Eli decided to stick around if only to get some more information about the research team. He listened patiently for Deittman to run out the clock answering questions, most of which were about how to go about getting into the field without having a research grant.

Just as he was about to run out of time, Deittman finally said, "If you are interested in learning the details about the research team, please remain. As mentioned, I am specifically looking for those who believe they have some extraordinary skill or a sixth sense, if you will. If you do not have that, I assure you, it will not be worth your while to go through the process. I thank you for your time. Good night."

The lecture hall emptied rather quickly. Many students eagerly began discussing the lecture as they filed through the door, leaving behind a handful of audience members to listen to the follow-up session. A few individuals walked to the front, exchanged words with Deittman, shook his hand, and quickly scurried away. In the end, only a half-dozen or so people remained to hear the details of Deittman's offer.

The woman on the floor was one of them. She stood once students started to leave and moved to take a seat some rows in front of Eli. She kicked her feet up, letting them rest on the chair in front of her.

"Eight of you," Deittman commented once he turned back to the remainder of his audience. "Impressive. Usually, we receive only three or four candidates. Very well. Tomorrow we will be conducting one-on-one interviews with interested individuals. I will assign each person a time slot. Fill out this form, hand it in, and report to the conference room just outside of this lecture hall at that designated time."

"That's it?" the woman in front of Eli said, her voice sharp. "Just... fill out this form and come back? You aren't going to give us any further details?"

Deittman frowned a bit and looked up at her from over the rim of his glasses. His eyes flicked over her, lingering on dirty boots, before responding in what Eli could only describe as a 'flat' tone.

"Yes. That is it. We do not provide any unnecessary information to those for whom we have no use. If we choose to accept you, then you will receive a more detailed explanation. If that bothers you, well, you certainly do not have to feel obligated to return."

"Oh, but then you'd be missing out," the woman replied with a cool tone and a bit of a wave.

It seemed Deittman wasn't going to dignify her with a response. Instead, he turned to his briefcase, which sat on the raised desk next to the laptop, and withdrew a handful of papers. He marked something down on each of them and then set them down on one of the student desks. One by one, everyone walked to the front to retrieve a paper and a pen while Deittman began to disconnect his laptop.

The form was rather basic, all things considered. It asked him for his contact information, current occupation, and availability. However, it also asked about any paranormal experiences and to describe any 'believed *extra senses* and/or *extraordinary abilities*'.

Eli was really, truly tempted to simply write down *I see dead people*, but he refrained. Instead, he merely listed out a brief description of his affliction. *Post-cognition. I see images of bad moments people have suffered—usually their deaths. It's not consistent. It comes and goes. Some days are worse than others. I want it gone.*

Good enough, he thought. He could explain the rest in person if they wanted. Eli wasn't the first to complete his paper, despite his brevity. Instead, it was the woman. She beat him to the front, slapped her paper down, and then headed towards the door. Eli followed her out, hands shoved into his jacket pockets.

He ended up walking behind her the entire way to the bus stop. They both stopped and turned to face the street. After a few moments of awkward silence—the woman turned to him, offering him a cigarette.

"No thanks," he said.

She shrugged and placed one between her lips. She pulled a small, brass lighter from her pocket and lit the tip. "So, you're going back for an interview tomorrow?"

Eli nodded. "Yeah. You too?" he asked her.

She puffed out a wave of smoke.

"Yup. They won't want to, but they'll take me."

"Confidence will get you far, I guess," Eli replied, fighting the urge to roll his eyes. The woman snorted.

"Sure, if that's what you want to call it. I'm Ash, by the way."

"Eli," he replied.

"My great *extra senses* tell me we'll be working together in the near future," Ash said and turned to face him fully. "I'm going to grab dinner. Want to join me?"

CHAPTER 5

It was after eight by the time they reached a dumpy bar and grill. Ash led the way, nudging Eli off at her stop and navigating a series of litter-covered alleyways. There might have been a sign above the establishment once upon a time, but now there was nothing but the rusted-out bolts where it should have been. Why, of all places, was this the one that the woman opted to patron? Eli couldn't say. The place was dingy and had only been open for a few hours according to the faded sticker plastered to the exterior of the door.

As she sauntered in, she gave a wave to the older man behind the bar and went to a high-top table by the back window. She threw her jacket off and over the back of the chair in one smooth motion before hoisting herself onto it as if she had done it a million times. She must have been a regular.

Ash flipped her mess of black hair over her shoulders and adjusted the fitted black tee shirt that rode up at her waist before nodding to the seat across from her. Eli hesitated, his throat tightening as he tried to swallow down the nerves that suddenly bubbled up within him.

He wasn't sure why he did it, and the pit in his stomach told him that he would regret it later, but he slipped his wedding ring off before taking his hand out of his pocket and hanging up his jacket as well.

He tried not to think about it—tried not to feel guilty. It was Sophia, after all, who had kicked him out of the house. She was the one who said she was done with him. Everything else in his life was terrible—what was one more mistake?

Before Eli had a chance to look at the menu, the gentleman from behind the bar—dressed in well-worn black pants and a stained white shirt, rolled up to the elbows—dropped off two bottles of beer. Eli opened his mouth to decline since he was trying to cut back on his alcohol consumption but immediately changed his mind. The server had a grizzled look to him that Eli found rather intimidating. Ash spoke, though not in English.

Once the man walked away, he looked back at the woman who had already started into one of the bottles.

"So… you come here often?" he asked, mentally chiding himself for defaulting to the world's worst pickup line.

The corners of the woman's mouth twitched upward into a small smirk. "Yeah, whenever I'm in town. The food's not horrible, and I drink for free--well, at least this cheap stuff. I'll take a free drink wherever I can find it."

Well, free was free. Eli grabbed the other beer. He took a few swigs as they sat in a somewhat awkward silence.

"Is 'Ash' short for 'Ashley', or something?" he finally asked, having nothing else to talk about.

"No," she replied with a chuckle. "Natasha. I picked up the name 'Ash' as a kid, living in an immigrant community. There were a few others with the same name. Is your name short for something?"

Eli hummed and nodded. "Yeah, it's Elijah. No one but my grandmother calls me that though."

"I see…" She said, shifting to rest her elbow on the high window sill to her left as she brought her bottle up.

Eli raised a brow as knocked the drink back. The girl could drink, not that he was one to judge. Another set of beers appeared before them not a few moments later, though Eli gripped his a bit tighter. He refused to give in to the urge to keep up with her, even if the drinks were free.

"So, what do you think about Deittman and his adventure?" she asked him as she swapped out for her second beer.

He sighed as he ran a hand through his dark hair, tearing his eyes away from her. "I don't know. The guy doesn't come off as crazy, which is what I was expecting when I walked in. Just... seems too good to be true, you know? A potential job like this popping up right now..."

"Yeah, I get it. In my experience though, there is always someone willing to buy unique skills. You just have to find them. Also, in my experience, those people are either bags of crazy or awful excuses for human beings. I didn't actually think I would consider applying for this so-called job when I walked into the lecture hall, but hey, cash is cash."

Eli glanced over behind him to see that the server was behind the bar, off to the side by the grill. He was cooking something up despite neither of them having ordered.

"So, you can really do something then? You're an actual psychic?" Eli asked, turning his gaze back to her.

With a bitter smirk, she leaned back and crossed her legs and her arms. "Psychic? I guess, technically, as an umbrella term. Sure. But it isn't like reading minds or seeing the future, or some shit like that. Mine's more of... well, *active*. I can do some damage," Ash replied with a casual shrug.

Eli fought to keep his eyebrows from shooting upwards. Either this girl was serious, or she was delusional. The last thing he wanted was to find himself stuck around some psychotic woman who believed she could kill him with her mind or something.

"Uh-huh," he replied slowly, grabbing the menu that was in the middle of the little condiment boat and staring down at it intently. "So, what do you do then?"

When she didn't answer, Eli glanced up at her and found her staring at him coolly. She knew he didn't believe her.

As she stared at him with dark eyes rimmed with equally dark markup, a shiver went down his spine. For the second time, the word danger flashed through his head. For whatever reason, she reminded him of a bird of prey—as if she were watching him from afar and preparing to swoop in on him, ready to eat him alive. Though the woman sat slouched in her chair and looking completely relaxed, her presence didn't match. It was cliché, and he knew it, but there was more than met the eye with her.

It scared him.

His body tensed as he got caught in her gaze, unable to pull away. It was like something was drawing him in, and he didn't at all like it. For a moment, he could've sworn something flashed across Ash's eyes. But in the span of a heartbeat, she shrugged and turned her attention back to her drink.

"I don't show off for just anyone. You'll have to work for it if you want to see my tricks. God, I hate that I can't smoke in bars in this city."

Eli blinked and swallowed, sitting back a little bit to put a bit of space between them. He glanced to his left and found the sign for the restroom. Eli slid from his seat and took two steps away from their table. "I'll... be right back."

He tried not to run, tried not to show the sudden wave of anxiety that washed over him, but his brisk steps as he fled into one stall bathroom gave him away. His arms and legs felt like jelly, felt weak—like the first signs of sickness. He put his hands on either side of the sink and leaned against it to steady himself, and took a few deep breaths. After a few long moments, the discomfort began to fade and he was left with only his *normal* levels of anxiety.

"This is crazy," he muttered, looking up at his reflection. "I'm getting caught up in all this supernatural bullshit."

One more deep breath and he was standing again, adjusting his shirt. Despite his own ability—or curse, as he referred to it—it was *so very difficult* for Eli to believe in the paranormal and all of the frills that went along with it. To be honest, it was more like he simply refused to believe in it. If it were all real, if there was some entirely other world that lies just beyond the surface, did he really want to get himself involved? He had hidden his abilities for so long that it was the only way he knew how to live. He didn't think that finding others with possibly similar experiences would be so... bracing.

"I'm fine," he told himself as he washed his hands and splashed a bit of water on his neck. Eli's skin was hot and the air around him was stuffy. If his undershirt didn't have an obvious hole in it, he probably would've pulled off his thermal.

He swung the door open and started back to the table. To his relief, sitting on the table was a basket of food and some glasses of water. Ash was already munching on whatever it was in front of her. Once he sat down, she waved a hand at the basket.

"It's like a salty cheese. People eat it with beer—especially cheap beer," she said with a chuckle. "It'll dry you out though so drink some water."

Eli stared at the strips in the basket before reaching in to grab a piece. It was chewy and flavorful, which was brought out further when he took a deep swig of beer to wash it down. He wouldn't go so far as to say it was *great* but it was... something.

"So, what's good here?" Eli asked, returning his gaze to the menu despite the fact he couldn't read most of it. Ash laughed.

"Nothing, really. I mean, it's not bad, but... it's an acquired taste for the most part. I always get the lamb sausage, but that's mostly because it reminds me of what my mother used to make. She wasn't exactly a good cook though."

"She's not around anymore?" He reached in for more cheese strips. Like most pub food, they were dangerously addicting with each bite he took.

Ash shrugged and hummed curiously. "In a manner of speaking. I was kicked out at sixteen. I've been in touch with my younger sister, but I haven't seen my mother or stepfather in almost a decade."

Eli figured that made the woman younger than twenty-six— more than five years his junior. She looked older than that, though. Maybe it was the chain-smoking.

"Ah. Sorry to hear that," he said, though it was hardly sincere. He'd never been the empathic sort.

"No big deal. I've certainly lived an interesting life. What about you? Family in the area? You from here?" She waved down the server and pointed to her empty beer bottle.

"No," he replied. "I went to school here, dropped out, and stayed. I don't... I don't have any family around here." He clenched his jaw and swallowed a bit, deliberately failing to mention his wife and daughter who were just across the city.

"Sounds lonely," Ash said as she picked at some of the cheesy appetizers. "Do you know what you want to eat?"

Eli looked at the menu before him and shrugged. He had no idea what most of the dishes were. He settled on a sausage-looking item with a side of potatoes. Since he didn't know how to pronounce the foreign name, he chose to point at it. Ash craned her neck to see what he had picked, reading upside down and then shouted it over her shoulder along with her order. The cook muttered some sort of confirmation.

The two of them continued to chat throughout dinner. Ash politely asked him questions about himself, but Eli found himself at a loss. He felt... uninteresting. He hadn't done anything particularly exciting with his life. He had no stories to share, no adventures (or misadventures, even.) He felt... bland.

So, he asked about her life.

Which only made him feel worse about himself.

She was well-traveled. She was a bit of a drifter, putting herself in what he considered to be dangerous situations, especially for a woman traveling solo. But she had spent time in most of the country's major cities, and she had backpacked internationally. Ash laughed as she told him about a whirlwind love affair she had once had with a woman in Mexico that lasted all of a month before she ran off with the woman's brother.

"I don't know if I can ever go back to south Mexico... if either of them caught me again, I think they'd try to murder me," Ash said, smirking.

"Your life is..." Eli raised a hand, waving it a bit. "Well, it sounds so exciting."

Ash's smirk faded as looked down at her beer bottle. "Yeah, I guess it is. But having no ties... Well, it means no one ever misses you."

They fell into an awkward silence. Eli didn't know what to say. Was he supposed to say anything at all? He shifted a bit, hesitating. Ash laughed.

"So, you've been here a long time, right? What's in the area? What would a paranormal investigator want to check out? Whatever Deittman's looking into can't be too far away if he's looking for locals, right?" she asked, changing the subject much to his relief.

Eli wiped a hand through his dark hair and then grimaced. He shouldn't have done that—his hands were greasy from the cheese. "Honestly, I can only think of a few..." he hummed, digging through his local history knowledge for a possibility or two.

The subject change got them through dinner as they traded ghost stories and location speculation. By the end of their meal, he had learned more about Ash than he had learned about anyone else in the past five years. Had he made his first new friend in who knew how long?

The grizzly-looking cook appeared at their table, dropping two slips of paper in front of them. Drinks might have been free, but the food wasn't. Eli inwardly sighed as he quickly ran the numbers to figure out how much cash he had left from Lou and when his next rent payment was due. The cook said something to Ash and Eli was certain her lips twitched downward. She nodded and the man walked away.

"I need a cigarette," Ash finally said with a sigh and pulled out her wallet. She dropped a twenty and some small bills on the table then pulled her jacket on. Figuring that it was best he get moving too, Eli followed suit. He was a bit stingier on his tip... money was tight, and he could hardly read the writing on the bill he was given.

Eli trailed behind Ash as they walked outside. She walked at a quick pace, occasionally sparing a glance behind them.

"Something wrong?" Eli asked.

"Some people are heading in that I don't care for—just don't want to have to make pleasantries," she replied with a shrug. Once they were about two blocks away, in a rather eerily quiet part of town, she turned the corner, eventually stopping under a dim streetlight.

A few feet away from her, there was a gasping sound—gasping, and crying--though Ash didn't notice.

While Ash busied herself with digging her cigarettes out of her pockets, Eli dared to walk a few steps forward, emboldened by cheap alcohol in his system to cautiously craning his neck to glance around a parked delivery truck.

There was what appeared to be a teenager on the ground, wearing a helmet and trying to drag herself towards the sidewalk. She was sobbing as blood gushed down her face. She made a choking sound with each inch she managed to move, and one of her legs was bent the wrong way. Eli guessed that she was trying to call for help, but only a gurgling sound came out.

"Not here," Eli said, more to himself. "Not here..."

"What?" Ash replied, taking a few steps towards him.

"Can't stop here," he muttered. Without taking his eyes from the gruesome sight, he backed up, his arm outwards, until he touched Ash's arm. He grabbed it and pulled her forward, hurrying the two of them down the block away from the bloody girl.

CHAPTER 6

Eli released Ash as they crossed the street but didn't give her a chance to stop him. He squeezed his eyes closed a few times, trying to shake the image from his mind. However, it was never that easy—not without his medication. Ash trailed behind him, only trying to slow him after another two blocks, but he walked onwards until he reached familiar territory. Finally, he stopped, but not until he was at a railing overlooking the river on their side of town.

"So, uh, you okay?" Ash asked, eyes narrowed as she studied him from a safe distance away.

Eli wiped his hand across his brow and down the side of his face, then braced himself against the railing. "Yeah, sorry about that... I probably seem nuts."

Ash chuckled, relaxing as she resumed her search for her cigarettes. "I've seen crazy. You seemed more scared than anything else, at least to me."

Eli sighed. He was scared—he was always scared. He knew his visions couldn't hurt him, but it didn't stop human nature from taking over. The things he saw... they were terrible. They were *supposed* to scare people.

"Yeah, I guess so."

"Was that your *extraordinary ability*? Whatever *that* was?" She moved forward, one slow step at a time as if she were approaching

48

a skittish animal, and leaned against the railing next to him. Eli glanced at her and saw that her face was even, with perhaps a bit of curiosity shining through. She wasn't mocking him, she wasn't humoring him. Not a hint of skepticism. She was just passive. Eli reluctantly nodded, letting his head hang a bit. "Yeah. Yeah, it is... I've done some research. It's called post-cognition. I see things. Dead people, okay? I see dead people. Christ, I sound like a basket case..."

There was a pause and then Ash hummed.

"Technically..." she paused, thinking as she flicked her eyes over him. "Technically you don't though, right? I mean, post-cogs... It's... like an imprint, right? So, maybe they're dead, but maybe they're not?"

Eli blinked, his eyes shooting up to meet hers, surprised that she knew what a post-cognitive *was*. He had never spoken with someone else about the Echoes (with the exception of a psychologist, who did think he was crazy and medicated him). His face must have betrayed his surprise because Ash smiled and tapped the center of her chest.

"I'm literally filled with weird. You aren't weird. You're unique," she said with a shrug. It was so casual. He might as well have told her he liked a niche piece of media, rather than revealing his deepest, darkest secret. It was the most reassuring thing anyone could have done for him at that moment.

Eli gave her a slow nod and then exhaled, letting his body release the tension he had been holding. "Imprints. Yeah, that's true. It... It seems like it would always be the worst moment in a person's life. Like their negative emotions stick to an area and replay from time to time—and sometimes I'm around to witness them. I don't always see people die. I just ... assume they do. It's usually pretty bad. Sometimes, I guess, I just hope they died instead of living with what I saw."

"Dude, that sucks," Ash said and lit up the cigarette that she'd been struggling to have for the past twenty minutes. "My thing sucks, but I know when it's going to get bad. You might turn the corner and find someone getting dismembered. What a life."

"So, what is it that you... do?"

"Me?" she asked mildly, taking a drag from her cigarette. She glanced around them briefly to check for any onlookers before she raised her left index finger to the lit tip of her cigarette. She then pulled it away, wiggling her finger about in small circles. Eli had to blink a few times to be sure he was actually seeing what was in front of him.

Dancing around just above her finger was a small flame that grew by the second. Once it was big enough, she turned her hand palm up and a ball of fire hovered in it.

"You're... a pyrokinetic? I didn't think those were real, " he murmured, watching the flame.

Ash shrugged and closed her hand, extinguishing the flames as a couple started to near them on the walkway. "I've never met another and, as far as I know, there's never been any substantial research on it. I'm not keen on showing my skills off. Someone's bound to want to study me."

"Well, you're pretty much putting yourself out there with Deittman, aren't you?" Eli pointed out, raising a brow.

"Yeah," she sighed, putting the cigarette to her lips once more. She let out a puff of smoke. "Yeah, I am. But he's willing to pay. I need the money. Even if I think it's the second dumbest thing I've ever done in my life."

"I can relate."

"Alright, well, I need another drink," Ash said. She dropped her cigarette and snuffed it out with the toe of her shoes. "You brought us out here. Know of a good local place?"

Eli smiled and turned, glancing down the street to their left. "Well, I can't say it's good, but it is local."

"Sounds perfect, lead the way."

Shoving his hands into his jacket pocket, Eli pushed off the railing and started towards Burke Street Pub. He didn't like to think of himself as becoming a regular, but he had to admit he had been going more frequently than he should have these days. At the very least he figured he would return the favor of the few cheap beers she had scored him.

What was the worst that could happen?

Eli frowned as he watched the growing crowd of men forming around Ash. A few of them found her amusing—a few others decidedly did not. But the latter were the ones who had finished playing a round of pool with her, losing wads of cash in the process. No matter how many of them tried to puff themselves up and stand in her way, Ash was unbothered as she lined up her shots and continued her games. It helped that she was a taller woman, only a couple of inches shorter than Eli.

As a chorus of irritated groans came from the pool table, Eli licked his lips nervously. Ash snatched up the cash and slipped right passed the men to slink over to the barstool next to him.

"Looks like I'm buying the next round of drinks," she said with a smirk, slapping down a newly-won twenty. The bartender poured her another whiskey sour and gave Eli another beer. She let the bartender keep the change.

"Are you over there hustling guys at pool? Seriously, they don't look like they're taking it well. You might want to ease up," Eli sighed, shaking his head. Ash rolled her eyes and started in on her drink.

"Eli, look at me. I mean, really look at me. Do I look like the sort of girl who makes a living behind a desk? Huh? I've been doing this for a long time. I'm fine." She only stuck around with him for a few minutes before she slipped back into the crowd of patrons by the pool tables.

The bartender, Jack—who Eli had come to know rather well over the past few weeks—leaned forward and shook his head.

"Listen, man, I'm usually all for good-looking girls coming into the bar, but if this starts getting out of hand, I'm going to have to ask the two of you to leave. Those guys are regulars. I don't want to lose business 'cause some chick conned 'em out of some cash."

Eli sighed again and nodded, rubbing his temple. He brought the bottle to his mouth and chugged down the beer before gathering himself up. He walked towards the group of men and Ash, and tried to catch her attention. He tensed as one of the men grabbed her arm. She sternly pulled away, a frown planted on her face.

"C'mon," the man said, reaching back out for her. She swatted his hand away. The man's smirk—a toothy sort of smirk which revealed a few missing teeth—turned into a snarl. "We practically paid for you. The least you can do—"

"Paid for me?" Ash said coolly, her eyes narrowing. "I'm not *bought*. I'm not sure what women you're used to around here, but I assure you, I'm not one of them."

The man opened his large mouth and Eli imagined the words forming in his throat. Ash cocked her head to the side, and the man shut his mouth. The two stared at one another few moments, moments that felt long and very quiet, before the man took a step back.

"Fine. Ya fuckin' bitch…" He waved a few of his buddies over to the bar, leaving Ash standing with only two other guys.

"Hey, Ash," Eli called out to her, finally getting her attention. "Let's get out of here. It's getting late anyhow."

As she looked at him, it was as if she looked *through* him. It was… unnerving. But with a blink, the cold, piercing expression was gone and she was giving him a half-smile.

"Yeah, alright. I could use a smoke anyhow." She brought her glass to her mouth, throwing back the rest of her drink and slamming it down empty on the pool table. She haphazardly set her cue on the felt and approached Eli, letting him lead the way out of the bar.

Once they stepped out into the crisp night air, Eli let out a deep breath he hadn't realized he'd been holding.

"Christ, I thought that they were going to start swinging," he said, glancing over at her. Ash shrugged as she started digging around in her pockets for her cigarettes and lighter.

"Could've been fun if they had."

"Are you insane? Guys like them would kill us and not even bat an eye," he hissed at her. She only responded with a low chuckle.

Once they were a few blocks away from the bar, Eli stopped and leaned against the brick wall of a building. He let out a loud sigh but said nothing. Ash took a spot next to him, tossing the butt of her first cigarette and pulling out another. She flicked the lighter and he noticed she didn't bring it fully to the end of the cigarette. Instead, after bringing it close enough, she wiggled her finger. The flame practically jumped towards it, lighting the tip as the flame passed over it.

"Those things will kill you," he said, nodding to her cigarette. She let out a puff of air and let her head fall back against the dark red brick of the wall.

"We're all dying anyhow, some of us faster than others."

Eli wasn't sure exactly what to say. Should he push her? Was she hoping he would pry into whatever deeper meaning she had? If she did, she would be disappointed. Eli wasn't exactly eager to pry into someone else's past if she wasn't offering it up—especially someone he likely wouldn't run into again. He watched her for a bit, watched as the yellow street lights cast shadows over her, accentuating her sharp facial features. If his staring bothered her, she didn't say anything.

Finally, she glanced at him from the corner of her eye, her lips twitching upwards.

"Well?"

He shrugged and turned away. "Well, what?"

"You said we should get out of there, so we did. Was hoping you had something more interesting in mind. You did say your apartment was around here."

Eli's mouth ran dry. *Shit, shit, shit. What am I supposed to do?* He found himself fingering his wedding band in his jacket pocket. After a moment of thought, he dropped it and withdrew his hand. If there was ever going to be a time for him to try to embrace the part of his life he had suppressed, he supposed this was it.

"Yeah, a few blocks down. It's pretty awful though, just so you know," he said.

Ash laughed and smiled at him fully, sending a rush down his spine.

"I promise you I've seen worse. Lead the way."

When Eli awoke to his alarm in the morning, he had a terrible headache from a night spent drinking. It took him a little while to recall the events that led to him getting home. He panicked for a moment when he realized he was unclothed and searched for any signs of Ash. She was gone, and his front door was no longer deadbolted.

Though he was glad he was spared any awkward morning-after conversations—which he hadn't had to deal with in over a decade—he felt horrible. Eli leaned forward, his head in his hands and fingers in his hair, immensely regretting his decision. What was he thinking? Was it cheating if he and Sophia were separated? Were they ever really separated? And beyond that--Ash was dangerous. He knew it--he *felt* it. How could he have been so very *stupid?*

Eli didn't have time to dwell on the matter, however, because his phone soon started ringing, alerting him to his upcoming meeting with Deittman. He only had a few hours before he had to be back at the university.

CHAPTER 7

Eli slouched in his chair, watching the rather diverse group of people filling the limited space in the lobby of the psychology department. A few he recognized from the day before, a few he didn't. For the most part, what he saw was exactly what he expected from a gathering of psychics.

Crazies. He saw crazies.

There was a woman with frizzy, graying hair, wearing two colorful scarves and a hand-knit sweater covered with hanging stars. She had an oversized purse and carried a box likely holding tarot cards based on the symbols covering the wood. With a roll of his eyes, Eli shook his head and continued glancing down the line of chairs. Toward the end sat a man who looked rather... posh? That was the word popping into Eli's head. The man wore an expensive peacoat and a cashmere scarf wrapped around his neck. He sat with his legs crossed, bouncing his foot while he idly tapped a notebook. Eli raised his brow—was that a dowsing crystal in his other hand? All in all—not *too* weird. Of course, then the man started having a quiet conversation with someone who wasn't there. Eli wondered if perhaps the man had a wireless headset, but no. Nothing. He was talking to himself or someone he was calling 'Sam.'

And finally, there was a token creepy child with an equally creepy doll. She sat between a man and a woman, and they whispered to her in sharp tones. When the woman caught Eli watching, she narrowed her eyes at him and waved at the man and the child to move to the other side of the hallway, out of Eli's line of sight.

Outside the conference room door sat a young woman with pale blonde hair and fair skin. She also had a notebook in her lap, but she wasn't using it. Instead, she sat with her hands clasped on top of it, gazing off at the floor. Eli stared longer than he should have, but she was pretty. Almost doll-like. She caught him staring but only gave him a small smile before returning to gazing at the floor.

The door to the conference room opened and out stepped the young man who helped Deittman the night before. The young woman looked up at him, brows raised in curiosity, but he shook his head. She shrugged. Now that Eli saw him next to the seated woman, the resemblance was uncanny. They were nearly identical. Both had the same hair and complexion, and even their eyes were the same. Twins, certainly. Just when Eli thought he had found another 'normal' person, she had a gimmick. Twins were often unnerving by default, especially when they were similar as these two.

From within the room came a middle-aged woman in a fringed dress. She clutched a fabric bag with an image of a purple hand, with an eyeball in its palm, sewn in the middle. Eli heard her sniffling and upon closer inspection, she appeared to have been crying. After allowing her to pass by, the young man turned to what Eli assumed was the couple with the child, though he couldn't quite tell from where he was seated.

"I'm sorry," said the young man in a slightly accented tone Eli suspected was British, "but Dr. Deittman has made his choice. He will not meet her."

"Why not?" The woman hissed and stood, coming back into view. She practically stomped her foot and balled her hands into fists. "She's a real psychic!"

The young man shrugged. "That may be true—really, we aren't discrediting you. However, Dr. Deittman is not accepting children into his research study. The location is potentially dangerous due to the condition of the building alone, and he will not have a child's well-being to worry about. He has her name. Once she is eighteen, he recommends she contact him. But for now, that is all. You may go."

The woman continued to screech insults at the young man, but he kept his composure. After she continued her slew of insults for over a minute, he turned his back to her, ignoring her, and called out Eli's name. Eli pushed back his chair and walked over to who he assumed must have been Deittman's assistant. The young man gave Eli a nod and a polite smile before ushering him into the conference room. As he tried to close the door, however, the aggravated woman grabbed the edge and yanked it back.

"I want to talk to him!" she shouted from behind Eli's ear, causing him to scowl. "He should tell us himself—"

Eli glanced over to find that Deittman was, in fact, in the back of the room. He made no motion to calm the woman or even stand. The young man blocked the doorway with his body and stood straighter.

"Madam," he said, his voice distinctively icier than it had been moments before, "if you think you are the first guardian we have seen try to take advantage of a child, you are mistaken."

That shut the woman up.

"We have traveled around most of Europe and we see it often, especially in poorer areas," he added with some emphasis. The woman's face turned from shock to embarrassment. "As we've said, it's very possible your *niece* has some sort of ability. However, until she is old enough to make decisions *for herself*, we will not meet with her."

The woman released the door and he slowly pulled it shut in her face. Eli noted the lack of a lock. However, the woman didn't try to enter again.

"That's seriously a problem?" Eli asked, nodding towards the shut door. The young man shrugged.

"Unfortunately, it is," Deittman responded, drawing Eli's attention. "Spots on our research team are paid positions and many people are eager to do what they can to get at that money. The last thing I want is for a child to be forced into participating because of their greedy families. Now, please, if you will, have a seat." He extended his hand toward a chair across from him.

Eli shuffled around some of the chairs so he could squeeze through. The room wasn't as large as he had thought it was, and the table in the middle made the space almost claustrophobic.

"So, Eli Gehring, yes? I am Dr. Lennard Deittman, and this is Markus Valentinian. He is a member of the research team who has traveled with me from Europe. Now, tell me a bit about yourself."

Eli glanced between the two and then adjusted a bit. He didn't feel particularly comfortable in the room, but he couldn't quite place why that was. Maybe it was the way the old meeting room chair squeaked loudly under his weight and the fluorescent lights above him hummed.

"Uh, yeah, okay. So, yeah, I'm Eli Gehring. I'm thirty-one. I mostly do IT work. I worked for a big company in Manhattan but was laid off a few months ago—well, I guess it was almost a year ago, actually. I've been trying to hold down some work doing computer repairs, but it's been... difficult." He sighed and shifted again. When that didn't help make him more comfortable, he pulled off his jacket and set it on the chair next to him. It provided no relief. Instead, he started to feel an itch on his shoulder blade and the tag on his shirt scratched at his neck.

If they noticed his squirming, they didn't say anything.

"And family? Are you married?"

Instinctively, Eli looked down at his hand to show off his wedding ring. Then he remembered he'd taken it off the night before and hadn't put it back on.

"It's... complicated. We're separated for the time being."

"And why is that?" Deittman asked, reclining a bit in his chair and clasping his hands together.

Eli opened his mouth and then frowned. "I don't see why that's your business," he muttered, crossing his arms in front of him tightly.

Deittman smiled and chuckled softly. "I suppose you wouldn't. You do have to understand that my background is in psychology first and foremost. All of this," he said and waved his hand about the room, "is secondary. It is only logical that I give someone a psychological evaluation before taking them into a possibly stressful situation. I wouldn't want you to turn out to be a threat to my research."

That... was a fair reason, Eli supposed. However, he noticed Deittman said *research* rather than a threat to his *team*. He pushed the thought from his mind, instead focusing on the clinical nature of Deittman's questioning. Deittman and his team were more professional than he had initially thought. This wasn't like some ghost show on television.

"Drinking, mostly," he said and sighed. His head was feeling heavy. "After losing my job, I couldn't get the prescription medication I needed. It... kept me from seeing things. Once I started seeing them again, I started drinking. It suppresses them. I missed job interviews. I forgot to pick my daughter up from school. I even spent my anniversary passed out on the bathroom floor while my wife waited at the restaurant, assuring the servers I would be there soon... She waited for an hour and a half before coming home and putting me to bed."

He wasn't going to go into any of the physical altercations he had while he was at the bar. That would surely cut him from their list if nothing else did. Eli brought his hands to his face, pressing his palms into his eyes, trying to ease the tension forming behind them. When it didn't help, he sighed and dropped them to the table again.

Deittman didn't appear surprised or offended or anything at all. He merely nodded as if he were making mental notes.

"And what sort of things were you seeing? I'm sure you've been told that hallucinations can be part of a greater mental disability."

Eli smiled bitterly and looked away. "Oh yeah, I've been told. Many, many times. I spent time in and out of hospitals since I was fourteen years old. Everyone thought I was crazy. I thought I was crazy. Once I was put on anti-anxiety medication, I was fine. Stopped seeing things, for the most part. Lived a normal life. Every time I went off them, it all came back. Seems to only get worse as I get older."

He pinched the bridge of his nose and blinked. A headache was coming on. All he wanted was to go back to his crappy apartment and take a nap. He was starting to think this was all a terrible idea.

"Listen, I'm going to be blunt. Take it or leave it, I don't care," Eli said and sat up so he could rest his head against the cushioned chair. "I put down on my application--I'm a post-cognitive. You've got to know about them. That's the closest I can get to describing what I have. I see... Echoes. It isn't always someone's death, but it usually is. It's like... It's like I'm seeing the worst moment of someone's life. It's... residual energy or something." Deittman had used the term the previous day and Eli hoped he was using it correctly.

"Do you know how awful it is to walk down the street and watch someone get gunned down, and no one else notices? Or to be sitting in your living room, and suddenly, someone's hanging body appears in your stairwell as they choke to death? It's terrible. Anyone would go crazy having to witness that stuff. I can't control it. I can't control what I see or when I see it. It's not consistent." He put his head in his hands and rubbed his eyes with the pads of his hands. Eli stood up abruptly and grabbed his jacket. "This was a mistake. I have to go."

Markus practically leaped in front of him, blocking the door and raising his hand to encourage Eli to sit once more.

"Now just one moment," Deittman said. Eli glanced over, gritting his teeth. Deittman leaned over to the side of his chair and Eli heard something *'click.'* Within a few seconds, the headache started to disappear. "Forgive me for the annoyance I may have caused you. However, we did need to test you."

"Test me?"

Deittman nodded to Eli's seat, urging him to sit back down. With a loud sigh, Eli reluctantly did so.

"As you can imagine, there are far more people who believe they have psychic abilities than those who actually do," Deittman said. Markus pulled a briefcase onto the table and pulled out a handful of papers. He passed them over to Eli along with an expensive-looking pen. Eli raised a brow as he evaluated it—was that real gold?

"Frauds," Eli muttered and started to flip through the papers. They were pages upon pages of waivers and contracts.

Deittman shrugged. "No, not always. In my opinion, frauds are those who claim to have abilities when they knowingly do not. There are plenty of people who truly believe they are gifted with no way of truly verifying their skills. I have come up with a tentative way to test them." He slid his chair out and reached down again, this time placing a small device on the table. It looked like the exposed circuitry of a piece of equipment, rather than a piece in and of itself. "This piece here emits an uncommon frequency, one that is far too high-pitched for anyone to hear. However, it will affect those who have... extra senses, if you will. I modeled it off of the concept of a fear cage. Are you familiar with the concept of a fear cage?"

Eli shook his head.

"It's an area with an unusually high electromagnetic field reading. These are often common in old houses and buildings suffering from poor wiring or insulation. Exposure to high EMF will cause discomfort and feelings of anxiety or paranoia, more often than not. In this case, my device emits a frequency that I believe disrupts those 'extra senses.' Judging by your physical reaction, you do have those senses. If you did not, you would have likely sat here quite comfortably, if a bit warm."

Even as his eyes darted back and forth between the two men in the room, Eli was shocked. They believed him. It was one thing for Ash to believe him without much of a second thought—she had shown him her ability, so he believed her as well. It was entirely different for a pair of scientists, however unconventional they may be, to listen to him and not call him delusional. Still, it wasn't entirely comforting. He didn't like the idea of being considered 'special.' He had never wanted to be special—he just wanted to be normal.

"Have there been any others?" Eli asked slowly, hoping this wasn't all going to be an elaborate hoax. What if he was getting himself involved with con men? Would the University have hosted someone without proper credentials?

Deittman shook his head. "Not from this batch, unfortunately. At this time, we have a team of paranormal investigators who will be joining us, as well as a journalist who assures me she is only doing research for a novel. The only 'psychic' at the moment is Markus's twin sister, Isabella."

The woman outside the room was Isabella, Eli figured. He was not entirely surprised that she was believed to have an ability. She did fit the part, in a way.

"Isabella is what we call an automatic writer," Markus explained. "She has had the ability since we were children. Being born unable to speak seems to have gifted her with something else."

Eli nodded slowly and turned to the papers once more. "So, explain to me what's going on here. What am I signing and what is the job exactly?"

"We will be going to a location with a reputation for reported paranormal activity. You will not know the location details until we arrive, simply to ensure that no one is able to falsify their intuitive knowledge. We will be there for four days and three nights. You will leave your mobile behind, and it will be returned to you at the end of the investigation. We will be dropped off at the location and picked up at the end of the investigation. It will be quite like camping."

Eli glanced over the paperwork and read mostly general terms and conditions. However, there were a few other unique items, such as a statement declaring that Deittman and his affiliates were in no way liable in the event of possession. He raised a brow and looked at Deittman, who merely shrugged. It was likely that others had questioned the passage as well in the past. Separate from the terms and conditions was a half-completed contract—missing only his personal information. Included in the contract were the payment conditions.

"So, five thousand dollars?" Eli asked. It was awfully high for only a few days of work.

"Yes. That is our standard agreement for uniquely skilled individuals. You will be considered a contractor to my business and you will receive your payment in two parts—a deposit upon agreement and the balance at the end of our investigation," Deittman explained.

"Listen, I'm not complaining here, but I don't know many jobs offering that much outright—at least, legitimate jobs."

Deittman only chuckled. Eli was also probably not the first person who had said something along those lines.

"Of course. I understand any wariness you may have. However, I will be blunt. The pay is to lure you in and convince you to sign the contract before you can think about the matter further. Many people have reservations about going to a likely abandoned location and suffering a few days without modern conveniences. Also, you are signing away your ability to sue either myself or the property owners in case of injury."

Eli stared at Deittman with a bit of alarm.

"Well if you put it that way..."

"You seem like a smart man," Deittman said with a wave. "You would have thought of all of that yourself, I'm sure. Before you ask: no, it is non-negotiable. As I said, it is a standard agreement. We offer more for longer contracts, but this one is only three nights."

On the one hand, the price seemed a bit low if Deittman was freely admitting the danger. On the other hand, Eli really needed the money. Deittman knew that now, too, since Eli had already stated his inability to hold a job at the moment. That money would potentially be enough for him to pay for his shitty apartment for another few months and still give Sophia some to put towards Sarah's semester tuition payment. They were still a few grand short and he couldn't imagine Sophia had a plan to come up with the difference.

"Let's say something happens to me," Eli said cautiously. "Can the money be sent to my wife? I've got a kid to take care of."

"Of course. We will pay you or your spouse regardless of the outcome, so long as you do not voluntarily leave before the end of the investigation."

There had been a pit growing in Eli's stomach since he had entered the room. Unfortunately, it didn't seem to be a side effect of Deittman's device, which meant it was his own gut instinct telling him that this was a bad idea.

Well, five thousand dollars was five thousand dollars. He put pen to paper and signed his name.

CHAPTER 8

Eli quickly figured out why Deittman had intentionally put off interviews until just two days before the planned research trip. If there had been any more time, Eli may have reconsidered the entire offer and backed out completely. Even the money didn't seem worth putting himself into a position where he may be overloaded with visions of the past. By the time he started seriously reconsidering the matter, he was already piled into a small charter bus with a handful of other people.

The group had met at a loading dock on the University's campus at six thirty in the morning, much to Eli's dismay. The September weather was cooperating, but the sun had only just started to rise, and the chilly morning air was sure to linger. He wondered briefly if his jacket and long-sleeved shirts would be enough for the weekend.

Some of the other group members were probably wondering the same thing as they paced back and forth, trying to warm themselves. Eli remained silently to the side, leaning against a stone wall, observing the other members of their little group. Despite the sheer confidence Ash exuded a few nights earlier, she was nowhere to be found. Perhaps Deittman felt her abilities weren't worth the trouble of the loose canon. Perhaps she never showed up for her interview at all.

Deittman, Markus, and Isabella were, of course, in attendance. Once he had a good look at Isabella, he was almost a bit surprised she was going on a trip that Deittman had admitted may be dangerous. She was a petite, almost sickly-looking young woman. Eli was sure a strong breeze would knock her over. But there she stood, using sign language to communicate with her brother and Deittman. Did anyone else attending know enough sign language to communicate with the young woman? He certainly didn't.

There was a couple—were they a couple? Maybe they were co-workers? Regardless, there was a man and a woman who had quite a few bags. The woman stood in jeans, boots, a white blouse, and a grey blazer, pointing a finely manicured finger around her. As she gestured about the area, the man, who had somewhat spiky black hair and was dressed in jeans and a tight black tee shirt that screamed *asshole*, knelt and checked their bags as directed.

One of the bags resembled a heavy-duty camera bag. Reporters? The woman didn't strike Eli as the paranormal investigating sort, but then again, Deittman was proof that Eli didn't have a clue what to expect beyond what he saw on television.

Speaking of television…

Once the man stood up and faced Eli for a moment, Eli realized he *had* seen the man before. He was an Internet personality or something. He made videos documenting his own paranormal experiences and disproving others. Eli had stumbled across his series while researching his post-cognition and he was not at all impressed by the boisterous man.

This is shaping up to be a crack team…

To no one's surprise, there was quite a bit of resistance when Deittman insisted on collecting everyone's phones. Eli wasn't particularly eager to hand his phone over, even if it was going to be locked up, but he did it anyhow. He didn't exactly have a lot of people contacting him these days, and the only thing he may miss would be a call from a recruiter or something not nearly as pleasant.

With how things had been going for him, that would be just his luck. With a sigh, shut off his phone and placed it into the box with Markus's and Isabella's.

The nicely dressed woman attempted to persuade Deittman, but the man was steadfast. He stared her down until she turned off her phone, removed the battery, and placed her device into the box. The spiky-haired man also tried to convince Deittman, insisting his social media followers would be expecting him to check in—saying it would be good publicity for Deittman.

To Deittman's credit, he kept his face blank as the younger man spoke. Eli, on the other hand, couldn't help but give a low chuckle, which earned him a hard glare from Spikey Hair. One by one, the devices were placed away. Deittman locked the container with a key on his personal key ring and handed it over to Markus. Box in hand, Markus quickly walked into the University building.

A little while later, they loaded their bags into the undercarriage storage of the bus—Eli had a single duffle bag with some clothes since it was only going to be a few days—and then started to file on board. He had started to think that Ash wasn't coming after all, when she casually strolled around the corner, cigarette in hand and stuffed duffle bag at her side.

"You're late," Deittman said with a frown firmly in place.

"I don't get up this early for just anyone, you know," she said and stared back at Deittman over the rim of her sunglasses, tossing her cigarette butt to the asphalt and grinding it out under her heel. Since the storage area had already been closed up, she carried her bag on with her—not that it would take up much space. It was even smaller than Eli's.

"Mobile," Deittman said, blocking her way. He held out her hand. Ash reached into her jacket pocket and handed it over without any argument. She didn't bother turning it off.

She stepped onto the bus and gave Eli a nod before taking a seat behind him and putting her head against the window.

"We will be on our way in a few minutes," Deittman said from the front of the bus. "We should reach our destination at approximately one o'clock, barring any unforeseen circumstances. We will have a few stops along the way so that you may stretch and use the facilities, as well as eat lunch before our arrival."

Once Deittman was sitting, the driver pulled away from the curb and they were off.

Fifteen minutes in, Eli was wishing he had a pillow.

Getting through the city was, of course, awful. It took far too long for the bus to maneuver around the city through the stoplights and crosswalks, but eventually, they were on the highway heading north. As the scenery started to change from dense cityscape into the countryside landscape, Eli wondered where exactly they were going. So much for local. Was it even in-state? What was the condition of the location? It might be a hotel—they hadn't been told to pack pillows or blankets, so maybe the location was providing them. Was it a haunted mansion? That one actually sounded the most appealing.

Eli couldn't say he was well-versed in haunted house lore. For obvious reasons, it had never struck him as a fantastic idea to go visiting old, abandoned locations or places claiming ghostly activity. He knew Deittman was intentionally keeping their destination a secret so that no one could try to gain access to information ahead of time. Though he wasn't sure what difference it would make, he supposed perhaps Deittman was concerned about people faking paranormal activity based upon previous claims.

Now that he knew who his teammates were, Eli couldn't say he was surprised. He had no idea what the one woman's role was in the scheme of things beyond being the reporter working on a book, but he was sure the Internet personality was likely to go about making wild accusations—accusations that only Deittman, now, could confirm.

It was more difficult to claim that you're possessed by the spirit of an executed criminal when you're investigating... well, a theme park or something. The guy would look like a fool if he went around making assertions about an area that had never had any indication of paranormal activity.

After almost an hour and a half, Eli managed to nod off. Occasionally he was jolted awake when the bus hit a pothole or stopped too quickly, but he didn't fully rouse until they had stopped for a rest stop nearly three hours into the drive.

"We will remain for approximately ten minutes. Please be back promptly so that we may continue."

Deittman exited first, followed by Markus and Isabella. Eli let the others go off before him so he could reach back and give Ash a prod. She jumped a bit at his jab and squinted at him through her dark sunglasses.

"Rest stop," he said, rapping his knuckles against the window. "Dunno when we're stopping again. Figured you might want woken up."

"Thanks," she croaked out and climbed from her seat. Eli trailed behind, stepping off the bus and into the little rest station.

After Eli used the restroom, he found Ash staring blankly at the one vending machine in the building.

"If you stare at it hard enough, do you think it will give you a free drink?" Eli asked and shoved his hands into his pockets. No use feeling awkward around each other just because he had taken her home with him on a whim.

Ash sighed loudly. "Even if it did, it only has root beer. I hate root beer."

Eli hummed and shrugged in response. They stood for a moment longer before he turned and stared out the sprawling window of the rest stop. Deittman was already back and waiting at the bus's door.

"We should probably head back..."

"We have a few more minutes," she replied.

Well, she wasn't wrong. He hoped to go back and fall asleep to avoid any conversation with the other traveling companions. Then again, standing and stretching wasn't a bad thing. He didn't know how much longer he would have to sit in his small space. At least no one was in the seat next to him. If Ash decided to try to move into his seat, he was willing to push her right back out.

He liked his personal space. Sitting too close to someone for too long tended to make his skin crawl. It had taken him ages to comfortably sleep next to Sophia every night.

"Have you met the rest of our team?" Ash asked and finally took a few steps towards the door.

"Not really," Eli replied and passed her, opening the door first. "I recognize that guy though. I think he makes ghost videos or something."

"Yeah, that seems familiar," she said with a nod. "Maybe I've seen him. He gave me a smirk when he passed me. Didn't like it. I don't like his face. I have the urge to punch it."

Eli cracked a grin before wiping it from his face again. As he glanced at her, he saw she was serious. To be fair, the guy did have a punchable face, what with his permeant smugness and the cocky tilt of his chin. While Eli may not have been confrontational, he suspected Ash might not have the same reservations.

The pair climbed into the bus once more, and to Eli's relief, Ash had no interest in sharing a seat with him.

Ash, however, wasn't as lucky as to remain unbothered. Though Markus and Isabella were content enough to keep to themselves, the douchey ghost guy on board was not. When he walked back onto the bus, he dropped himself right next to Ash, much to her visible dismay—she didn't attempt to hide her disgust as her lips curled up in a sneer and she pulled her arm away from him.

"Hey, so, you two," he started, including Eli in his attempt at conversation, "are the psychics, right? So, like, what can you do? Talk to ghosts? Move things with your mind?"

"I will move you with my body if you don't find another seat," Ash said, scowling deeper.

That wasn't enough for the man. He smirked irritatingly at her and tried to nudge her with his shoulder, but she elbowed him in his bulky bicep. "Fuck off."

His expression faltered for a moment as he slipped into a glower. A heartbeat later it was gone, and his grin was wider than before. Eli's knuckles whitened as he grasped the back of the bus seat tighter.

"C'mon, don't be like that! We're going to be around each other for a few days! Might as well get to know each other. That's my partner, Marina," he said, nodding towards the well-dressed woman a few seats away. "And I'm Jackson Cohen—I'm pretty much an expert on the paranormal. I know my way around this sort of gig. If you stick with me, I can assure you, it'll be worth your while."

"I'm good—really," Ash replied and sunk down in her seat. She turned up her jacket collar, ending their exchange.

When Jackson realized he wasn't going to get any further interaction, the smirk wiped from his face and he clenched his jaw. He stared down at the woman before flicking his eyes up to meet Eli's suspicious gaze. With a sniff and a shrug, Jack roughly pushed himself up from the seat, making it a point to bump against Ash as he did. She didn't crack an eye.

Once they drove through the trees, everyone, including Deittman, sat forward a bit, straining their necks to get a look at the building as it came into sight.

If Eli had thought it was a bad idea for him to accept the research position before... Well, he began to wonder if he could make it back into town if he started walking at that very moment.

The building ahead of them was an imposing, dark brown brick structure akin to a castle, if not for the clinical nature of its design. The bus slowed to a crawl as the driver worked to navigate the long, unkempt driveway that began just beyond a set of dented, iron gates roughly pushed open for their arrival. With each long second of their approach, the building filled more and more of their vision until it was nearly all the passengers could see beyond the mass of trees behind them.

The entryway was made up of a large set of stone steps leading to a covered front porch—the top of it might've been a balcony, though most of the upper railing had crumbled over the years. Further above was a tower, a high spire topping it off. The building had two wings meeting at a center structure where two, imposing double doors awaited them. Though it was difficult to tell because the top floors of the wings didn't appear to be consistently built, Eli counted four floors.

What was most interesting, however, was the sleek black utility van already parked out front, its back doors wide open. A red SUV sat parked a few yards away from the van as well. It seemed there were other people already there and waiting for them.

It was still early in the afternoon, and the autumn sun was bright overhead. Even with ample sunlight cascading over the building, however, it was ominous. What could only be described as a dark aura pulsed from the structure, washing over him in a way that made his skin crawl.

Eli couldn't help but clench his jaw and dig his fingers deeper into the cushioned seat ahead of him.

Five thousand dollars was not enough, not for what this building was going to put him through.

"And so, I welcome you to Maple Hill Asylum," Deittman said, still staring straight ahead. "I hope that it holds good things in store for us."

Eli grimaced. Somehow, he figured his idea of 'good things' varied drastically from Deittman's.

CHAPTER 9

Once the bus was parked, everyone rushed into the aisles to scurry out the door. Deittman wore a joyous smile as he crossed the driveway to stand in front of the building, hands on his hips in admiration. Isabella practically skipped to his side as a breeze rustled through the trees, tousling her blonde locks—Markus was right on her heels, making sure she didn't disappear too far down the slope leading away from the asylum.

Jackson and Marina also headed towards the front entrance, pushing past Eli as they did so. He heard them muttering about how they would need to get their equipment running immediately—and how much they missed their phones.

Eli wandered down the driveway so he could take in the whole structure as he pleased. A shiver went down his spine, and though the wind was blowing, it was colder--deeper than the air itself. The entire atmosphere of the building made him uncomfortable. He had felt it a few times before, mostly instances when he was at a hospital. It was almost as if... as if there was a charge in the air, something he felt physically in a way most other people wouldn't understand.

Sure, there were worse places-- places of extreme tragedy and horror. Places so vile their histories left permeant marks upon the earth and against the so-called veil to the other side. But a hospital--an *asylum*--brought back so many memories of his youth that he could not help but feel as though the malicious energy radiating from the structure was targeting him in particular. There was so much negativity around him, so much lingering ill will, that he felt as if he were on the verge of stepping over a cliff. Instead of falling, however, he would be crossing over into a world meant to remain unseen if he took one wrong step.

Ninety-six hours. I just have to make it ninety-six hours. Then the money is mine.

The bus driver popped the storage area, and one by one they all filtered over to grab their belongings. Ash, since she already had her duffle bag, was standing far off to the side, smoking a cigarette and staring up at a window on the second floor. Eli grabbed his own duffle and was about to approach her when Deittman began ushering everyone together.

"Come along now, you must meet the other team members. They have only just arrived as well if I am not mistaken. I am sure that they will be eager to check in with us."

Eli followed after their designated group leader as they entered the building. The massive double doors were already open for them, but based on the dirt and leaves gathered in the foyer, they had likely been stuck open for some time prior to their arrival. The entryway floor was made up of grimy marble tiles which met thick planks of wood in the surrounding rooms. The one-white plaster walls were discolored from water damage with spider-web cracking every so many feet from years of the building settling. Though the foundation seemed sturdy enough, Eli's eyes flicked upward to watch for any wayward ceiling tiles.

Deittman led them through the foyer and then off to the right, down a hallway littered with small rooms—offices?—until they reached a much larger, open space. The ceiling reached up to the second story where there was a half-rotted wooden railing.

Three men were already standing in the room, clipboards in hand as they conversed. Upon further inspection, however, Eli realized there were two men and one *teenager*. The figure had his back to Eli, but once he shifted, Eli guessed the scrawny boy couldn't have been older than twenty. He was tan with short, dark, curly hair and wore a black hoodie.

The other two men noticed Deittman enter and gave him a nod before wrapping up their conversation. Looking at them side by side, the two men were polar opposites. Though they were both similar heights, one of them was bulky and dark with close-cropped black hair that reminded Eli of a military cut. He wore a plain black, long-sleeved shirt and utility pants with a walkie-talkie clipped to his belt. He was the one who seemed to do the majority of the talking.

His counterpart was lanky and pale, with brushed back, golden-blond hair and thick-rimmed glasses. He was wearing jeans and a button-down, and for whatever reason, Eli imagined that the man was the sort to wear vests as well.

"Everyone," Deittman said, waving the group into the room and motioning for them to join up with the others, "I would like to introduce the rest of our team."

Everyone filed into the spacious room and stood around cluttered folding tables haphazardly set about as if they were in the middle of set-up. Eli glanced over his shoulder to find Ash leaning against the doorway, still puffing on her cigarette. Though Deittman spared her an annoyed look, he let her continue. Eli supposed that if anything were to catch fire, Ash would at least be able to handle it.

Probably...
Maybe?

Eli had only seen her toy with a baseball-sized flame. Surely, she couldn't take on an inferno. He hoped he would never have to find out.

"I would like you to meet Christopher Stevens, Garrett Davies, and... I am so sorry, my dear boy, I have forgotten your name," Deittman said, looking at the youngest member of the team.

"Carlos. Carlos Torres," he said and gave a small wave to Eli and the other newly arrived members. "I'm only an intern."

"Good afternoon," said Christopher Stevens. Yes, he had definitely been in the military if the way he put his hands behind his back before he spoke was any indication. "Call me Stevens. I am one of the founding members of PTGS Paranormal. You may have heard of us, but probably not. We are serious investigators. We aren't interested in a TV deal, not interested in social media followers—"

Eli swore the man looked directly at Jackson when he said that last part.

"—We are only interested in scientifically-documented cases of true paranormal activity. We would rather come into a place like this and debunk all incidents than walk away with something questionable. I am a veteran, honorably discharged for a leg injury. I have seen true horror, and I can tell you, it doesn't come from abandoned buildings such as this. If you're expecting this to be like you watch on TV—or in web videos—you'll be disappointed. Stay calm and everything will go smoothly."

Though the man was certainly a hardened and intimidating sort, Eli found his presence to be comforting. He was like an immovable rock in a rushing river of negative energy. Eli hoped that if he did his best to follow directions and stay out of the man's way, they could get along just fine.

"I'm Garrett," said the put-together blond man. "My background is primarily in engineering. Some of the equipment we're using I have developed myself. I use our investigations as opportunities to field test my devices. I helped Dr. Deittman design some of his tech as well. Because they are rather finicky and not easily fixed or replaced at this time, please avoid touching any of my equipment. There are plenty of other things about for you to use, if you are so inclined. We have voice recorders, thermal cameras, K-IIs, EMF readers, laser grids, and MagLites, among other things. We will teach you as we go so that you're all comfortable with the equipment and can use everything when conduct our research in separate groups."

Garrett was agreeable as well. He reminded him of many of his former co-workers—people who preferred to be left alone with their computer rather than interact with people. Carlos didn't say anything more, but then, he was an intern—probably a student going along with the investigation for college credit, or something. Really, out of everyone, the only two people Eli wasn't particularly keen on were Marina and Jackson, but they didn't seem awfully keen on anyone else either.

Jackson was puffed up, taking personal offense to Stevens's words, which he rightly should since Stevens hadn't bothered to hide his distaste for the internet personality. Marina practically had her nose stuck up in the area, as if she were above everyone else.

"Let us go about and introduce ourselves as well, yes?" Deittman said. "Myself excluded, since we have all met. Markus, would you care to go first?"

"Of course," he said, "my name is Markus Valentinian, and this is my sister, Isabella." He placed a hand on her shoulder, and she smiled sweetly. "We are from Italy, though we spent most of our youth with our mother in England. I have a business degree myself, but I am a full-time employee of Dr. Deittman's firm, as is my sister. Now, I fully expect many of you to be skeptical, but my sister is what many people would consider to be a psychic. She is an 'automatic writer,' if you will, sometimes called a psychograph. We believe that because she is unable to speak, she was born with an extra sense and has a connection to whatever other world might exist."

Isabella clutched the notebook she was holding to her chest a bit tighter, as if she were expecting some sort of backlash. Skepticism flashed across Stevens and Garrett's faces, but they said nothing.

Jackson snorted and nudged Marina in the side.

"Of course, one of the abilities that's impossible to verify. Surprise, surprise," he said. Marina scowled and jabbed him with her elbow, shushing him.

Eli glanced back at Markus and found the soft-spoken young man was staring coolly at Jackson, though Jackson didn't notice.

Because Eli was standing next to Isabella, everyone turned to him next.

"Hey," he said, shoving his hands into his pockets and shifting in his spot. He didn't enjoy being the center of attention. "My name is Eli Gehring. Used to work in IT, now I guess I don't work in anything. I'm what people would call a post-cog. I see... imprints, I guess. 'Echoes' are what I sort of call them. Terrible moments in someone's life—like when they violently die. I figure in moments of trauma, some of our energy gets stuck in place, leaving people like me to witness it—even when I really don't want to."

"So..." Garrett started slowly, raising a brow at Eli, "you see ghosts?"

"I guess. I don't know," Eli said with a shrug. "They never interact with me or try to communicate or anything. It's literally just like watching a movie."

"That sounds like a ghost to me." Carlos hummed, interested.

"Maybe. Whatever. Who's next?" Eli said with a sigh.

Annoyingly, the next person to go was Jackson.

"My name is Jackson Cohen, and you probably recognize me from my channel *The Void Stares Back*." He waited to receive some sort of recognition for his work, but no one so much as batted an eye. Either no one had heard of him, or no one was impressed by him; Eli was willing to venture to guess it was the latter. Jackson scowled before clearing his throat slightly. "So, yeah, I'm a well-known paranormal investigator. I can pretty much guarantee that weird things will happen when— "

Eli didn't listen to the rest of whatever Jackson was saying. From the corner of his eye, he caught movement from atop of the balcony. He barely had time to sidestep, pulling Isabella with him to avoid a collision with an Echo. He hadn't had a clear view, but he thought the poor being had been pushed from the balcony.

"Excuse me?" Markus snapped, quickly stepping over to remove Eli's hands from Isabella's shoulders. Eli didn't bother to look up as the woman was pulled away from him.

He stared down at the floor, watching as blood pooled around the contorted body of what might have been a nurse based upon her white outfit and little hat. He had to step away to avoid getting blood on his shoes as it pooled underneath her. He was sure it wouldn't have actually stained the black cloth of his shoes, but it wasn't a risk he was willing to take.

It wasn't until he heard a beeping next to him that he was pulled from his thoughts.

Garrett crouched down, holding a small device at the area in front of Eli and watching as it's lights flared to life. Its beeping wasn't particularly loud, but it certainly seemed louder in the silence of the room.

"Are you seeing something?" Deittman asked curiously, ignoring Jackson's protests that he hadn't finished talking.

Eli squeezed his eyes shut for a moment and ran a hand through his dark hair. He took a few steps backwards until he hit one of the equipment tables. His words caught in his throat, and he cleared it a few times before speaking. He glanced down at the form but tried not to look too closely.

"A woman. Might've been a nurse or something. It's hard to tell because she's on her stomach—I can only see her back. A lot of blood—but she's still alive. She's gasping for air and... No, she's dead now. She's gone." The flashing lights and beeping on Garrett's device stopped at the same moment.

"Eli, can you please recount for us what you experienced?" Markus asked as Isabella opened her notebook. At the same time, Stevens fiddled with a recorder. Again, all eyes were on him. Eli clenched his jaw and frowned.

"I only glimpsed it out of the corner of my eye. I saw something go over the balcony, so I moved in case it was a real person. It's hard to tell sometimes—a lot of the time, actually. Can't do anything about it when it happens. Just gotta let it play out, I guess. I don't stay to watch if I can avoid it. Once they die, that's it. It goes away. Honestly, I won't be surprised if I see that one again if this is going to be our headquarters. Like I said earlier, it's a loop. It'll happen whether or not anyone's here to witness it. Sometimes they're every day at the same time, sometimes it's only one day a year. I don't know what rules they follow. I just know I see them," he explained with a shrug, shoving his hands back into his pocket. He glanced over at Isabella. "Sorry for grabbing you. Reflex, I guess."

She smiled and shook her head.

"I will admit, though I'm skeptical of your abilities, you certainly gave us something to help prove your credibility. Do not be offended if I am inclined to gather further research," Garrett said and hurried to mark down a few notes on a pad that was sitting out on one of the tables.

"I'm not offended at all."

After everyone settled down once more, Marina stepped forward from her spot along the side and directly to where the Echo woman's head had been moments before. Eli winced at the woman's callousness, even if she couldn't have known what she was doing. Marina cleared her throat, catching everyone's attention.

"My name is Marina Martelli. Until recently I was a reporter for GWN News. I've decided to move onto other ventures. Currently, I'm working on an editorial piece about old facilities left to deteriorate. This location will surely make for a good basis for my book," she said and flipped some of her brown hair over her shoulder. She smiled at everyone, perhaps expecting someone to ask a question of her.

No one did.

Eli figured no one particularly cared about some journalist. Then again, maybe he should care—he gave his full name to a reporter. What if she used him in her piece? Could she do that without his permission? Did the waivers he signed for Deittman give her permission? He should have read those contracts closer instead of focusing on the payment section.

If anyone else was concerned, they didn't let on. Surely he was blowing it out of proportion.

Once she had finished, everyone turned toward at Ash, who was still leaning against the door frame. Her cigarette had gone out, though the smoke still wafted through the room.

"My name is Ash and I am also one of the lovely psychic bunch," she said with a bored sigh. She pulled her lighter out of her pocket and clicked it open. "I don't see or talk to ghosts, I'm just here to be a battery and bail you out if you come across something nasty. People call me a pyrokinetic--"

"*Bullshit,*" Jackson said, crossing his arms. "Ghosts are one thing. No one's ever proved that anyone's had some sort of kinetic anything."

Ash rolled her eyes. "No one you know. Most of us like to keep ourselves out of the public eye. Don't want to be a lab rat in a government facility. Do you really think I would stand here and claim to be a pyrokinetic without being prepared to back it up?"

There were some murmurs through the group, but nothing from Deittman, Markus, or Isabella.

83

Presumably, all three of them had already seen examples of her abilities.

Ash placed her hand over the lighter and the small flame rose. She pulled her hand away and the flame was hovering just a bit above her palm, as Eli had seen before. Quickly, Ash pocketed the lighter and then put her free hand out. She made a motion with the flame that reminded Eli of someone idly toying with a ball before she willed the flame into her other hand. To Eli's amazement, the flame actually grew. For a few more moments, she juggled the fire back and forth in her hands, increasing its size until it reached almost the size of a basketball.

"No," Jackson said, incredulous, shaking his head, "It's gotta be a trick. You've probably got something up your sleeve or something."

Ash shrugged and balanced the large ball of fire in one hand so she could use her other to slide up her sleeve. She moved to the other hand and did the same—but did so gingerly. Eli wondered if the flames grew harder to control the larger they became. "Believe me or don't. I don't care." She moved her hands together slowly, and the ball began to shrink until she was able to clasp her hands together, extinguishing it completely.

"That's amazing!"

Eli jumped when a new voice spoke from behind him. He and a few others turned on their heels to see who had spoken.

Standing in the second entrance of their room was a man who might have been Eli's age, or perhaps a few years older. He had short brown hair, dark eyes, and a wide smile. At the very least, Eli was relieved to find the others also looking at him, so he was very much real.

"I didn't mean to startle you guys! I'm so sorry! I just got back from getting the water turned on in this part of the building," he said with a laugh.

"Ah, Mr. Colton, I presume," Deittman said. He stepped forward, extending a hand. The man took it and shook it.

"Yup, and you must be Dr. Deittman. Sorry for not being here to greet you—I helped these guys get in," he said, jabbing his thumb towards Stevens and Garrett, "and then went to get the water turned on for you. It should be fine, but it'll be cold, and I wouldn't recommend drinking it. I'm sure it's fine for using the facilities or showing though. The U-Haul with the cots left right before you got here. I'd be surprised if you guys didn't pass him on the way out. You're all taken care of."

"Ah, wonderful, wonderful," Deittman replied. "May we visit that area first so that everyone may stow their luggage?"

"Sure, of course, follow me."

The group of ten followed after the man, down the hallway and through another door. This new area was done up a bit differently—it had hideous, peeling yellow wallpaper and some dusty old furniture. There was even an old vending machine, still stocked with long-expired candy.

The man turned to face the group and cleared his throat, clasping his hands in front of himself, rocking on his heels almost excitedly.

"So, everyone, I'm Vincent Colton. I now own the lovely Maple Hill. I've only recently inherited it, so I can't say I know every detail. I've done my research though to help you before I head out. This area here is the nurses' station. Each floor has one, but this one is the nicest since this is where nurses brought visitors. At Dr. Deittman's request I've brought in cots for everyone and set up two rooms—one for the men, and one for the women. Ladies, I do apologize, your little room is a bit cramped, but I was told there were only three of you, so I figured it was better to keep you all in one area, rather than spreading you out. If you'll follow me..." he said, gesturing, before turning to continue walking.

They entered into a sitting room and turned left into the first room with seven cots awkwardly spaced about the room. Eli grimaced as he appraised them. They weren't very long, and he was rather tall. They didn't look particularly comfortable either, nor did the thin excuse for a pillow. He really should have thought to bring his own. Through another open doorway on the left side of the room was an area that may have once been an attached office. Actually, he was sure he spied drag marks leading out of the doorway. Definitely and office, once upon a time.

"I left some emergency candles and flashlights, just in case," Vincent explained, pointing to a pile on one of the ladies' beds. "I know you have your own stuff, but I figured better safe than sorry, right?"

One by one, the girls started to claim their beds. Though Ash had been steps behind Isabella, Marina maneuvered her way into the room to claim the bed in its own little nook. She glared over at Ash and Isabella, daring them to object to her choice. Isabella merely raised her brows Ash who shrugged and shook her head.

"I really don't care. I'm up all night anyhow so I probably won't be here with you most of the time."

Isabella moved to take the one furthest from the door. She set her little purse down as Markus stepped around Ash's cot to set down Isabella's bag. The first thing she did was unzip her stuffed suitcase—a suitcase bearing a foreign designer logo—and pull out a blanket that was crammed in on top.

Smart girl.

The men went about picking their spots, though everyone wisely chose to let Deittman choose his bed first. Even Stevens and Garrett, who had been there before them and could have put their belongings out when they arrived, waited until Deittman had set his things down. He chose the cot closest to the entrance. Eli would have thought Markus would have chosen the cot next to Deittman, but he did not. He hurried to put his belongings on the cot next to the ladies' little room, much to Jackson's dismay, to be nearer to Isabella.

Vincent walked through the sitting area once more and then through the remaining door.

"Over here is the washroom," he said, pointing to the door out to the group. Eli didn't bother to try to get into the small room. He could see most of it from the open door, and besides, it was a bathroom—what else was there to know? "There's a towel and washcloth for each of you. It isn't much, really, sorry. It's extremely difficult to get water in the place, I found out. I'm mostly hoping everything just makes it for the few days you're here. The shower was a decontamination shower, so there isn't a curtain or anything. You'll have to lock the door," he said with a shrug.

Marina tsk-ed from in front of Eli, but hey, what did she expect when she signed up to go to an abandoned building? It was *abandoned*. A hot shower simply wasn't going to be one of the amenities for four days.

Vincent shuffled out of the bathroom and stood before them, hands clasped.

"So... any questions?" he asked, looking around. They all looked to one another, shaking their heads. "Great! Let's start the tour. I'll show you which areas I think are unsafe and some of the stories I know. I don't know many, unfortunately, but hopefully I can give you some ideas of the hot spots."

CHAPTER 10

They hadn't even made it the entire way up the stairs to the second floor before Eli's heart started to race. He knew something bad had happened in the stairwell. Since a place like Maple Hill was such a new experience for him, he wasn't quite sure what to make of the tingling sensation creeping up his spine. It had happened before when he was experiencing an Echo, but there was nothing around, at least, not that he could see.

"Now, bear in mind: Vincent will only provide enough basic details for us to begin our investigation. No names—we would like to try to gather information to verify *after* the fact to aid in the authenticity of our research," Deittman explained, following a few steps behind their 'tour guide.'

Eli wondered what the point was of Deittman collecting their phones if they were going to be given information anyhow. Surely whatever they would be told might be enough to fake recordings, or something. But, Eli supposed, they all needed to have an idea of where to start. The sprawling building, with its dozens upon dozens of rooms and narrow side corridors, was simply too much to cover organically.

"Okay, if everyone would pause here for a moment," Vincent said from their right. The stairs wrapped around, and he was standing on the platform between the floors, just a bit above everyone else. "From what I understand, there is a death certificate for an elderly patient who fell down this flight of stairs. I don't know the exact details, but Maple Hill had been converted into a retirement home for close to a decade. From 1983 to 1994, only about half of the building was in use—this half. The other wing was closed down after a fire broke out in 1976. The building was evacuated and sat unused for about four years before the owners chose to reopen it with a new function. We'll get to that part of the building, but I honestly don't recommend anyone go wandering around, since it did suffer structural damage. Most of the real dangerous areas were torn down or closed off. It wouldn't do to have an elderly patient wander over and fall through the floor."

"If I may," Markus said, once Vincent had finished, "we've visited similar facilities in the past. Many people would have likely died here. Does this death in particular stand out from the others?"

Vincent shrugged. "I'm not really sure. This happened to be one I found marked down in a former employee's journal. The death was ruled accidental because they believed the woman was in a wheelchair and mistakenly turned down the stairs— she probably had dementia. However, staff reported seeing a figure resembling an elderly woman in the area after the fact, so I think that's why this incident was memorable."

Vincent turned from them and continued onto the next floor.

Unlike the first floor, which was rather bright because most of the rooms only had empty door frames, the second floor was quite a bit darker. Most of the patient room doors with shut, with only a handful cracked open to provide thin slivers of daylight from the rooms' windows.

"Alright," Vincent said, turning around to begin walking backward. "So, if you take a peek in the rooms, you'll notice they're still mostly furnished with what was here when the building closed down in the early 90's. From what I gather, the government funding had essentially stopped because the condition of the building had deteriorated, along with a handful of abuse reports. It turned into a private institution for a very short period, but residency had drastically decreased. In the end, only about fifty-five patients remained, most of whom had family who wanted to be 'hands-off' in their care. The institution ran out of funding and pretty much shut down overnight. A few patients who were within driving distance of families were dropped off on doorsteps with a box of their things and those who weren't were sent to the closest care facility, which was Valley View Manor across the state at the time."

"That can't be legal!" Marina said with a gasp.

Vincent shook his head. "Well, no, it probably wasn't. But by then, the owners were bankrupt, and any legal action would've been civil, so no one could really get anything out of them."

Their group continued onward. The hallways were spacious enough to fit four of them shoulder-to-shoulder without any issue getting through, though they frequently had to sidestep miscellaneous items littering the hallways. Some beds had been pulled out of the rooms, a few filing cabinets lay sprawled across the floor, and of course, the stereotypical dusty wheelchair sat smack dab in the middle of the hall. Eli found that to be the worst— he kept staring at it, expecting it to move across the floor on its own.

Once they made it about halfway down the hallway, they arrived at the balcony overlooking their little headquarters. He craned his neck to peer down without getting too close and found he had a perfect view of the cluttered equipment tables.

"This floor, back when this was an asylum, was primarily for the mildest cases—nonviolent, to be sure. I don't know who thought putting a balcony in a looney bin was a good idea. To no one's surprise, we know of at least one case of a nurse going over the side."

The group turned and looked at Eli, giving him approving nods. He stared straight ahead at Vincent and ignored them.

"It was boarded up after the incident, but when it was turned into a retirement home, it was converted again. You can tell that the balcony railing is higher than normal. That's so none of the patients could go over without deliberately trying. Over there," he pointed to a desk a few feet away from them, "was a nurses' station, so I guess that's why they didn't usually have too many problems."

"Don't you think it's more likely that the nurse was pushed over?" Jackson asked, crossing his arms. "I mean, it seems pretty unlikely that a normal person just 'whoops, went over the side.'"

"I'm not sure. Maybe the railing was damaged? Who knows? I wish I had more info for you, but I'm not much of a tour guide," Vincent said with a laugh, rubbing the back of his head. "I've only owned this place for a few months myself."

As they walked by the nurses' station, Eli noticed papers scattered about the area—some on the desk, some in open drawers, some around the floor. He stopped and picked one of them up. "This is a patient record," he commented, surprised to see that it was left behind. It had a name, birthday, and social security number listed.

"You'll find them all over the place," Vincent replied. He sighed and ran his hand over his nearly bald head. "I've got no idea if I have some sort of legal obligation to do something with them since HIPAA didn't exist when it closed. The previous owners didn't bother doing anything with it once it was closed. Well, that was the state, technically, so maybe that's why? I don't know. Obviously when my aunt and uncle didn't do anything either once purchased this place... Do me a favor and don't, like, steal the information or anything. I... might get in trouble."

Eli shook his head and set the paper back down on the desk counter. The desk itself was inset around the counter, which was raised to be at a comfortable level for anyone standing. Pens, pencils, a cracked mug, and even an old clipboard with a shift rotation schedule still covered the surface, abandoned by their owners. Maple Hill had truly shut down overnight, with everything left in its place until probably trespassers got to it.

He wondered about his own records. He had been in hospitals similar to this as a kid when he went through his suicidal phases. Were his own records sitting around somewhere for someone to find? Hopefully, they were all digital by the time he had gone through.

"Okay, so here you'll find the stairs split off."

There was an open doorway just ahead of them, leading to a set of stairs which went straight down to the first floor—further back in the entryway Eli suspected, based on the flooding sunlight and mass amounts of leaves he saw at the foot of the steps. To the right of the stairwell entrance was a small set of stairs that led upwards to a nicely carved wooden door.

"This style of asylum, called a Kirkbride facility, had this central area in the middle with the two wings. Each wing had additional sections staggered in a way to maximize sunlight exposure and fresh air, which doctors believed were key in healing the majority of the patients. Now, this main area here was used for the head doctor and his family. It was actually locked when I got here so I had to go through all of the keys to find the right one. It took almost half an hour." Vincent said and stepped up to the door. He reached out to open it, but it was locked.

Again, apparently.

He sighed loudly and *thunked* his head against the door. "Give me a few minutes. You can all... explore or something."

Vincent pulled an antique ring of keys from his pocket and started sliding through them, looking for whichever one opened the door.

Eli wasn't particularly eager to go snooping about. He was sure he would have plenty of time to do that later when Deittman inevitably made him go out to test his abilities. Honestly, he hoped if someone was chosen it would be Ash—someone to give a charge to the paranormal air, without being expected to do anything. He doubted they would let him off the hook, especially after he had already shown his hand down below.

He walked back and leaned against the nurse's station, staring down the hallway. Ash was still lingering nearby as well, leaning on the rotted-out balcony—which Eli thought was unwise, but she seemed at ease.

Garrett and Stevens walked to the end, little devices in hand. Carlos trailed behind them, making notes as they directed him. They carried masking tape as they went, marking down Xs on the floor or the door frames. They placed one in the stairwell before walking back, making a note in one of the patient rooms, and putting an X on the door frame. They made their way back up and put one at the balcony railing as well, asking Ash to move. She didn't, saying there was another two yards of balcony for them to mark off, they didn't need her spot.

He half-listened to their squabble as he stared off. He realized then how incredibly drained he felt. It wasn't like total exhaustion, but it was a fatigue he associated with staring at his work computer for a few hours on end without a break. As he became aware of it, Eli could practically feel the pressure and stiffness that had built up in his neck and shoulders from the uncomfortable bus ride.

He sighed and gazed down the hallway. After a few even breaths, his vision began to blur. Blinking, he tried to shake away the shapes that had started to move in his peripherals to disappear. They did not. They instead crossed into his normal vision.

Then he realized they weren't just crossing his vision, they were *crossing the hallway*. He was seeing spheres of light casually amble down the hallway and into or out of rooms. He squeezed his eyes shut and tucked his chin down, pinching the bridge of his nose.

"You okay?" Ash asked him, causing him to jump. He looked up at her and then down the hallway. Gone. All gone.

"Yeah, fine," he lied and turned from her, walking down to join Deittman, Markus, and Isabella. He was only a few steps away when Vincent let out a cheerful, "*ah-ha!*"

As Vincent pushed the door open, a rush of air burst out, flowing down the hallway, rustling the patients' records sitting halfway down the hall at the nurse's station.

Everyone fell silent as a breeze—which was more like moist, warm breath rather than the cool fall air to which they were becoming acclimated—washed over their bodies.

"It's, er, a bit stuffy up here because all of the windows are closed," Vincent said and slowly moved forward. Though he tried to put on a brave face, Eli watched the man carefully stretch his head forward before taking a tentative step into the room.

Garrett and Stevens were quick to rush to the front of the group, holding their investigating devices ahead of them like weapons. When they moved past Jackson, he hissed at them, causing Stevens to stop and size up the other man.

"You want to go in first?" Stevens asked, narrowing his eyes at Jackson.

Jackson, to his credit, did his best to meet the man's alpha male challenge, but he couldn't quite make it. Stevens had an air of authority Jackson could only imitate. "*Pfft*, well you're already ahead of me, so *by all means*," Jackson said, trying to save face. He over-dramatically swept his arms to the side with a mock bow.

With a deepened frown, Stevens went forward and followed after Vincent and Garrett.

From his spot behind the rest of the group, Eli caught Deittman giving Markus a look, who responded with a knowing shake of the head. This was certainly going to cause problems throughout the duration of their trip.

Eli had to wonder why, exactly, Jackson had been allowed to join the group. Had he sought Deittman out? Did he pay Deittman to let him come along? Maybe that was how Deittman funded his expeditions—charging non-essential members for their spot in his hopeful glory.

"I would put money on the likelihood of Jackson getting his face beat in by the end of all this," Ash muttered from next to Eli. He glanced at her and nodded in agreement. As he did, his eyes were drawn to her hand, where she was clicking her brass lighter open and close, open and close.

He took a few steps towards the door but then stopped and turned to her, putting his hand on her arm to cause her to pause. Once they were the only two left in the hallway he spoke. "Hey... theoretically, if there was something... *bad*... here. Would you be able to... I don't know... fight it?"

Ash stopped clicking her lighter and stared back at him. She raised a brow as a slight smirk danced on her lips. "I imagine Deittman is hoping we'll find out."

She pulled away from him and started up the small set of steps. Just before entering, she looked back at him over her shoulder.

"I'll tell you this—if shit goes down here, and I have a feeling it will, one way or another... It won't be Stevens you'll want with you."

The middle area on the second floor looked unlike anything else they had seen so far. Eli had to wonder why, exactly, they weren't staying in *this* area.

It was certainly musty, and the room showed its age. Whereas the rest of the building looked as though it was crumbling and covered in a layer of dirt, however, this area was covered in a visible layer of dust. As Vincent said, it was a bit stuffy and Eli had to cover his mouth to stop from coughing. Carlos had a sneezing fit, causing dust to scatter about him and cover the device in Garrett's hand.

That being said, it was... quite lovely. It had dark, stained hardwood floors, beautiful woven throw rugs, and a couch right out of a 1950's home magazine. Wooden furniture was placed strategically about the primary sitting area—a coffee table, writing desk, and even a dining table still showcasing place mats and a vase filled with fake flowers. There was a kitchenette towards the front of the building, on one side of the table, and a small bedroom on the other. In the back of the area was a bathroom, equipped with an incredible clawfoot tub. Across from it was what appeared to be a master bedroom.

Eli found it a bit strange that everything was in such well-kept condition, down to the bedding still made in the back rooms. Had trespassers never made their way into the Doctor's Quarters? Was it so well insulated that not even a stray squirrel or raccoon managed to make themselves at home? It was eerie; it was all *too* well preserved.

"This would be so much more comfortable than the rooms downstairs," Marina muttered, staring at the modest master bed.

"Well," Vincent said, wiping his hand down his face and neck. "Well, two things. I couldn't get water up here. Only one of the pipe systems is still working, so you wouldn't have been able to use the bathroom here. But, more than that..."

He sighed and let his arms flop to his sides.

"I don't like the feel of this area. This is the only way into the old asylum area—that door over there," he pointed to a door directly opposite of the one they had entered across the room. "That's the only one *not* completely sealed off from this side of the building when it reopened. I did check and you can unlock it. I'll tell you what I've heard and then we'll keep going."

Everyone stood in a semi-circle around Vincent. The room was eerily silent and when any of them shifted, the creaking of the wood echoed loudly through the air.

"This was where the head doctor and his family would stay, and it had been that way since expansions started in the late eighteen hundreds. This area was barely updated through the decades, as you can tell. The last one to live here during his full tenure was a doctor who was here in the forties. He's probably the most notorious individual to be associated with Maple Hill. His name was Dr. Bernard Pollock, and he was responsible for the death of a great many patients here."

Eli stiffened as he swore he felt hot breath on the back of his neck. His first instinct was to twirl around and see if anyone was behind him, but he refused simply because there was a chance he might see an unwanted Echo.

Deittman *tsk'd* loudly and shook his head, an annoyed frown planted firmly in place. "As I said, you are not to use any names during our tour."

Vincent shook his head. "Damn, I'm sorry. I wasn't thinking. It's the story I know best out of everything, so I just started my spiel. Sorry about that. I hope it won't mess up too many things for you."

Deittman opened his mouth, as if to list out the reasons why Vincent had put a dent in their investigation plans, when Markus spoke. Eli got the sense Markus was often the peacekeeper in Deittman's entourage.

"Did he die here?" Markus asked.

Vincent shook his head. "He did not. His wife and young daughter did die in the building though. After a young nurse anonymously tipped off the authorities, it was discovered he had been faking death certificates in order to avoid unwanted attention. Dr. Pollock was never convicted for the numerous deaths—which are speculated to be in the hundreds—because he had done it all in the name of medical research. He claimed to be working to find a cure for mental illness, which was a noble cause of course, but as we know, impossible because there are so many different forms of illness. Regardless, this was at a time when the United States needed every able-bodied man they could get because of World War Two, so when he said he was hoping to give the military those needed individuals, they let him slide. His medical license was eventually revoked."

Eli saw Garrett and Stevens share skeptical glances.

"One moment," Garrett said, raising his hand. "Now, Stevens and I did our research on this place ahead of time—we, of course, were told the location ahead of time as professionals."

Jackson scowled and huffed, looking away.

"We did find a bit of information on Dr. Pollock, but we did not find those details anywhere. How can you be sure what you said is true? We did not find that his daughter and wife died here, only the year of their deaths."

Vincent shrugged and shifted about uncomfortably. "That's because it was my grandmother who was the anonymous source."

There was a collective creaking in the room, starting at the door to the asylum, then a rumbling through the floorboards. Everyone quickly turned from their spots to look around them as Garrett's device started beeping and Stevens's gave off a high-pitched beeping. From the corner of his eye, Eli watched as the door back to the hospital side, as he dubbed it, slowly started to close.

CHAPTER 11

Eli was completely bewildered. Despite all he'd seen, he'd never actually experienced something interacting with the physical world. He didn't know what to do. Neither did anyone else, for that matter. Everyone was staring at the door in shock—though Deittman, Garrett, and Stevens were hurriedly scribbling notes and raising devices.

It was only Ash, who was standing closest to the door, with the wherewithal to spring over and grab it to keep it from closing them in.

Much to Eli's horror, it pulled her forward.

When it didn't stop once she grabbed it, Ash threw her body between the door and the frame, letting out a pained cry as it continued to try to close despite the obstruction. Eli was next to reach the door, grabbing at it before he even realized it. He placed one foot against the frame and putting his entire weight into pulling the door open. Markus was next, followed by Jackson—much to Eli's surprise. It took all three of the men to wrench the door open. Ash stumbled out of the doorway, falling down the small set of stairs and then remaining on the ground, her arms wrapped around her torso and waist in pain.

Isabella slipped through next, running down to help Ash. The others followed while Eli, Markus, and Jackson awkwardly maneuvered around the door so that none of them let go until they were all on the other side of the door.

It slammed shut behind them.

And then... the lock clicked from the other side after he reached the steps.

"Holy shit," Jackson said, voice raspy, once they were all standing at the bottom. Most of them had spread out down the hallway, gathering around the balcony to stand in the sunlight pouring through the windows, drawing comfort from the gentle warmth. Jackson clutched his head in his hands, pacing around. "Holy shit, that was *real*."

"I thought you were used to the paranormal," Stevens snapped. His face was twisted in anger moreso than terror, but perhaps it was his defense mechanism.

Jackson opened his mouth to reply but then thought better of it and shut it again, continuing to pace around. "Not like that, I'm not!"

Eli was surprised to find himself shaking. After a lifetime of being forced to witness terrible things, he thought nothing could be worse. Turns out--he was wrong. Experiencing something he *couldn't* see trying to lock them in a room was *so much worse.*

Once Ash was standing, her back facing the rest of them, she lifted her shirt to let Isabella assess the damage from the door, revealing the edges of a sprawling back tattoo. Isabella furrowed her brows and gingerly ran her hands along the other woman's rib cage. She gently tapped Ash's waist and gave her a reassuring smile, tugging her shirt down. Ash nodded, letting out a puff of air and groaning.

Vincent released his grip on the counter to the nurse's desk and let out a loud exhale. "Should we... continue?"

"Oh, why yes, certainly!" Deittman said, an amused smile on his face. "This is what I've paid to experience, after all."

100

"We shouldn't stay here!" Marina shrieked, running a nervous hand through her hair. "This—this isn't what we signed up for!"

Deittman shrugged, "oh? Well, you are free to leave. You'll have a difficult time doing so, though—the bus has departed. I suppose you could leave with Vincent here when it is time."

Eli couldn't blame their guide for not planning to stay with them. He gave Vincent credit just for doing the work to the building prepared for the team. Who knew what he had to deal with when he was walking around alone? Eli himself was thinking of taking the offer to leave despite the forfeiture of the money…

"You've got to be crazy to want to stay here!" Marina turned towards Ash and tossed up her arms. "Look at you! You're actually hurt from this! What if you had broken something? You can't be thinking of sticking around!"

Ash adjusted her shirt and rubbed the center of her rib cage with a bit of a grimace.

"What I'm thinking is that I'm glad I have a bottle of whiskey in my bag. I'll be fine. Next time you all see a door shutting on its own, don't just stare at it, 'kay?"

Eli caught Markus's eyes lingering on Ash for a few moments with a faint, approving smile on his face. Deittman was unsurprised by the sudden activity, and neither Markus nor Isabella appeared upset by it. Perhaps their team had seen or experienced more than they let on.

"So, we continue on, yes? I should like to hear more about this doctor," Markus said lightly as Isabella approached him. They stared at Vincent until he reluctantly nodded.

"Yeah, alright," Vincent sighed, "but I'll tell you more about the doctor when we're back downstairs. I don't want to talk about him now."

Before they continued back to the stairwell to go up to the next floor, Carlos marked off an X at the foot of the stairs to the Doctor's Quarters.

101

The group was on heightened alert as they slowly made their way to the third floor.

"Okay, so I don't know much about this section. I've found records from staff who saying there was a little boy who liked to play with marbles in this room—" he pointed at room 312, "—but some say it was a little girl who liked dolls. I'm not sure which, so if you have any toys maybe you can figure out what they prefer."

Vincent seemed to have lost his luster. He was walking briskly from room to room, giving them less of a chance to look around. For the most part, the hallway looked very similar to the one below them. Light filtered in from the small windows, highlighting the peeling paint and wallpaper. One of the rooms Eli passed had cut-outs of flowers pasted to the walls, most of which were barely clinging onto the surface. More cut-outs littered the floor.

"Ladies, you may not like it up here. Supposedly there's an old man on this floor who likes to pinch behinds and grab hair. Guys are usually left alone, but sometimes they feel like someone pinches their arms. Again, this is from staff reports in the nineties," Vincent said.

Unlike the floor below, which had the Doctor's Quarters in the center, this one did not have a separate middle section. The end of the hallway led to a stairwell leading up to the next floor and down the entire way to the entryway. "It won't be a problem right now but be careful using these steps at night. I'm pretty sure we have bats."

They didn't head straight for the stairwell, but instead to a small set of steps, like the ones below, that led to a slightly raised area. Next to the stairs was a short ramp which Eli imagined was to allow gurneys or wheelchairs access. After they reached the platform, he saw a closed elevator door to the right.

"There are two elevators on this side of the building. This one went to the fourth floor, this floor, the main floor, and the basement. The floor below us had its own elevator as a private lift to the Doctor's Quarters. It would have been weird for the rest of the staff to have access, I guess. Be really careful around the elevator. Obviously, they don't work, but you'll notice the one upstairs is stuck open. You don't want to fall down it."

Vincent pulled a small flashlight from his back pocket and clicked it on before heading up the stairs. Garrett, Stevens, Carlos, and Deittman also had the foresight to bring flashlights with them. They staged themselves between the other members of the group so no one would be left in the dark as they climbed the stairs to the fourth floor.

There was squeaking above them; there were indeed bats.

The fourth floor was different from the others. The ceiling was lower, and it was very warm despite it being a cool September day. The floors were entirely wooden with discoloration from a leaky roof. Though Eli didn't believe he was going to fall through, everyone subconsciously made an effort to spread themselves out, just in case in the floorboards were weak.

The rooms were small, but they all had closets and tiny windows. They also had no overhead lights, unlike the rooms on the other floors. Some of the rooms were painted in different colors, though the paint was chipping.

"We aren't too far from a little town, and many of the employees were residents of it. However, \quite a few staff members lived on site and these were their quarters. You can see that they're tight. There were rooms on the other side as well, the asylum side, but the entire fourth floor is gone. Because the floors were wooden, the fire destroyed it all. Story is that there were four deaths up here. One was an overdose in the sixties, and one was a double murder-suicide in the 1920s. A nurse was having an affair with a doctor who lived up here. Her husband found out, snuck in, and when the guy came back after his shift—*bam*. Head blown off. When the nurse came in to 'visit' the doctor, the husband killed her as well, then himself."

Vincent stepped up to one of the rooms—407—and held out three fingers signaling the number of deaths, then stepped further down to 416 and held out one finger.

Eli walked down the hallway and stopped at 414 when he heard a sigh coming from the room. He braced himself and peered inside.

There was a person floating in the room. Eli assumed that at some point there had been a bed where the body was horizontally hovering above, needle in hand.

"You sure it wasn't 414 and not 416?" he asked, staring into the room. The man, who wore something akin to an older style of scrubs, blinked for a few moments before his head rolled to the side. He seemed to stare at Eli until the body disappeared.

Neither Garrett nor Stevens made it in time to check for any energy signatures on their handheld devices. They shook their heads and turned back at Eli.

"Trust me, if you're gonna monitor a room, do this one," Eli said, and the group continued down the hall.

"I don't like this hallway," Carlos said once he reached the end and looked back. "I don't know what it is. It's not like it's got a bad atmosphere or anything—I mean, I guess it should, if such awful things happened here—but it's not that. I just can't put my finger on it."

Isabella strolled over curiously and stood next to Carlos, looking down the hallway as well, her head tilted to the side. After a moment, she opened her notebook and wrote something, showing Carlos.

He nodded thoughtfully. "Oh, yeah, I guess that's more like it."

Once Carlos noticed a few people staring at him, a bit of red creeped up his neck.

"Um, she said it's like a funhouse. I think that's accurate. I think it's something about the height of the ceiling and the open doors— it plays tricks on your eyes."

After Garrett, Stevens, and Carlos finished taping off their markers and making notes, the group went down the stairwell to the bottom, exiting into the atrium. This stairwell was mostly wood and creaked loudly, unlike the one they had taken up. That one, the one on the far side of the wing, was newer.

"Keep use of this stairwell to a minimum," Deittman said as he stepped down into the atrium. "Too much noise contamination."

"Before we go any further," Vincent said, glancing out the front door, "does anyone want to take a break? Maybe go outside for a few minutes? We'll want to grab more lights before we go down to the basement anyhow."

"I think that would be for the best," Deittman said. "If you have not already picked up a flashlight, please take one and keep it on your person at all times."

Nearly everyone started to head towards the headquarters, their shuffling footsteps echoing down the abandoned halls. Ash, however, chose to go straight outside, a cigarette already in hand.

Once back in headquarters, Garrett opened a worn canvas bag in need of unpacking. He handed Eli one of the smaller flashlights with a clip on the side to attach to his collar. "I'm going to go step outside too," Eli said to Garrett, who nodded.

Eli ventured back down the hallway on his own, hoping that taking a break from the negative energy in the building would help ease his tense shoulders and neck. As soon as he was out in the sunlight, the effects were almost immediate, and he let out a sigh of relief. Looking around, he saw Ash sitting on the lawn, gazing out into the trees surrounding the asylum. Eli walked over and joined her without invitation, sitting down in the overgrown grass a few feet away.

"Hey, are you sure you're okay?" he asked when she didn't spare him a glance. "I know I'm pretty freaked out, and I wasn't the one pinned by a door."

She let out a puff of smoke and shook her head. "It's not a big deal. I'm not easily rattled."

He stared at her for a few moments, furrowing his brows. It was one thing to act tough—it was another to stupidly ignore the fact they were in danger.

"I get that... But what happened was... extreme. I think anyone would agree. I feel like it's only going to get worse. What happens if something like that happens again but no one else is around to pry the door open? You've trailed behind everyone else since we got in. If someone's going to get hurt, it's going to be you."

Ash smiled, to his surprise. It wasn't snarky—not a smirk or a grin. Just a smile.

"Listen, it's awfully sweet of you to be concerned for me, but if something like that happens again and I'm alone, you'll have bigger problems than door-closing ghosts."

"What do you mean?"

She shook her head and looked away, returning to puffing on her cigarette. "Nothing. Don't worry about it. It'll be fine."

They sat in comfortable silence for a few more moments, soaking up the sun. Jackson, Marina, and Isabella joined them in the grass. They stayed outside until Deittman called them back in. They responded with a collective reluctant sigh.

CHAPTER 12

"Okay, just a few quick things before we go down," Vincent said, standing against the metal door with his hand on the busted latch. "The basement isn't split into wings like the upper floors, so we'll be under the asylum wing as well. The door into the asylum was blocked off, making the basement inaccessible and also marking it safe from structural damage during the fire. It's got a lot of crap in it though, and a lot of dark corners, so be careful."

He focused on the floor for a few moments and shook his head.

"As you can see, this door might be the newest thing in this entire building. This was only replaced in the past decade, not long before my aunt and uncle bought the property. It had been broken into at some point. A guy kidnapped a little girl and.... well, police found her body in the basement. I don't know where—I didn't go looking. But from what I read online, it was... bad. If you're investigating, you may... find the spot. Just be careful. Or don't go down at all—that's what I recommend."

Eli took a step back, bumping into Jackson.

"Watch it man," Jackson growled.

"Sorry... sorry." Eli continued to move backward, putting more space between him and door.

"Eli?" Deittman called out to him, causing Eli to start shaking his head.

"I'm not going down there," he said sternly. "Absolutely not. I can't."

Jackson snorted, "scared?"

Eli frowned and shook his head, surprised it wasn't obvious to the group. "If a guy murdered a girl... You guys might experience cold spots or movement or something, but I might have to *see* it. You can't put that on me."

Deittman looked at him in contemplation but ultimately nodded. "Given the circumstances and the fact that you have already started to exhibit your abilities, I will allow you to remain behind. You should not be alone, however."

It didn't seem as though everyone was eager to go to the basement, but no one wanted to stay alone with a stranger either. Eli whipped his head over toward Ash to plead with his eyes. She started to open her mouth when Garrett spoke up instead.

"I'll stay," he said and adjusted his glasses. "All three of my team don't have to go. I can go investigate with them later."

Eli nodded his head in thanks and Garrett stepped aside to let the others go in front of him.

Eli watched as the rest of the group disappeared down the dark mouth that was the basement stairs. The door remained open even after they all entered, the darkness staring back at him as the shadows threatened to draw him in. He shut his eyes, trying to shake the discomfort creeping up on him.

"Eli, if you don't mind, I'd like to head back to base. I can continue unpacking until they're back."

Eli opened his eyes and nodded, "yeah, sure, let's go. Let me know what I can do to help."

Their walk back to the dayroom-turned-home base was quiet. Once they were in, Eli dropped into one of the seats and shoved his hands into his pocket with a sigh.

"Are you starting to reconsider what you've gotten yourself into?" Garrett asked, looking at Eli from over the rim of his glasses.

Eli shrugged and nodded slowly. "I knew it wasn't a good idea. I just didn't realize how *bad* of an idea it was until I got here."

"Are you thinking about leaving?"

It took Eli a few moments to answer. He tilted his head back and stared up at the balcony, trying to guess where the Echo had come from earlier. "I don't know. I guess. I could really use the money, though. Ninety-six hours can't be that bad, can it?"

"I suppose it depends on your personal tolerance. I imagine it would be harder on you than it would be on someone else. Do you mind if I ask you some personal questions about your ability? If it's too personal, I understand if you don't want to talk about it."

Eli rolled his head over to look at Garrett, who was setting a laptop down on one of the tables.

At least the guy was considerate. Eli appreciated that.

"Depends, are you going to name me in any of your research or whatever?"

"Do you want to be named?"

"Not at all," Eli replied. "I don't want people knowing who I am. I don't want people I know thinking I'm crazy. It's one thing for you to be here with me, seeing or at least experiencing what I do in a way. Someone reading or listening to it though—they'd never buy it. They'd think I'm nuts."

Garrett nodded. "You are correct. They would. As I said, I'm not yet convinced but I also don't necessarily think you're crazy. I've seen far too much in this world to write you off entirely."

"Can I ask how *you* got involved in all of this? You seem like a normal guy—Stevens too. You guys aren't what I imagined when I pictured ghost hunters," Eli said, causing Garrett to chuckle.

"You imagined someone more like our *friend* Jackson, I imagine," he replied and moved a monitor to the table next to the laptop.

Eli shrugged. "Well… yeah actually."

"Unfortunately, that's the reputation we get, what with the reality TV boom. Believe it or not, I've been doing this on and off for over a decade. I started as a hobbyist with some friends, and then once I got into engineering, I started looking at it from a different perspective. I've been following Deittman's career for some years, actually. There are only a handful of professional paranormal investigators in the world, and I strive to be one of them." He started to pull a handful of cords out of his bag.

"Are you setting up a split screen? Let me do it."

Garrett's face lit up, then he nodded. "That would be helpful, thank you. It's a lot for one person. You're under no obligation though."

"Please--tell me what I can help with. Happy to stay distracted."

Eli moved over to the table and started booting the laptop up while he ran some cables from the generator sitting unpacked on the side of the room. It would have to be set up near an open window in the next room. The two men fell into an easy silence, which actually helped Eli relax. The atmosphere was decidedly more comfortable, and it was nice to do some familiar work without worrying about the legality of it all. It was doing wonders for his dampened mood.

"My interest in the paranormal started when I was about seventeen," Garrett said as he moved on to withdrawing numerous little cameras from their cushioned storage. "I had my first experience then. I was terrified and bewildered. Mostly terrified. There was another guy my age who had committed suicide. I was devastated—I believed it was my fault. We were... involved... and of course that led to a great deal of unwanted attention. He couldn't handle it. During the weeks after, I had considered... following him. One night, when I was ready to pull the trigger, so to speak, he came to me. He begged me not to, said it wasn't my fault. And, well, I'm still here."

Eli looked over at Garrett, surprised that the man had shared such a personal story with him. Garrett deliberately avoided his eye contact.

"Guess we have something in common then," Eli replied, but then realized what was implied when Garrett raised a brow at him. His cheeks turned red and he quickly shook his head. "Not that, I mean… Not that there's anything wrong—I meant…"

He ran his hands through his hair nervously.

"My abilities drove me to a suicide attempt. I was in and out of places like this," he waved his hand around the room, "for a few years when I was a young teenager. That's how I figured out how to suppress them. There's a particular brand of anti-anxiety medication that works better than others, and I can't easily get it anymore because of losing my job and my new insurance won't pay for it. It's made my life hell—ruined my marriage and everything. Trust me, if I could get rid of seeing these things forever, I would do it in a heartbeat."

"It's a unique gift," Garrett said as if trying to supply Eli with a positive.

"Unique and *terrible*. It…It really messes with me. Leads me to doing stupid things like accepting dangerous research jobs in abandoned asylums," Eli muttered, shaking his head.

"Do you remember when you first started experiencing your visions?"

Eli sat down at the laptop and clicked around to set up the split screen. "I think my earliest was eight years old or so? They got worse once I went through puberty, I think. Then again, I had an Echo in my childhood home, so that didn't help either."

"An echo?" Garrett asked. He wasn't taking notes, which was a plus.

"Yeah, an Echo. That's… what call them, I guess. Because they're like a shadow of a person, just a residual echo of a past trauma. It's stupid."

111

"No," Garrett replied, "no, I think that's rather appropriate. It makes sense."

"What's Stevens's deal?" Eli asked.

"You'll have to ask him. In my experience, these sorts of things are deeply personal, so it's best not to talk about someone else's, you know?"

Eli nodded, "yeah, makes sense. So, what do you think of this place? You aren't afraid of it?"

"It's surprisingly active for so early in the investigation but no, I'm not. When you do this long enough, you become immune to the atmosphere. I'm sure it will be fine—active, but fine."

The two continued to set up the base until the rest of the group returned. When they did, everyone seemed unbothered—not as unnerved as Eli would have expected. In fact, most of the members were chatting amicably as they entered again.

That soon ended as everyone rushed to find open seats.

Markus grabbed one of the folding chairs and slid it over to the side for Isabella while he stood next to her. Ash slid down the wall and sat against it on the floor, disregarding the dirt she immediately covering her pants and jacket. Garrett gave his seat over to Deittman, and Marina got the last one in the room. Stevens leaned against the window sill and rubbed his knee.

"So, that's everything I planned to show you. I'll take you to the entrance of the asylum and I'll leave you with the keys. I understand that you've all signed a waiver so if you do anything stupid, that's all on you. The first floor is... mostly stable, but you've got to make sure nothing's going to fall *on* you. I think you can reach the second floor, but I don't recommend it because that was the area where the fire broke out in the late seventies," Vincent said, clapping his hands together.

"Tell us more about the doctor," Marina insisted.

Vincent sighed and his shoulders slumped. "Alright, alright. But then I'm getting out of here. I'd like to be back at my hotel with enough time to get cleaned up for dinner. So... Dr. Pollock. He was a fairly young man when he was here in the forties. He was newly married when he started, and his daughter was actually delivered in the asylum since, you know, he was a doctor and there were enough fully trained staff here. Lots of kids were born here, believe it or not. Not to the doctors, so much. But sometimes women came here pregnant or became pregnant...."

"You're deviating," Deittman interrupted.

"Sorry. Pollock did an absurd number of experiments, the extent of which is still unknown. However, eyewitness accounts say it might as well have been torture. He killed every patient he tested on in the end. They said he had a way of moving the bodies without others noticing, so it went on for a while. Since he was the one who filled out the death certificates, he would wait a little bit between deaths to fill out the form so no one would be suspicious when three patients died within a few days of one another," Vincent said.

"So, what happened to his family?" Eli asked.

Vincent frowned. "Well, as you saw, the only way to get in and out of the Doctor's Quarters if the elevator is down is to actually go through the asylum. Remember, at the time, the whole building was an asylum. One morning, when Pollock's wife, Dianna, was leaving to go into town, two male patients grabbed her. They dragged her into a room, suffocated the baby with a pillow, and strangled Dianna."

Eli's mind flashed to Sophia and Sarah, and he shifted uncomfortably in his chair. If someone did something to his wife, he might be inclined to extract some terrible revenge as well.

"No one knows why they did it. Most people attribute it to them being crazy. Some people think it might have been because their friends were ill-fated patients—or maybe they were being tested on themselves. It's hard to say. Pollock actually remained here for another two years before he was removed," Vincent said.

"What happened to him? Surely, he's still not alive today," Markus said.

"No," Vincent replied and shook his head. "He moved to California, remarried…. I think he died some years ago. I imagine he kept his head down and led a relatively quiet life."

"And you know this because your grandmother worked here?" Garrett asked, marking a few notes down.

"That's right. She left here, got married, and the rest is history. She always said this place was evil—or so I hear. To be honest, I don't remember her very well. She died when I was a kid. Said if she had the chance, she would buy this place and condemn it so no one else would ever come here. Tear it down, even."

"And yet, here we are," Ash muttered, putting her head back against the wall.

Vincent shrugged. "My aunt and uncle tried to honor her wishes when this place went up for auction. No one wanted it—especially with the death of that little girl fresh in their minds. They got a bargain for the property. But tearing it all down is incredibly expensive—too expensive. I'm probably going to have to just sell this to be rid of it. I don't have the money to sink into demolition," he said with a nervous laugh.

"What can you tell us about the fire? I've done some research, but the information available was rather minimal. Seems like the town did their hardest to keep this place out of the news," Stevens said.

"I think you're right," Vincent agreed. "Though Maple Hill was their primary employer, it's a black spot for them. Lots of abuse for many, many years. The fire broke out in a patient's room. The origins of the fire are unknown—anyone around to say was killed in the fire. It was a disaster. They lost pretty much everyone on the third and fourth floor, and some on the second floor. A few people lived. Most of them with terrible scarring. Some died on the first floor when the ceiling caved in on them. This wing was unaffected because of how the building is segmented. The fact that the staff didn't attempt to evacuate any patients, even the non-violent, finally brought attention to the poor care here, which is why it closed down as an asylum after."

"But we can go into the asylum section of the building, correct?" Garrett asked.

Vincent nodded and shrugged. "At your own risk, as I said. Just be very careful. Are you guys ready to go to the entrance? Besides the door in the Doctor's Quarters, this is the only way you can get in. You'll have to go outside and around to the end of the other wing."

The group took a moment to have a breather from the basement and grab a few water bottles from a case provided by the equipment rental company. In addition to Garrett and Stevens's own equipment, Deittman had paid to have supplies carted over along with the cots. Back together as one group, they left through the main entrance of the building and headed across the front lawn to the far end of the wing.

Eli spied movement in the windows to the asylum—on the fourth floor, no less, which apparently had no floor. It had been brief but enough to cause him to stop. When Garrett noticed he had stopped, Garrett also paused.

"Something up there?"

Eli shrugged and shook his head. "I don't know. I thought I saw something, but it's gone now." Regardless, he still felt the sensation of something watching them, even if he couldn't quite pick out where it was coming from. From ahead, Isabella was also constantly looking up at the windows as if she was expecting to see something. Perhaps her own *extra senses* made her feel the same.

Once upon a time, there had been a walkway leading from the building's large double doors to the side entrances, each with its own small overhang to protect visitors from the elements. While the one leading to the hospital side had been repaved at some point, the one leading to the asylum was little more than a set of cracked and broken blocks left to deteriorate for nearly half a century. Marina would have faceplanted after getting her boot caught in between the uneven pads had Ash's hand not shot out to grab her by the back of her jacket.

When they reached the door, Vincent tentatively tested the handle. This door was older than the basement door but newer than most of the others they had seen in the building. It had probably been replaced at some point to keep anyone from trying to break into the dangerous section of the asylum. This time, the door opened without any resistance.

"I checked this earlier," Vincent said, audibly exhaling in relief. Maybe he had expected it to be locked again like the Doctor's Quarters. "I'm only going to go in a little bit. I don't have any intention of wandering around in there."

Vincent clicked his flashlight, illuminating the hazy interior, and walked inside with Deittman following close behind.

The interior was much darker than the other side of the building. Though the hospital side had been abandoned for over two decades, this side had sat for over four and it showed. The windows were covered in grime which kept the sunlight from filling the area, despite the layout being nearly identical to the other side. Spiderwebs and insect casings littered the corners, a long dead bird sat rotting below one of the broken windows, and the odor of mold hung in the air. Eli was starting to hope Deittman had a set of masks in his supplies pile, especially if they were going to be expected to spend any time investigating the hazardous space.

Eli stepped into one of the first rooms on his left and scanned the area with his flashlight. It looked as though everything had been removed—salvaged so it could be put back into use elsewhere, perhaps. The room was the same size as the others, but the walls were very plain. There was no paint, no wallpaper... only brown blotches that made him wonder if they had been made before or

116

after the room had been vacated. What stuck out to him most were the little hooks jutting out from the upper ends of the walls. The bottom had metal pieces bolted into place as well.

"Those were for chaining unruly patients in place," Markus said from behind him, causing Eli to jump a bit. Markus gave him an apologetic smile. "We've seen them before in other mental institutions. If a patient was in danger of harming themselves or someone else, the physicians would have them strung up by their arms and legs, naked. And they would simply remain there. It was a terrible, terrible practice. It would have certainly not been used by the time the fire broke out, but it seems no one took care to remove the bolts, which is dangerous. A resourceful patient might find a way to injure themselves with them, despite the bolts being near the ceiling."

Eli grimaced. The thought of such horrific practices being used at all was simply devastating. How could humans be so cruel to one another?

"Here's what I know," Vincent said from his spot about five rooms down from the hall. Eli and Markus backed out of the room and moved to rejoin the group. "I can't give you terribly accurate information. You'll have to sort of figure out as best you can. First, you'll notice that there are no bars on the front of the building. The back of the building, however, does still have all of the bars in place on this wing. Once it was converted, the owners didn't want the bars to scare away potential customers, so they removed them from the front and from the hospital wing. During the removal, a worker died. He was on scaffolding removing a set from the second floor when he fell. It was ruled accidental," Vincent said.

Jackson nudged Marina and smirked. "He was probably pushed by a ghost."

She only frowned at him, clearly not amused.

"A patient on this floor was killed in the bathroom," Vincent said and pointed to a door down the hall from him, "when another inmate started bashing his head against the tile wall. He lived for a little while, but he died when the doctors tried to move him for treatment. You'll find the observation ward on the second floor, which was essentially a row of cages so doctors could monitor everything a patient did. The second floor is where Pollock's wife and daughter died and where the fire broke out. I'm sure there are more stories, but obviously a lot wasn't reported, and there aren't as many staff reports about experiences since most of what we're told came after this part was decommissioned."

"Excuse me," Deittman said, drawing Vincent's attention. "Now, a building such as this would surely have had a hydrotherapy or an electro-shock therapy section—possibly both. Where would those have been here?"

Eli could have sworn he saw Vincent's brow twitch at the comment as he pressed his lips in a thin line. "I'm not sure. Maybe they were removed or converted after the practice was deemed barbaric. They might've been in the other section and then removed before the elderly care patients started to arrive."

"I suppose you're right," Deittman said lightly and turned away, continuing to inspect one of the bedrooms.

"I'm going to step outside. Take your time though. I'll be leaving shortly and can see myself out if need be," Vincent said, walking down the length of the hallway, past Eli and the others.

Eli was about to turn and leave the building when he noticed Ash standing in one of the rooms, staring up at the ceiling. He shoved his hands in his pockets and walked in, stepping over some crumbled plaster. Once inside, he found a gaping hole in the ceiling. He joined her in staring into said hole.

"There's something Not Good up there," she muttered. He heard a slight clicking noise and figured she was opening and closing her lighter—Eli was starting to think it was a nervous habit.

"This place just feels bad in general," he replied.

Ash shook her head. "There's a lot of bad too, but there's more than 'good' and 'bad.' Some things are 'neither'."

Eli turned to look at her curiously. Her brows were furrowed as she stared up with an uncertain look. Thus far, it was an expression he hadn't seen cross her face. "So... is it like a ghost?"

Ash looked away and sighed. "No idea. I'm not the type of *psychic* who usually sees things. I've...I've found some Not Good things before, but it doesn't really make a lot of sense for something like that to be here..."

"I think there's a lot of things that shouldn't be here that *are* here."

"Maybe. I dunno. I can't explain it," she said with a frown.

Eli got the distinct feeling that it wasn't so much that she wasn't able to explain so much as she was *unwilling.*

The group filtered back out of the building and Vincent shut the door behind them, locking it. "I'll leave the keys, but you should keep this locked when you aren't investigating here. I don't think it's likely anyone will sneak around the property while you're here, but you can't be too sure."

They were about to turn and walk away when Markus wandered towards the back of the building. "Vincent," he called out before they could get too far away from him. "What is that building?"

It hadn't actually occurred to anyone to check out the back of the property, Eli realized. They stopped and slowly turned around, walking towards the back. There was, in fact, a building, two stories high, that looked more like a renovated farmhouse than a hospital facility.

"Oh, that," Vincent replied and waved it off. "Not sure actually. I think it was the original building on the property—or one of them. I think there were two. That one and the one that was turned into the asylum. When this opened in the mid-1800s, it was a home for the destitute. Once this building got into full swing, there was no need for the original anymore. It's been sealed up for... I don't even know how long. Before the seventies, definitely. I haven't found a way in. I imagine it's in poor condition. Probably rotted out. There are no-stories that I'm aware of, so I wouldn't worry about it. You've got your work cut out for you as it is."

Stevens, Deittman, and Markus all continued to give the building a long look before exchanging glances. They would probably go check it out for themselves after Vincent was gone, just to be sure, Eli guessed.

"That's all I've got for you," Vincent said as they reached the front of the building. "I'm going to head out. You can call me if you really need me, though reception is poor and I would prefer not to come back until I have to lock up. Being here all day has reminded me why I want to get rid of it as quickly as possible." He gave them a sheepish smile and rubbed the back of his neck.

"I think we should be able to manage for a mere three nights," Deittman assured him and extended his hand. Vincent took it, followed by handshakes from both Stevens and Garrett.

"I sure hope so! Best of luck; it's all yours," he said, handing over the keys. He gave a wave to the rest of the group before heading over to his vehicle.

Eli glanced around. No one tried to stop him—no one chased him down, asking to leave with him. It seemed that even after their fright, everyone was now in for the long haul.

They watched as Vincent adjusted his seat and mirror, then pulled away with one last wave. The sound of his car on the gravel of the driveway echoed through the air almost ominously, as if it were mocking them for deciding to stay.

"Well now," Deittman said with a smile and clapped his hands together. "This has all been quite exciting and informative. Let's all work together to set up the equipment so everything is ready before nightfall."

CHAPTER 13

Stevens and Garrett took over directing the equipment setup. Deittman and Markus were trusted with the cameras, having enough experience to assure the other investigators that they wouldn't break anything. Isabella checked every device for fresh batteries and organized their workstation. Eli was able to help set up the monitors and test connections while Carlos ran and taped down cables. Jackson and Marina were quick to disappear on their own since they had their own cameras.

The fact that Jackson planned to set up a few of his own had caused a bit of an argument to break out, but ultimately Deittman had the final word and he allowed for it so long as it didn't disrupt any of the other equipment.

It was actually a much harder task than Eli had expected. There was a method behind the stationing of the cameras to maximize space coverage with their limited resources. However, there was a bit of an issue as the group finished hooking up their first generator, which could only hold so many devices while being expected to last the entire weekend.

"What do you *mean* we're missing a generator?"

The intern visibly swallowed and shrugged. "I mean... there are two. There are only two of them."

Stevens wiped his hand down his face and turned around. "You've got to be fucking kidding me," he said, sighing loudly. He paced around before turning to face Carlos again. "How does a generator just *disappear?* You took inventory when we got in. There were *three.* I saw the inventory sheet. There were *three* of them. Those things are fucking huge! Someone couldn't have just walked off with one without anyone knowing about it."

Eli watched the scene unfold from the doorway. He wondered if he should interfere for the poor kid's sake, but he decided against it. It wasn't his business. He had nothing to do with the technical bits and pieces of this investigation, though he was sure he would be able to help during the weekend. But hey, what did he know about hunting ghosts? He didn't have to look for them after all—they usually found *him.*

"Well, actually, we might not have had three of them when we got here. I only opened one of the cases to make sure they were the generators we ordered and—"

He had to give the kid some credit. He was holding up pretty well under the other man's fury. Carlos stood patiently, waiting for Stevens to finish his slew of curses. Eli ventured to guess this wasn't the first time Carlos had to sit back and take a verbal beating from his supervisor. Apparently, his job wasn't all that different from a typical office job after all.

"Deittman's not going to be happy about this," Stevens finally said as he leaned forward on the folding table, his palms flat against the surface. "We're going to lose coverage of one of the major areas. We're going to have to choose what to investigate now. Either that or we don't have power in half of our base. We can try to stretch this as long as possible, but I don't think two will cover everything for the entire weekend..." He shook his head and looked down, losing himself in his thoughts.

Carlos stood by idly until Stevens was done with him.

Eli chose to make himself busy once Stevens made the situation known to Deittman who was, in fact, not happy.

Ultimately, it was decided that the basement would not be covered. They didn't have much to put into the asylum section since it was hardly accessible anyhow, so they didn't need to rely on the generator. They would need to continuously swap out batteries to keep cameras running at all times since they would no longer be able to rely on power cords running from the generators.

They also wouldn't have any power in their sleeping quarters or bathroom, which meant everyone would be using their flashlights and lanterns once nightfall hit—now only an hour away, once they finished getting everything ready.

Dinner would consist of hot dogs from a cooler Stevens and Garrett brought with them during travel. Because they didn't have any refrigerator access, they would be all eating chips and sandwiches for the next few days, not that Eli minded. With his lack of cooking skills, that had been his diet anyhow over the last few months. They did have multiple cans of soup, as well as camping equipment to cook it over a fire for those so inclined.

Deittman assigned Ash to the task of monitoring their campfire, which was on the stone steps of the front porch. Though Eli wasn't sure it was the best idea given the proximity to the building, no one was eager to wander too far off in the dark. Besides the wooden door, there was only stone around the fire and nothing to catch alight at the very least.

Even if something did manage to accidentally go ablaze, Ash assured them she'd handle it.

Once nightfall settled in, the building took on a life of its own. Eli noticed a great deal more creaking and rattling throughout the building, despite the air outside remaining unchanged. Logic told him it was only the building settling—cooling down after being in the sun all day.

Logic didn't count in Maple Hill, however.

When he became too restless, he went to join Ash and Isabella by the fire as they cooked the last of the hot dogs. With a groan, Eli dropped to the ground and leaned against the wall next to the opened double doors. watching as Isabella

"Isabella," Eli said, tearing his eyes away from the hypnotic dance of the flames. "Would it be too difficult to ask you some questions about your experiences in other places?"

The young woman looked up and smiled at him, shaking her head. She tapped the notebook sitting next to her. She was prepared.

"I was just wondering if you think this is the worst place you've been to. I mean, it seems like you and your brother have gone to a lot of places with Deittman."

She nodded and set the hot dog prong on the edge of two rocks Ash had lugged up from the driveway. She took a few moments to scribble down a response and pass it over to Eli.

No. It's certainly one of the more uncomfortable locations, but I've been to worse. Castles with actual torture chambers. Sites of mass execution. War ravaged cities. There's an oppressive energy here, but it comes and goes.

Eli bobbed his head in agreement, though he really couldn't actually fathom being in a place that felt worse than Maple Hill at the moment. As he gazed off into the distance and listened to the wind rustles the towering trees, he felt Isabella's on him. Perhaps she had questions of her own, or perhaps she was merely waiting for him to ask something else. After a few moments of silence, she stood, pat Ash on the shoulder, and entered the building once more.

"Because Ms. Martelli and Mr. Cohen are eager to begin in the asylum, we are going to begin our investigation on this side of the building," Deittman explained once everyone gathered about the

headquarters. "Now, to keep noise contamination between the first and the second floor to a minimum, I am going to request whoever remains behind to monitor the cameras do their best to be absolutely silent. We will need to have someone awake at all times in headquarters so that if something interesting takes place, we can mark it or investigate on the spot."

"Garrett and I are generally able to switch off for most of the night, and Carlos will join one of us. It's the last shift—four until six or seven—that no one wants," Stevens said.

"I'll take it," Ash said immediately, much to the rest of the group's surprise. She shrugged and rolled her eyes. "I usually don't go to bed until then anyhow. Won't be much of a struggle for me."

"So long as we are not required to be investigating during the later shifts and can get some sleep, Isabella and I don't mind relieving Ash so that the rest of you can sleep for a while longer," Markus offered. Eli figured it made sense that the two of them would stick together since Isabella couldn't exactly call for anyone if she needed something.

"As long as I'm up, I can fill in wherever," Eli said with a shrug. If no one was going to push him into a rigid schedule, then he wasn't going to volunteer for it.

Deittman smiled and clapped his hands together. "Wonderful. Now, let us settle on some investigating teams. Ms. Martelli and Mr. Cohen are likely to jump in with us at some point, but they made it clear that they are here for their own purposes, and as they were never meant to be part of our core team anyhow, that is perfectly fine. Eight is plenty for a thorough investigation."

Once again, Eli wondered why Marina and Jackson were even with Deittman. They must have paid him to bring them along. Eli saw no other plausible option.

"Stevens and I would like to be separated, if you don't mind," Garrett said, "so we can supervise the use of our equipment."

For a moment, it looked as though Deittman may have been offended by the implication that he or his own team members would be careless or inept. In the end, he shrugged and nodded. "Yes, that would be fine, I think. It would be best if Markus and Isabella remain with me as I can also read sign language. Stevens, would you like to join us?"

The man gave a nod. "Yes. We can take the first investigation shift and rotate once we have covered the second and third floors. We should at least do a sweep of the asylum by the end of the night, but we can save the investigation until tomorrow if necessary."

Stevens started to give an overview of the equipment, but Deittman quickly stopped him. Unless they were using something unusual, Deittman's team was well versed in investigating tools. Markus and Isabella went straight for the voice recorders, and each of them took either a KII or an EMF detector. Deittman was partial to an infrared camera he had brought with him. Stevens picked up voice recorder, an EMF detector, a mag light, and his own thermal imaging camera. Garrett and Carlos took seats behind monitors, preparing to scour footage for anomalies and to be on call in the event equipment needed quick repairs.

Because of the need for silence, Eli was given the go-ahead to go back to their little 'residency' quarters and nap until he was needed. A poor night's sleep and an early morning had him feeling completely wiped out by eight o'clock. Ash also retreated from the headquarters to go back outside and smoke without bothering anyone—though Garrett did insist she take a walkie talkie with her so they could grab her if she was needed without having to go wander around after her.

Eli didn't think it was a particularly good idea to go outside alone, but Ash wasted no time disappearing into the darkness. She didn't even bother to click on a flashlight. Sighing, Eli turned to head off for his nap. If Ash wasn't nervous about the prospect of trekking around a haunted hospital, who was he to question her?

Eli jolted awake shortly after he put his head down on his shockingly comfortable cot. Or, at least, it *felt* like just after. He quickly sat upright, nearly smacking skulls with Garrett. Garrett stumbled backward and fell onto his own cot.

"Sorry to wake you, but the other team is back. We're up now. We're going to go straight to the third floor so we can investigate, then switch off with Jackson and Marina. They've finished whatever they were doing and are planning to take a little break before continuing," Garrett said, choosing to keep his voice low. Eli appreciated it as he stifled a yawn.

"Okay," he croaked out and threw his legs over the side to slide his shoes back on. He would have gladly gone ahead and slept through the night if he had the option.

The two men walked from the room—well, Eli more *trudged* than walked—and down the dark hallway toward their little base. Eli could hear voices, even from a distance. He wondered if Stevens was going to get after any of them for noise pollution since the echoing would surely make any recordings on the first or second floor useless.

After Eli was given a brief explanation of the equipment, he took the KII and a voice recorder. He wasn't at all interested in carrying a camera around, but that was mostly because he saw enough without a len. At least with a KII, it easily fit into one hand and the worst it would show him might be some flashing lights at an energy spike. Eli wasn't particularly eager to hear ghost voices, but the recorder was simple enough to use and do a playback if needed.

Ash stubbornly fought each attempt to put a piece of equipment in her hand, declaring she didn't want to be responsible for anything. But as tired voices began to rise, she snatched an EMF detector from the table and shoved it in her back pocket. Eli doubted she would pull it out again.

It was almost midnight by the time they finally ventured off to the third floor. Though the building had been quiet during the day, it was now so silent, it was near deafening. Eli swore he heard movement, but it could have been anything—a mouse looking to raid their food bin, a droplet of condensation from the cooling temperatures, a piece of disturbed plaster loosened by their vibrations... It could have been nothing at all, with his ears instead playing tricks on him as he strained for some sort, *any sort*, of sound in the silence.

He was tense as they started up the staircase, so tense that his jaw *hurt* from being so tightly locked.

Just before his group reached the entrance to the third floor, Eli heard a loud ***bang!***, and then nothing. He jumped and the KII slipped from his grasp. He wore a wristband, so it didn't go very far, though it did smack off the metal stairwell railing, startling the others in his group.

His teammates stopped and stared at him.

"You... didn't hear that?" he asked and swallowed. He received headshakes in return. Eli nodded slowly, and he waved toward the door. "An Echo-loop is starting. Probably the guy who killed the cheating doctor and nurse on the fourth floor."

The idea of paranormal or psychic energy starting up certainly slowed Eli down, but Garrett and Carlos practically sprinted up the stairs. Eli didn't follow right away, but he heard the two investigators exchanging words excitedly as they scaled the last flight of stairs. Their devices were going off in a cacophony of buzzing and beeping and screeching. Eli winced at the high-pitched noises as he walked up their stairs, his pace no more than a crawl. Just as suddenly as it all started, however, it stopped.

Ash stared at him, her eyes glittering in the dark from the dim light spreading from Carlos's flashlight in the hallway a few steps above them.

"I'm fine," he said, even though she hadn't asked. "The noise startled me, that's all."

With one heavy step after another, Eli joined the other two investigators on the floor.

Eli didn't see anything in the room that supposedly housed the double-murder-suicide, but he still felt an intense energy lingering in the air even if none of the investigation equipment picked up on it. Maybe it was the leftover energy of the killer, lying in wait for the Echo of his next victim to show up. If they remained long enough, Eli figured he might have to witness that too.

Garrett and Carlos walked from room to room, taking readings with their devices and marking them down. Ash stood around idly, trying her best not to sigh in boredom. Whenever Garrett would peek out of the room at her, she would hold up her EMF detector and at least look like she was paying attention to it.

Eli didn't get much enjoyment out of ghost hunting. He found it all rather boring. Despite the heavy atmosphere and his initial scare, nothing happened. They stood around, occasionally asking questions to the air in hopes of getting a response—*is someone there, can you give us a sign, how old are you, did you die here, did you work here…* Carlos and Garrett rattled off questions consistently, giving a few second pause between their words. Once they had decided they had enough readings, the two investigators sat down on the dusty wooden floor.

Garrett sat opposite of room believed to have been the murders-suicide scene while Carlos sat and stared into the room Eli had suggested they watch earlier.

"We're going dark, so I suggest you find a spot and settle in, then turn off your flashlight."

Eli heeded Garrett's advice and sat down near the door to the stairs while Ash crossed the length of the hallway and sat down far away from them. She had said she would be up all night, but he wouldn't blame her if she took a snooze in the dark. Hell, he was tempted to do it too.

And that's exactly what he did, albeit unintentionally. He hadn't even realized he dozed off in the end. The fourth floor was rather warm compared to the rest of the building and thus surprisingly comfortable. After a while, he stopped noticing the heaviness in the air as well.

Then he heard a woman scream and another loud **bang**.

He jumped up and pointed to the room across from Garrett but there was no need. Garrett's device, which he had left sitting just in the entryway of the room, was lighting up and beeping again.

One of the things Eli disliked was the fact that no matter how dark it was he could always see an Echo—perhaps because he wasn't seeing them with his eyes, so much as he *saw* with an extraordinary sense. Eli imagined that was what Deittman would tell him, at least.

The man's body was already disappearing, proving he had died almost immediately after turning his gun on himself. The woman, on the other hand, lay twitching for nearly a minute after Eli started watching her. She had chunks blown out of her head, with pieces of skull scattered about the room. Eli tasted the bile as it started to rise in his mouth. He had to turn and stagger away, putting his back to the horrific scene in the room and bracing himself against a nearby doorframe.

Garrett and Carlos once again diligently took notes and attempted to film the area to see if they could get any activity. Though they didn't think they caught anything, they were eager to check out the enhanced footage—whatever that meant.

"You know, Eli," Garrett said, pushing his glasses a bit further up on the bridge of his nose, "when this is all over, I think I would like to talk to you about your availability. It would be incredibly useful to have someone around who can hear something we can't and point us in the right direction."

Eli wasn't sure if Garrett could see him grimace in the dark, but if he did, Garrett simply ignored it. Eli didn't think he would be interested in signing on for any more haunted locations anytime in the near future.

Or ever.

CHAPTER 14

No matter how hard he tried, Eli wasn't able to sleep as long as he would have liked. The dirty windows of their sleeping quarters let in just enough light to be annoying after being up for most of the night. Though Markus and Isabella had quietly navigated the room to go relieve Ash as dawn began to break, Ash had not been so courteous. She had tripped over something when she entered the room and cursed under her breath—loudly enough to wake Eli and Jackson.

"*Shut up*," Jackson moaned into his pillow, only causing Ash to mutter under her breath more.

"*Both* of you shut up," Garrett snapped from his corner. Eli cracked an eye to see that Ash was scowling and making a face as she silently mimicked their words. She didn't say anything further as she entered the women's little room.

Eli tried his best to go back to sleep, to no avail. He found himself flip-flopping on the cot, causing quite a bit of squeaking and earning him his own share of groans. Finally, he decided it was best just to get up. He slipped his shoes on and grabbed his bag, deciding to take advantage of the horribly cold bathroom before anyone else was awake.

Waking up in an abandoned building was certainly new for him, and not something he looked forward to experiencing again anytime soon, he thought as he trudged into their little bathroom.

Eli scrunched his nose as he looked around the old room and tried to push the door quietly closed behind him. His effort was useless with the old hinges, however, and he heard a fresh wave of groaning and cursing as the metal screeched before he latched the door. The bathroom was far more disgusting in the early morning light flooding in through the grimy window panes. The day before, in the afternoon's half-light, much of the film of dust and dirt could be overlooked.

In the end, Eli was only able to muster the courage to wash his face. It was too damned cold with absolutely no hot water. He'd go as long as possible before braving the freezing shower. Still, washing his face, brushing his teeth with a bottle of water (since they were advised against drinking anything), and changing into fresh clothes helped brighten his spirits along with the bright morning. He felt almost cheery—at least until he opened the door and heard a loud *bang* from somewhere up the stairwell.

Eli stopped and turned towards the entrance to the stairs, wondering if he should check it out. With a sigh, he chose to ignore it. He had seen enough horror movies to know not to go investigating.

Eli wondered if it was safe for him to be wandering around the building by himself but figured there was probably little danger in the daylight. What was the worst that could happen? A *ghost* appearing and dragging him, kicking and screaming, down the hallway? Eli snorted to himself as he stepped around a dirty and broken wicker chair. He figured it was more likely he would see an unwanted Echo that would send him scurrying down the hallway.

As he neared the closer of the two doorways to their base, he heard voices.

When Eli walked into the headquarters area, he saw Stevens up and about. He was dressed and leaning over a monitor, shaking his head. It appeared as though one of their cameras had lost its connection—the little square where footage should have been playing was completely dark.

"We can go take a look if you want," Markus said from next to him, "but Garrett did ask us not to touch his equipment."

Stevens stood, running a hand over his shortly cropped hair. Eli had to admit, he was a bit impressed at how alert the man appeared for how early it was—especially given the late night that they had all had. Had he managed to horde a secret stash of coffee from the rest of them?

Eli doubted it. Stevens was just *disciplined*.

"Let's hope it's salvageable. Eli, you're techy, aren't you?"

Eli shrugged, setting his toiletry bag down off to the side of the entryway. He would take it back when everyone else wasn't sleeping—he was fairly certain that Jackson or Garrett would throw something at him if he so much as turned the creaky door handle.

"Yeah, IT networking and repair. Why?"

Stevens grabbed a small tool bag from the cluttered equipment table, muttering something about Carlos needing to do a better job of cleaning up, and gave him a wave as he started out of the other entrance to the headquarters. "Something fell on the third floor—one of Garrett's custom-made pieces. I want to see if I can fix it before he's awake. He tends to get worked up when his things break." he explained, gesturing for Eli to follow him. "Wouldn't mind some help."

Though Eli may have wanted to argue—wanted to insist on getting a breakfast bar in his stomach at the very least—he figured it was best not to argue with the man. Stevens had quite the presence to him, and Eli was rather certain the tall, ex-military man could break him in half if he really tried. Eli nodded and put his hands into his jacket pockets, following after Stevens as they headed for the stairwell off of the atrium.

Up they went, Eli trailing behind Stevens. Now that he was moving so close to him, Eli noticed Stevens's unusual gait as they climbed the stairs, though Eli figured it would be rude to bring it up.

When they reached the third floor, Eli's spotted a small Go-Pro camera had fallen from its mount. It had been rigged up above a door frame, focused on the room where a child's spirit was supposedly seen. Eli hadn't witnessed any sort of Echo to confirm that, but then again, were many children kept on this property? It seemed unlikely to him. If there was a ghost child, he hoped beyond hope he wouldn't have to witness its Echo. Few things were more heartbreaking than being forced to witness a traumatic experience involving a child.

The camera was sitting in the dead center of the hallway floor still pointing at the room marked with a duct-taped X.

"Damn," Stevens muttered. He picked up the camera as he set down his tool bag, evaluating the damage. "Well, the exterior looks fine. I wonder if anything is broken inside."

"I can take a look," Eli said and put his hand out. Stevens handed it over to Eli, who flipped it about in his hands. Finding the backing, he sat down on the dirty ground. It basic infrared camera--a trail cam most likely--with a few modifications. Eli wasn't sure if he could repair much of the custom work, but he could tell if it would still record.

Eli pulled the tool bag towards him until he found a little screwdriver to help him with the camera casing. Stevens used that time to do a sweep of the rooms, looking for any unusual signatures.

"Hey Stevens," Eli called out, his attention still on the camera in his hands. The other man started to wander away, down towards the other side of the hallway.

"Yeah?"

"I was just wondering how you got into all of this. My experience with military guys leads me to believe they'd never go for all of this haunted shit," he said, pulling off the backing of the camera and examining the interior. A few cords disconnected they were easy fixes.

Stevens gave a sort of mix between a laugh and a huff. "Then you haven't met enough *military guys*," he replied, letting his arm drop to his side. "Everyone I know, at least, everyone who's ever had to do an active duty tour, they've all seen something. So much death and horror… It's a breeding ground for the paranormal. The unknown."

Eli hummed and wondered if he should press his luck. Stevens was intimidating enough without being irritated. Would pushing for more information set the man off?

"One of my buddies died while I was in Afghanistan," Stevens said after a few moments without further prompting. He continued his EMF sweep as he spoke. "A lot of them did. But this guy, he was the best man at my wedding. We grew up together. He was family. We were ambushed while clearing out a building and he was shot. Died in my arms. One of the worst days of my life— wondering why I lived, and he didn't. You wonder that a lot, over there."

He turned his back to Eli and then reached into one of the pockets of his cargo pants, pulling out a little notebook and a pen. He clicked it and started making a few notes before moving onto the other side of the hallway.

"Anyhow, I saw him everywhere I went. Obviously, people thought it was PTSD—which was understandable. But one night I woke up and he was just standing at the foot of my bunk, staring at me. He didn't look dead. He was wearing his tux from my wedding, complete with the fresh boutonniere… It was different from the other times I'd been seeing him. He just stood there, staring at me.

I stared back all night long. In the morning I went to the medic to get help. I felt crazy."

He finished his sweep and went to stand over Eli, arms crossed. Eli didn't much care for someone looking over his shoulder while he worked, but Stevens wasn't looking at him at all, gazing ahead towards the stairwell they had come through.

"They held me for evaluation for a few days. My unit went out on a mission. None of them came back. Might seem crazy to you— well, maybe not, you've seen things. I swear to all that is holy, my buddy had come back to warn me. I would've been with my unit if not for him, and I'd be dead."

Eli finished fixing the loose wiring and clicked the case closed, starting to screw it back together. "That sort of sounds like what Garrett said about his experience."

Stevens nodded and stepped away, giving Eli some space again. "Yeah, similar. That's how we ended up working together. We met online, looking for answers. We realized we had similar mentalities and weren't total nut jobs like some of the others on the forums with us... Spent some time doing research, jumping around with other teams, then formed our own. Figured we'd get better results that way."

Eli stood and handed the camera back to Stevens, who promptly began to rig it back up above the doorway like it'd been before. "You don't like other teams, I take it?" Eli said with a quick smirk. It was hard to imagine Stevens putting up with guys like Jackson on the regular.

Stevens snorted. "Deittman seems alright. But he's one of the first *legit* guys I've met. People try too hard to get famous from their work, and they're willing to fake evidence or take what little they might 'find' and run with it. That doesn't answer the questions I have, so there's no point dealing with them. Alright, we're set."

With the camera snapped back in place, Eli gathered up the tools he had been using and stood once more. Settling into a comfortable silence, the two men started back down the stairs. Stevens had such an air of confidence and command about him that Eli managed to forget where he was, at least for a little while. His aura was almost infectious, and Eli couldn't help but feel a little more reassured about the weekend, knowing a guy like Stevens was on their team.

CHAPTER 15

"You look distraught," Eli said as he walked into the base to relieve Garrett of his watch. Ash was once again outside watching the fire, keeping it a roaring blaze hot enough to warm their canned soup lunch. It certainly wasn't much but Eli was glad for the hot food. It had grown much chillier in the building. He was certain he would be able to see his breath soon if the temperature kept dropping. If only he'd thought to pack heavier socks and some gloves...

Everyone had slept as late as they could in the morning. Garrett took the shift to relieve Markus and Isabella, who were currently napping. It was almost eleven and Deittman's team members were only beginning to shuffle about.

Garrett's eyes flicked up over the rim of his glasses at Eli, perhaps with a bit of annoyance. He sighed and slapped a composition notebook shut. "Just irritated that we can't get Internet access up here. Deittman insisted we keep our phones shut off so as not to interfere with any equipment. I triple-checked all of my notes and, though I can mostly validate the stories from Vincent, I absolutely cannot find anything on the little girl in the basement. Now, granted, I certainly didn't have access to the details like he did, but I feel like I would have come across that one during our research. I found nearly everything else."

Eli nodded slowly, trying to think of a reason why Garrett and Stevens wouldn't have been able to find a record of such an incident--such a terrible tragedy that surely would have made the news. "Yeah, I get why you're frustrated. I guess you'll have to go along with it, right? And double-check the accuracy later?"

"I suppose so," Garrett muttered and pulled off his glasses. He rubbed his eyes a bit before sliding them back on. "Are you going to sit here and watch the monitors?"

"Yup," Eli replied. He was a bit relieved to find Garrett had pulled an extra blanket out from his truck and had kept it in the observation seat. The base was colder than some of the other areas they were in—partially because of the open second-story area, and partially because of the numerous glass windows along the outside wall. They were poorly sealed and let air seep in through the corners.

Garrett stretched and stood. "It's all yours. Hope they left me some food. Oh, and don't be alarmed if you pick up activity in the basement. Jackson and Marina have been going down all morning. If they've finished eating, I won't be surprised if they go back. Unfortunately, it seems we won't be able to record any reliable footage from our sole basement camera because of whatever they're doing, but at least we don't have too many reports from the area besides the girl and the boiler man."

"The boiler man?" Eli asked, brows furrowed.

"Yeah, the boiler man—at least, that's what staff called him, I guess." Garrett frowned. "He was someone who was in and out of here, most likely for schizophrenia, a mild case of it. He would drink and start talking to no one, mostly. Sometimes he was dangerous; most times he wasn't. Anyhow, after one drinking incident, the local police picked him up and dropped him off here. Basically, they didn't want to deal with him. It was the middle of winter, in the middle of the night, and no one noticed him passed out at the front door. When someone did, hours after he had been left outside, they took him down to the boiler room to let him sleep it off instead of checking him in. Whoever it was probably thought they were doing him a favor, letting him sleep near the warm boiler so he could leave in the morning instead of opening an official case. But unfortunately, the man died from hypothermia. Now people report seeing and hearing him. He generally leaves the women alone, but he can be violent against the men who enter the room," Garrett explained.

Eli nodded and hummed with interest. "I see. And we haven't caught anything down there yet? Or even if we did, you're saying it's unreliable because of Jackson and Marina's contamination?"

"Exactly. Very annoying. I wish they had been more upfront with Deittman before he accepted their money for this trip. He never would have agreed, had he known they would cause such trouble…" Garrett trailed off and waved, signaling that he was done talking. "Right. Well, I'll be back after a nice nap."

Taking the extra blanket, Eli settled into the folding canvas chair. With a poor-tasting, instant coffee in his hand, courtesy of Ash's boiling water at the campfire, Eli almost felt right at home in front of the monitors. It was like being back at his old desk job. He was just starting to think that the day would be better despite the cold when he caught movement at the balcony above him.

Eli could only sigh and try to stare at the screen as the Echo of the nurse fell from the balcony played out her final few moments— though this time he witnessed enough to think maybe she *had* been pushed.

Never mind, Eli thought, *this is going to be just as bad as yesterday. Maybe worse.*

Everyone gathered around the base during their early dinner time. Even Garrett was awake after his few hours of afternoon sleep to grab a peanut butter sandwich, an apple, and a bag of chips. It wasn't exactly filling but it was much better than what Eli had been eating since he had moved into his crappy apartment anyhow. The base was too crammed without enough seating for everyone, so Eli slipped away to sit out on the front steps, enjoying the sunshine and the clear, albeit cold, evening.

He stretched out his legs on the stone steps and groaned as his tense muscles finally relaxed. Spending most of the day and night walking up and down steps and standing on the hard hospital flooring had caused more than a few aches and pains. Though the cot wasn't horrifically uncomfortable, Eli had needed to scrunch up a bit so his legs would fit on the bed and under the blankets. It did nothing to help his stiff knees.

"I'm getting old," he muttered to himself.

After he finished eating, Eli simply sat with his arms on either side of him propping himself up, his eyes closed. With the sun beating down on him, warming him, and a breeze that smelled like autumn, Eli felt content for a few moments.

Of course, his contentment didn't last, much to his dismay.

"Hey man," Jackson said from behind Eli.

Eli clenched his jaw and held in a groan.

Without invitation, Jackson sat down next to him, munching on a bag of chips. "So, I was hoping you'd come down to the boiler room with me."

Eli looked at Jackson from the corner of his eye before pressing his mouth into a thin line and shaking his head. "I'm not going down to the basement."

"C'mon, really? You plan to be here the whole weekend without setting foot in the basement? That's the best area in this whole place!"

"Best area? No, I think that's the Doctor's Quarters," Eli replied. "At least something's *happened* in there."

"We've caught stuff," Jackson insisted.

Eli rolled his eyes. "Dude, you know you're on the camera, right? We're watching as you try to set things up to move 'on their own.'"

That shut Jackson up. Maybe the guy was truly an idiot who thought they didn't all know why he and Marina had broken off from the group with their own camera and microphone. Deittman didn't seem to care so long as he and his team weren't on camera.

The hair on the back of Eli's neck stood on end as Jackson's eyes bore into him, and when he turned to meet the man's gaze, he was met with a hard, darkening stare.

"If you don't come and do your psychic thing in the basement, me and Marina will release your name. Good luck finding a real job then," Jackson said, quite seriously.

"You can't," Eli replied cautiously after a moment. "We signed confidentiality agreements."

Jackson smirked. "No, we signed agreements saying we wouldn't release any information about PTGS Paranormal or Deittman and his team. You and Ash are consultants and don't count."

"Seriously? You're fucking blackmailing me? I've got a kid, you know. The last thing I want is for her hearing that her dad is a crazy person because of something someone saw in a magazine or on fucking YouTube," Eli said with disgust.

"Well then you'd best come down, do your thing, and be on your way then."

And with that, Eli ended up angrily stomping down the stairs of the basement, trying his hardest to put on a brave face despite whatever he may have to see and hear. He couldn't let his family find out about him seeing Echoes—he just couldn't, especially because of *Jackson-Fucking-Cohen*.

The basement was much larger than he had expected. It spanned the entire way under the building with a series of rooms and support beams holding up the foundation. There was a lot of … junk. Junk everywhere. It was dusty and damp, and it reeked of mildewy cellar.

The area certainly made him feel uncomfortable, but not because of the atmosphere—it was because of all the nooks and crannies that Eli imagined someone could have easily been hiding in between the shadows, and he would never had known.

Cobwebs covered spare wheelchair parts and gurneys lined the walls, some looking ready to collapse if anyone so much as breathed on them. Piles of unlaundered towels and sheets still sitting next to a series of retro industrial washers and dryers. Mops, buckets, brooms, and other cleaning supplies were lumped up in half-sorted stacks as if someone had abandoned their task mid-way. Then, of course, there were the items that reminded Eli of the building's terrible past—crates of padded restraints, bits, and straight jackets. Eli couldn't help but feel like he was walking through a paid-admission, Halloween haunted house.

But besides all of that, besides the creepy anatomy dolls and suitcases filled with pilfered belongings, the basement was the most normal place in the entire facility. He didn't feel anything unnatural at all.

"You getting anything?" Jackson asked, turning his camera on Eli.

Eli frowned and held his hand out to cover his face. "Putting my face in one of your damned videos is a hell of a lot worse than you releasing my name to the public."

Jackson snickered. "Don't be so uptight. Everyone looks a lot different in night vision—like *a lot* different. We'll distort your face a bit if need be but no one's gonna know it's you. Anything?"

Eli groaned loudly and shook his head. "Nothing. Absolutely no activity down here. Just like I said."

"The boiler room is down here, come on," Marina said, causing Eli to jump at the sound of her voice. She waved at him, drawing Eli's attention to a cramped walkway leading back towards the asylum side. She knew right where to lead them through the chaos of littered items. They went back into a small room with an open door, leading down to another level of the basement.

Upon descending to the next level, which was barely a fourth of the size of the first basement floor, the air immediately changed. It only took him a moment to pinpoint what was different—the presence of an Echo.

"There," he said, pointing to an area around a large water tank.

Jackson and Marina carefully crept over, their flashlights pointing where Eli indicated.

"I don't see anything," Marina said with a disappointed sigh.

"Well, of course you don't," Eli replied, shoving his hands into his pocket. "Remember, I don't see like ghosts or anything. It's like... like, set images. If you had some of Garrett or Deittman's equipment, you might get a reading or something. But I can't just like... Make something happen."

"At least tell us what you're witnessing—is it terrifying?" Marina pressed.

Eli furrowed his brows at her in confusion. "...No? It's just a guy who looks like he's sleeping. He's in brown pants, they're patched up, and a dirty blue button-down. He has suspenders. If this is the boiler room man, he died of hypothermia. He looks like a normal, sleeping guy. It's sad."

Jackson exhaled loudly as if frustrated with a child. "C'mon, give us something to work with. Make something up, act more like those mediums on that British ghost show."

"No," Eli replied sharply. "I'm not having you twist my words after the fact and making me sound like a fraud. That's worse than being called crazy. I'm not a medium. I don't talk to ghosts. I see loops that don't interact with anything in the current timeline. It's not something anyone can really use to their advantage."

"Seriously though, what if we throw some money your way?" Jackson asked, causing Marina to *tsk* loudly. "Deittman's paying you. We'd pay you for a few lines."

"*No*," Eli snapped. "I don't want anyone seeing me. You may be in this for some sort of online fame, but I'm not." Without a further word, Eli turned and stormed up the steps. He knew that going off in a fury was probably a bad idea, but he didn't want to stick around and listen to so much as another '*but.*'

However, it wasn't long before Eli found himself turned around in the basement. He had his little penlight on him, but all he saw were piles of junk around him, creating a labyrinth for him to navigate. He worked on pushing forward, back toward the center where the steps leading up to the first floor were located, but it was difficult. Everything looked the same, especially in the dim light. Add in all the little rooms, Eli couldn't even find a solid wall to follow.

Finally, he stopped and glanced around, his muscles tightening as he tried not to panic.

He had no idea where he was.

Was that...? It was. Movement somewhere to his left. Eli whirled around with his flashlight, trying to find the source. At first, he thought he was going to witness an Echo, but instead found one of the old wheelchairs, one tipped onto its side, had a wheel spinning.

Definitely not an Echo.

Eli backed up a bit, jumping as he bumped into one of the anatomy dummies. He turned quickly and his heart racing as his eyes met the fake, skeletal face.

"Jesus Christ," he muttered, his hand on his chest as his heart pounded. Shaking his head, he moved the light away and swept it over the rest of the room.

He cursed under his breath. He could have sworn he saw someone, or something, move back against the far wall. He had grazed over it too quickly with his flashlight, and when he pointed it back in the general direction, it was gone.

"I'm fucking out of here," Eli said, desperately continuing down the through the piled-up crap.

To his relief, he saw the light from the open door in the distance. He still needed to figure out how to reach it, but he sharply inhaled as he pressed on.

Movement resumed behind Eli. This time, he didn't stop. He started walking faster. It was getting closer.

He was nearly there—almost close enough that he could start plowing through the boxes if he had to in order to get to the stairs. Whatever it was behind him seemed to be a row over to his left—it was so close, and—

"Eli?"

It was Ash's voice calling down from the top of the stairs.

"I'm down here!" he shouted back up, panic lacing his words—more panic than he cared to show.

Perhaps she sensed the urgency in his voice, as not a heartbeat later, Ash's heavy boots were thundering down the stairs to meet him at the bottom.

Whatever had been following him stopped moving. Eli, however, did not so much as pause until he grabbed onto her to steady himself. Once he did, he turned around, his eyes frantically searching for whatever had been chasing him in the dark.

"I—I thought—"

"I can go have a look," Ash said seriously, genuine concern in her eyes.

Part of Eli was relieved that she wasn't mocking him, while another part of him was embarrassed that the woman felt the need to go check for monsters for him.

"No, nothing, never mind," he said and shook his head, "it was probably nothing. I need to get out of here."

He didn't hesitate to go up the stairs.

Once he reached the top, he looked down to find her still standing at the bottom without a flashlight, staring into the dark. She had one foot ahead of her as if to brace herself, with her lighter clicked open in her hand. She stood completely still for a moment--a moment that seemed to last forever in Eli's mind.

Whatever comfortable atmosphere he had experienced upon walking down was gone, and all he wanted was for Ash to get back up with him into the light.

Finally, she turned around and casually walked up the stairs, almost as if she was daring something to try to come up after her.

"Jackson and Marina still down there?" she asked, popping a cigarette between her lips. Eli was sort of feeling like he could go for one himself.

"Yeah. How did you know--?"

Ash nodded to her left, toward the base. "Saw you on the basement camera. You looked freaked out."

He cracked a smile and nodded. Now that he was standing in the sunlight pouring in from the open front doors, his tension began to melt away. "I guess I was. Pretty stupid. I see dead people, and there I was, getting myself worked up over the dark."

She didn't look amused. "You *should* be afraid of the things lurking in the dark."

CHAPTER 16

Eli did not envy the life of an intern.

He was lucky enough to have never been in the position. Even back when he was in school, he remembered how his friends complained of the long hours with no pay, and all the ways they were taken advantage of in the name of experience or exposure. He was glad to have missed it. Though he thought Carlos was on the lucky side to end up with such an interesting gig, Eli had to laugh as Carlos went around cleaning up their headquarters after dinner. Once the sun began to drop below the tree line, the young man was forced to scurry about, trying to collect all of the trash before darkness set in.

"Grunt work, huh?" Eli commented, leaning against the doorframe and crossing his arms. The chillier weather caused Eli to wear his coat at all times, keeping his hands stuffed in his pockets for warmth. Carlos only had on a thick hoodie, but he didn't seem to mind.

Carlos sighed and shrugged. "I guess. Can't be fun and games all the time. It could be worse. I could be working in customer service cleaning up *real* messes."

Eli chuckled, knowing the truth of that claim, and reached down to pick up two soda cans and three water bottles that he had left behind the day before.

"This going in the room off the atrium?" he asked as he dropped the bottles into Carlos's bag.

"Yeah, but I still have to clean up around the fire next and check for any dead batteries in the equipment."

"I'll come with you. I think the others went off to investigate, so I'm probably supposed to stay with you," Eli said, glancing about. Indeed, no one was around, leaving him to watch the monitors. He didn't think Carlos should be walking around by himself though, so the monitors would have to wait.

"Oh, thanks," Carlos said, his shoulders relaxing, visibly relieved at not having to walk around alone.

The two of them started down the hallway to the building entrance, picking up other bits of their trash they found along the way. Eli accidentally kicked a piece of plaster, sending it skidding into one of the rooms, and Carlos jumped.

"You seem a bit... skittish," Eli said, raising a brow. "I'm beginning to think you don't actually like being here."

Carlos laughed nervously. "No, no, I do. Seriously. I think it's a lot of fun—cool stories after, you know? I'm just... twitchy, I guess. I've done other locations with Garrett and Stevens, but this is the first time we're somewhere so remote for so long." He grimaced. "I think I've been psyching myself out about it. Well, that and the door thing yesterday kind of freaked me out."

Eli hummed thoughtfully. "Oh really? I figured you guys would be used to that sort of stuff."

"No," Carlos said, shaking his head, his curly hair bouncing as he did. "Not for me, at least. Maybe the other guys have seen more. I've never actually experienced anything. The only weird thing that's ever happened to me was that I knew when my parents died. I just... *knew,* and I told my gram, but she didn't believe me. Then she got the call. Super weird, but not like, ghostly."

"Oh. I'm... sorry to hear about your parents," Eli said as they stepped through the front doors. It was still fairly sunny out, but clouds were starting to roll in. The team might have to start planning for some bad weather if the gray in the distance was any indication.

"Thanks, but it was over a decade ago. I barely remember them—I grew up with my gram. Obviously, I would rather have my parents back, but their life insurance policies are putting me through school, so there's that."

The two of them fell into a silence as they straightened up their little cooking area. Eli separated the clean cookware from the dirty, which Carlos took from him, saying he'd figure out how to clean the dirty ones. They reset the stones around their makeshift fire pit and tossed any wrappers.

"So," Eli said as they finished, and Carlos tied off his bag. They didn't want any rodents getting into it and they had already seen a dozen or so. "Is it because of your parents that you got into all of this?" Eli asked, gesturing toward the building above them. Carlos laughed, a wide smile on his face.

"Well, *technically,* yeah. My parents were both in the Air Force— they died in a car accident, not on duty—and my gram and I would attend events for veterans and their families in my town. A lot of my parents' friends looked after me growing up. Anyhow, Stevens was at one such event, and we just got to talking. After a while, he told me about his team, and that was it. It took some convincing, but he let me join. He's…" Carlos paused, and Eli swore that he spied a bit of red creeping up Carlos's neck, even in the growing darkness.

The intern's eyes around, making sure that no one was in earshot, and that there were no recording devices nearby.

Carlos tilted his head down and lowered his voice. "Alright, this is super embarrassing, so don't say anything. When I met Stevens, he kind of reminded me of my dad. At least how I remember my dad, anyway. So, working with him is like how I would imagine working with my dad would be," he sighed. "Yeah, I know. Weird, right? But it's fun. And Garrett's pretty cool too. I'm studying

Computer Science right now, but if I can get my shit together, maybe I'll switch to an engineering field so I can work on paranormal devices too. It would be awesome if I could come up with something good and make it rich."

As his voice picked up again, Carlos went on to ramble about his school work and how he hoped to apply it to the paranormal investigation fields. Eli half-listened with a soft smile on his face. Carlos, with his happy innocence, was "too precious for this world". At least that's what Sophia would say if she were here with them.

Thinking about his wife made Eli sigh and wonder what he would do if Sarah had told him she was taking up ghost hunting. He'd probably try to lock her in her room to protect her from the paranormal. He couldn't imagine her having to face the things he saw. Or maybe it wouldn't be so bad. After all, for people like Carlos, places like Maple Hill weren't all *that* dangerous.

So long as they avoid falling plaster and the occasional haunted door, right?

Eli shoved his hands back in his pockets as they turned towards headquarters once more—Deittman's accented tones flit down the hallway, indicating that the others had returned.

"Now that we are together again, let us organize our equipment and plan for the next step," Deittman said as everyone searched for a seat in the headquarters. Eli noticed that Ash was holding a stack of files and a few bound books as she looked for a place to put them. Eventually, after not finding a spot, she huffed and dropped them on the floor with a startling *smack,* causing nearly everyone to jump. The group eyed her in annoyance, but she ignored them.

"I think we will need to drag Jackson and Marina out of the basement eventually," Garrett sighed, taking his glasses off and rubbing them with the edge of his button-down. "Stevens and I tried to get them to rotate but they refused. They keep saying they aren't done with what they're doing. I'm inclined to let them do whatever it is if only for the sake of convenience. We can investigate tomorrow. I have an inkling they aren't getting anything worthwhile."

Eli nodded though Markus and Deittman shared a skeptical look. "I don't think there's much activity. Boiler Man, maybe. But it was just, well, dead," Eli said with a shrug. It might have been cliché, but it was true. And after his last trip down, he absolutely did not want to go back—even if it was nothing.

"Agreed," Ash chimed in from her spot on the ground. She had her back to them, sorting through the files.

Deittman sighed. "I suppose you're right. If there's nothing worth investigating, it will be easier to exclude the basement from our research presentations, and we will be able to discredit any of their falsified evidence. This is the last time I let individuals buy their way onto my team…"

"Well, shall we continue?" Markus suggested. "Eli, we were hoping you would join us in the Asylum. We'd like to sweep the second floor—your post-cog abilities might be useful," Markus said with a small smile that Isabella mimicked from next to him. It was a tad creepy, but it at least looked endearing on the young woman.

Eli had hoped to avoid the asylum for as long as possible but figured it would only be a matter of time before he had to go check it out in a small group. "If you think it's safe…"

"Perfectly safe!" Deittman said, clapping his hands together and rubbing them—part in excitement but also perhaps also for warmth. "Now, everyone check your torch batteries and we shall be off."

Now that Eli knew what to expect out of the asylum side, or, at least, he hoped he did, he noticed a few other details when Deittman opened the heavy metal door. The odor inside was drastically different than that of the hospital side. It was a smell of decaying wood with a strong, smoky scent imbedded into every slab of stone that built the massive facility. Water damage from a half-repaired roof left rot and mildew to permeate the air. Isabella brought a mask with her this time around.

Eli doubted it was safe to spend much time there. If the floors of the second level didn't collapse on them then whatever they were breathing in might shave some years off their lives. They *all* should have been wearing masks as they mucked about, kicking up dirt and dust particles with each step.

The team entered and began investigating the first floor. Eli tried his best not to touch anything, as he couldn't help but find the entire area disgusting. Markus and Deittman would stop sporadically and ask questions to the air while holding out a voice recorder and an EMF detector. They would wait a minute or so before asking something else. They were clearly hoping for a response as Eli noticed that Markus had in earphones so he could listen back in real-time.

"Eli, would you like to ask anything?" Deittman prodded, perhaps hopeful that Eli would participate.

Eli shifted uncomfortably. "Um, no, thanks. I see enough as it is, so I'm not exactly hoping to find anything else if I can help it."

Deittman muttered in disappointment but he didn't force Eli to contribute. After they had finished some thirty minutes or so later, they started to move.

"Shall we move onto the next floor?" Deittman asked. Markus kept the recorder going, but Eli figured he couldn't hear much. Since they all made so much noise moving through the rubble-covered hallway there would be too much noise contamination.

As they started to make their way up to the second floor, a dizziness began to come over Eli. At first, he assumed it was from the amount of sheer *crap* he was inhaling, but soon his vision started to tunnel, and faint orbs started to bob in front of his eyes. He hated that he thought of them as *orbs* because it was a paranormal term and he thought it was *stupid*. But orbs they were, and as the group continued on, the orbs started to grow into *shapes*.

Frantic movement surrounded him, and his heart started to race—he was afraid, terrified. At the same time, Markus stopped and shushed everyone, holding up a hand. He stared at the recorder and then pressed his hand to his earphones as if it would help him listen.

One of the shapes passed through Eli and he began to sway. "I think I'm going to—"

"Shh!!"

Eli felt a hand on his back, and he jumped, looking at his left. It was Isabella. She had stepped down to meet him without him noticing. She placed one hand on his back and another on his arm, standing with her legs splayed on the steps. This braced her weight and, in turn, helped her brace his.

His swaying stopped and then his vision slowly returned to normal. He blinked and shook his head. Everything was gone—well, everything unusual at least.

"It stopped," Markus said, pulling the earphones out and shaking his head. "We'll have to do a playback on the stereo, but it sounded like... well, chaos. Moans, groans, screams... but it was all rather faint. Perhaps it's only a bit of apophenia, and I'm making the building sounds into what I wanted to hear."

Eli wasn't so sure about that. He was sure a surge of energy had descended upon them.

"Could you see that?" he asked Isabella. She shook her head and tapped her chest a few times. "But you could feel it?

She nodded.

"What's what?" Deittman asked Eli from the top of the stairs.

Eli sighed. He had no idea how to explain what happened. "My vision started to sort of narrow and tunnel. I saw these weird orbs—faintly glowing floating balls, I guess—that turned into--into vaguely person-shaped masses. I felt, well, scared. Then really sick. I thought I was going to pass out...actually, I think I need to sit down..." he muttered with a faint groan.

Isabella helped him up the stairs, apparently not quite as ill as he. When they reached the top Eli promptly sat down against the door to the Doctor's Quarters, the newest, cleanest, and sturdiest thing side of the building had, and focused on calming himself.

Deittman and Markus continued down the hallway, gingerly testing the floor before putting their full weight on it, careful to step around any weak areas. Isabella stayed with Eli, standing to the side of him and leaning against the wall. Though Eli was glad to not be left alone, there was something mildly unsettling about the silent woman. She was so pale—her skin, her hair, even her light, white and pastel clothes... Markus matched her and Eli watched the man's light figure moving about, despite his distance away. Both of the twins were a stark contrast to the hazy atmosphere, almost like spirits hovering in the dark.

Eli gently laid his head back on the door, trying to be soft so that Deittman's recorder wouldn't pick up any sound. He closed his eyes, hoping his wave of discomfort would pass.

Just as he was starting to feel like the room wasn't spinning, he heard movement behind him. Eli opened his eyes again but remained frozen in place.

It sounded like scratching, and then some sort of dragging. It was coming from the Doctor's Quarters.

Must be rats, he told himself. It had to be the mice or rats they had already seen about the area. Eli had no desire to investigate the Doctor's Quarters again, so he told himself *fuck that* and kept his mouth shut. He sat forward so that his ears weren't quite so close to the door. He glanced up at Isabella, who was still watching Deittman and her brother. She showed no signs of hearing anything.

The ceiling above them was partially intact. There were a few broken sections above Eli but as the hallway went on, the third-floor area looked worse and worse. Eli wondered how much of the fourth floor was still around since Vincent had said most of it had collapsed.

"We can't get to the stairs over here," Markus called down the hallway. "The floor is too unstable. We're going to come back." He and Deittman turned their flashlights toward Eli and Isabella, causing Eli to squeeze an eye shut and raise his hands to block out the light.

Deittman began to move toward them, but after only a few paces, the soft creaking grew louder until there was a violent *crack!* from below the doctor. He halted and Markus carefully faced him while wearing a concerned frown. Deittman took another step forward and his foot started to go through the floor. Markus's hands darted out and caught him before he could put any more weight forward. Isabella pushed off the wall, ready to run down to help, but stopped.

"We're fine!" Deittman called out to assure them. He grabbed onto Markus fully and managed to dislodge himself. He regained his footing and brushed himself off. "Well, I had hoped to go to the third floor at least and take a look, but that seems unwise. Eli? You do not see anything?"

Eli shook his head. "No, at least not now. But I can't control when the Echoes come."

Deittman sighed and reluctantly resumed his return.

Eli and Isabella held their breath until the pair made it back safely to the sturdier section of the floor. Once they were all together, they did not hesitate to go back downstairs and then exit the building. As they did, Eli felt his shoulders drop as he released a mass of tension he hadn't realized he had been holding. He did not like the asylum. Echoes or no Echoes, he was sure something lying in wait for them.

CHAPTER 17

After his stint in the asylum, Eli decided he deserved a break outside by the fire. Isabella joined him, relieving Ash, who had been waiting for someone else to come be responsible before she left it. Isabella stoked the flames with a gentle prod and rubbed the back of her neck for a few minutes. Eli wondered if she was also trying to shake horrible feelings from the asylum. She only remained for about ten minutes before giving him a wave and heading back to headquarters.

Eli returned the wave and pulled up one of Stevens's canvas ballpark chairs. He eyed up the soda cans left on the corner of the porch for anyone to take, before deciding it was too chilly for a cold drink. He settled into the seat and rubbed his arms in attempt to generate warmth, but it seemed useless with the permanent chill radiating through his body.

"Eli," called a voice from behind him. He inwardly groaned and turned around, struggling to keep a scowl off his face. Marina stood before him, her arms across her chest. "I wanted to catch you—to talk to you about earlier."

"Leave me out of your filming. I don't want any part of it. I'm just trying to get through this weekend and get paid."

Marina sighed and shook her head, a frown forming. "I know. About that—I just wanted to... *apologize*... for Jackson's behavior.

I'm not going to use anyone's real names in my books, beyond whatever Deittman signs off on for his team. And Jackson has an entire production team combing through his stuff—he's not the one who gets to choose what footage they use. It's doubtful they'll use your footage."

Eli shuffled and nodded, but he didn't say anything else. He didn't have much to say to the woman at all—she and Jackson had kept to themselves without bothering with anyone else.

"Can I join you? It's pretty chilly," she said, gesturing to the fire.

"Oh, uh... yeah, sure."

Eli wasn't exactly eager to spend any more time than necessary with Marina, especially not after Jackson's pushiness in the basement. However, he supposed her apology was fine enough and it was at least slightly reassuring to learn his name and image weren't likely to be used on some stupid web series.

Marina took the seat Isabella had dragged out and leaned forward to warm her hands over the flames, her manicured fingernails reflected the light of the fire. Eli raised a brow.

She looked so... out of place. While Deittman, Markus, and Isabella all dressed for afternoon tea most of the time, they still had an air of professionalism about them. They knew exactly what to do and when to do it. Marina, however, looked like she was waiting to jump in front of a camera to talk about the breaking news.

Well, she had been a reporter, so that was no surprise.

"Are you... having fun?" Eli asked, figuring he should make some casual conversation. It had to be better than the awkward silence between them.

Marina opened her mouth to respond but was interrupted when the tall grass some distance behind her began to rustle. She twisted in her seat and peered over the stone railing of the porch. Eli also craned his neck, but it was too dark to spot anything without a flashlight. Marina turned back to the fire and shifted her chair so she was sitting closer to the entrance of the building.

"Well, it's been an interesting time," she said with a nervous laugh. "You really don't think the basement is haunted besides that Boiler Man?"

Eli shrugged, half wondering if she had a recording device in her pocket. "No idea. Like I said, it isn't like I see *ghosts*."

Marina sighed and put her head in her hands, brushing back some of her dark hair. Her olive skin shone in the fire's flickering light, her dark eyes reflecting the flames. "Yeah, I know. It's just..."

She trailed off. Eli waited, before prompting, "just what?"

Marina shook her head and closed her eyes. "I keep trying to convince Jackson to come back up, to rejoin the group, but he's *so stubborn*. I don't like it down there. It feels like we're being watched."

"Well, you *are* on Deittman's camera. We can see what you guys are doing." That is to say, Eli knew they were faking their evidence, just as he had told Jackson. All of Deittman's crew knew what they were doing.

"No, it isn't that," she said with a sigh. "There's weird movement. I swear I keep hearing footsteps, but it's just too dark. Weird squeaking, like a door, but the only unlocked door is the one up here, and it isn't that... It would be nice if we all stayed together, especially at night..."

Eli stared at the woman for a few moments. With furrowed brows and pursed lips, she may have actually been frightened. Though, he supposed, it was possible it was all an act to rope someone else into their little scheme.

"Nothing's stopping you. You could jump in with our smaller groups at any time. It would be easier on everyone if you did. There's less noise pollution if we have one less group wandering around this place."

The longer he sat with her, the more he started to pity her. She hadn't slept well, judging by the circles under her eyes and the tension in her shoulders. Not that any of them had slept much the previous night. He even swore she was quivering—maybe from the cold or maybe from being so tightly wound from fear for so many hours.

"I wish I could. Jackson won't stop filming for his stupid channel though, and right now, I'm signed on with the same entertainment company. I really *am* writing a book about historical locations left to crumble, but I need to have something to supplement my income while I wait," Marina said, grimacing. Eli figured there was a story there—one he could probably relate to as he navigated the bureaucracy of unemployment.

He gave her a sympathetic nod. "I know how that is."

Marina returned the nod and sat back with a groan, stuffing her manicured hands into the pockets of her puffy white winter jacket. She had been one of the smart ones when packing. "I'm granted an appearance fee for being a guest on this episode. He and his manager are hoping to use it as a launching point for a full-fledged TV series. That's why the company was willing to dish out the money to Deittman for access to the building and some interviews."

"Oh," Eli replied, grabbing the thick stick Isabella had used to stoke the fire. He gave it a few prods and tossed another few sticks onto it. "Yeah, I think some of us were wondering how Jackson managed to get on the team. Deittman, uh, doesn't seem like the type to appreciate *influencers*."

Marina gave a soft laugh and smiled. Eli realized then that she was a very attractive woman. He had been put off by her stern attitude because whereas Ash was rough around the edges, Marina felt too refined. He instinctively put himself on guard in fear of judgment. It hadn't been fair of him to jump to conclusions. "I'll tell you a secret—neither am I."

Eli cracked a smile. Alright, so Marina wasn't half bad. In fact, he would dare to say she could be the most *normal* person in their ten-person gang, giving Stevens a run for his money.

"Well, at least we're all on the same page," Eli said before starting to stand up. "I should really head back in. I think I'm supposed to be relieving someone in the headquarters."

"Yeah, I suppose I should go back downstairs… Guess I was hoping to sit out here for a while longer," she replied, her expression dropping.

Eli had been about to stand when he paused. He glanced into the entryway, down towards the dark basement doorway, before relaxing again and grabbing an unopened soda from a line of cans behind him.

"Actually, I'm sure they'll come find me when they need me. I think I'll sit a little longer and caffeinate… do you want a soda?"

"Oh, yes, please. Is there something diet?"

Eli grabbed a diet soda and handed it over. She accepted it, visibly relieved to have more time at the fire. She opened her can and dove into stories about some of the other locations she had on her research list after Maple Hill. Eli half-listened as she spoke; the other part of his attention was straining to hear what sounded like movement. It had started from somewhere behind Marina in the direction of Stevens's parked van.

Though he never saw anything, Eli swore the rustling crept closer, as if to watching them from the shadows.

"What are you doing?" Eli asked Ash as he walked back into the base and dropped into his designated seat. The fire had only done so much to soothe him. He needed painkillers or a stiff drink. Or both. Both would be nice. He would be staring at the monitors in the dark for a while now that his 'shift' had started, and the eye strain was destined to bring about a headache.

Ash sat in the corner of the room between the outside wall and one of the folding tables littered with equipment. She had her cheap pillow behind her, an unlit cigarette in her mouth, and a bottle of soda sitting next to a flask a few inches away from her crossed legs. She had a stack of folders and books scattered about.

She hummed and put her head back, rubbing her own eyes. "Garrett asked me to go through some of the records we pulled out of the basement. Looking for death certificates or anything to put names to the incidents. Guess they think it'll drum up some better activity if they can connect or something."

"And did you find anything?" Eli asked.

Ash shrugged. "No, not really. I don't even want to be doing this. But it isn't like I have anything else to do here. This place is so boring. Was really hoping for something more. Here, take a look at this though. Tell me if you noticed the same thing I did."

She pulled a book off the top of one of the piles and slid it over to Eli, which hit his foot after it skidded across the floor. It was old and dusty, and it looked as if some moisture had caused damage to chunks of pages. Glancing it over, it seemed like it was a compendium of staff who worked in Maple Hill in the early forties. Eli picked it up and flipped the book open to a dog-eared page.

It was hard to see in the dimming light of the room, so Eli grabbed a penlight from the table and clicked it on.

"It's a staff photo," Eli replied. What he noticed right away was the fact that the nurse's uniforms were the same as the one the Echo falling from the balcony had been wearing. Ash couldn't have known that, however, so it must have been something else. He flicked his eyes over to her to find her gaze on him—possibly evaluating if he was as observant as she.

Eli sighed, "alright, alright. Let me see…. Maple Hill Staff, 1944… Oh. That's the doctor—Doctor Pollock. Okay… Nurse Colton, that must be Vincent's grandmother or whatever."

"Anything else you notice?"

"She's… pregnant?"

Ash nodded. "Yup. Her last name was Colton already and she's pregnant in the forties. I'm willing to guess she was Vincent's great-grandmother."

Eli shrugged. "Okay, yeah, maybe."

She stared at him and waved her hand a bit, as if to say '*and…?*'

"I don't get it. What are you getting at?"

Ash exhaled in frustration, removing the cigarette from her mouth and twirling it between her fingers. "You don't find it at all *weird* that the guy knew enough about this place to give us some incredibly detailed stories, but he didn't know that it was his great-grandmother, and not his grandmother, who ratted the doctor out? Or that she was already married when she worked here? He specifically said that she married *after* she quit here."

Eli shrugged and moved the book to one of the tables, leaving it open for the others to see when they came in. "I guess. I don't know. I don't know that much about my grandparents. You're making assumptions on age here, I don't think that means anything."

Ash hummed loudly, displeased with Eli's answer. Without another word, she clicked on her own penlight and resumed flipping through the pages in front of her.

CHAPTER 18

"What is he doing...?" Garrett muttered and leaned forward, his face illuminated by the glow of the monitor.

Eli had finished his shift at the monitors and had opted to take a quick snooze in their sleeping room for an hour. He tossed and turned, unable to get more than a few minutes of shut-eye at a time. An irritating scratching from somewhere below him, possibly in the building's internal structuring itself between the first floor and the basement, kept him awake. Eli hoped it was rats and thought nothing more of it. Eventually, Isabella came and gave him a few gentle prods to indicate it was time for him to return.

He had groaned with a sense of defeat and followed her out to headquarters, just in time to see Garrett's bewilderment.

"What's wrong?" Markus asked and walked around the table to stand behind Garrett, his brows furrowing as he tilted his head in confusion.

Garrett glanced between the monitors and the balcony on the second floor. "Carlos. He was just supposed to switch out the batteries in the voice recorders above us. I don't know why he's even in the Doctor's Quarters—"

"You deliberately sent him upstairs alone?" Markus interrupted, his voice sharp.

Garrett pressed his mouth into a thin line and looked up at Markus over the rim of his glasses. "I thought he would be fine since he was just going to be on the second floor," he said, pointing to the balcony above them, "and we'd be able to hear him if he needed help. The door to the Doctor's Quarters has been locked since it shut earlier, but we couldn't tell until now when Carlos adjusted the camera."

Markus pointed at the monitor that showed the new camera angle. Carlos had turned the second-floor camera to point directly into the open door of the Doctor's Quarters. The camera faced straight down the hall into the previously locked area. Eli saw from the feed that *both* of the Doctor's Quarters' doors were open.

"That locked asylum door is open—" Markus started to say, but he was cut off when they heard a *slam!* echo down from the hallway above them.

"And the door into the Doctor's Quarters just closed!" Garrett said with palpable alarm, jumping up and sending his seat clattering backward. There was a scramble as both he and Markus tried to rush to Carlos as fast as possible while grabbing flashlights. "Someone find Deittman! He's got the keys!"

Within minutes, most of the group was at the asylum door on the second floor. Stevens was leading the push to try to force the door open. Deittman appeared shortly after with Ash and Isabella, breathing heavily as he fumbled to pull Maple Hill's keyring from his pocket.

Deittman was struggling to find the key in the dark. The seconds seemed to last for hours as they waited until, with an 'Aha!', he put it into the lock. *Click.* But despite the door being clearly unlocked...

They could not push the door open.

Deittman and Stevens heaved, putting their entire weight into the door, trying and struggling to force it to move. Dread boiled up in his gut, remembering the difficulty they had prying the door open as it crushed. After considerable effort, the pair managed to gain some headway, creating a narrow opening into the Doctor's Quarters.

Though the gap was enough for Ash and Eli to squeeze through after Deittman, it slammed shut on the others despite Stevens's attempt to hold it open, the noise echoing ominously in Eli's ears.

Once inside, Eli immediately had to cover his face as he started to cough, hard—smoke was filling the room, wafting in from the open asylum door. To make matters worse, he heard screaming.

Lots of screaming.

Dozens of voices shrieked, begging for help, creating an overwhelming cacophony of agony and sound. He could barely make out shapes in the doorway, cloaked in thick, dark smoke, pounding on an invisible door to try to escape into the Doctor's Quarters but never crossing the threshold.

Eli glanced around at the other two of his teammates and found Deittman also coughing, covering his mouth with his arm. Eli's blood ran cold.

The smoke was *real*, even if the shapes of people beyond the haziness were not.

"There's too much smoke!" Deittman shouted, his voice muffled by his arm. "There is surely a growing fire—we mustn't remain!"

"What about Carlos?" Eli asked, thrusting his forearm to his face to cover his mouth and nose.

"I'll get him," Ash replied and let out a sigh—as if the prospect of it were simple and bothersome.

"You might be able to control some fire, but you can't take on an inferno!" Eli shouted after her.

She didn't so much as glance back at him as she responded coolly, "I'll be fine. You should get back to the other side fast... if you *can*."

Ash didn't seem at all bothered by the smoke in the room. She walked right through the cloud without so much as a sniffle as she left the two behind. Eli reached out to stop her but paused, watching as she strolled through the open door, colliding with the Echoes of screaming nurses and patients. To his surprise, they disappeared once she crossed through them. Usually the Echoes remained regardless of who or what entered their space.

"We cannot let her go alone," Deittman said determinedly, starting after her. "Even if she succeeds, she or Carlos could be injured, and we would never know!"

Eli reluctantly agreed. Deittman had a flashlight but the thick smoke made it hard to see despite the aid. They walked as slowly as they could afford to, watching their footing for any debris or weak flooring while remaining aware of the immediate danger the fire presented.

Eli knew that the hallway was as long as the other wing, so he moved with careful urgency. If Carlos had managed to wander down the entire length of the hallway, then they couldn't afford to go too slowly. But almost against his will, Eli found it becoming harder and harder to push on—not because of the smoke, but because of the sensation of experiencing so many Echoes all at once.

Eli had never been in an area of disaster before. It took a steely resolve to ignore the near-transparent people running around him. He knew they weren't real—Deittman didn't even flinch as a screaming nurse collided with him and then continued on *through* him. But for Eli, however, it wasn't so easy.

He could *smell* the burning flesh and hair as if it were real, the odor scorching his nose like an acid. He watched patients throwing themselves against the walls and floors as they desperately tried to smother the flames creeping up their pant legs or shirt arms. Eli stared at them in a mix of horror and pity, torn between wanting to try to run far away and to try to help snuff out the flames consuming the poor souls. The Echoes turned in his direction with pleading eyes, desperate for help, but Eli could do nothing other than step around them in hopes of saving someone still alive.

The further they went, the more the Echoes started to change—they had burned completely or had burning clothing. One man was trying to put out the flames burning his hair and scalp to no avail, his mouth twisted in a scream of agony. Eli wanted to scream himself, but he knew he couldn't—he would choke on the smoke. He pulled up the collar of his shirt and buried his nose and mouth in the fabric, using it as a filter. It helped him both breathe a bit better and hide the fact that Eli was trying not to be sick, the horrors of people being roasted alive turning his stomach over and over with nausea.

Once Deittman and Eli were about halfway down the hallway, marked by the charred nurses' station, they began to follow the glow of flames. The fire was in one of the patient rooms—possibly even the one that had been the epicenter of the 1970s inferno. The only reason so much of the floor had remained was because the original building was almost entirely stone, and it hadn't had much vulnerable structure. Still, the decay was enough to make the areas around them weak after forty years and the floorboards creaked ominously around Eli as if to warn him of the weaknesses in the floor.

They felt the heat before they reached the door and he turned his face away. Deittman, too, covered his face to shield himself from the intense heat radiating towards them, sweat beading on his forehead. Eli saw from his squinted eyes that Deittman had crouched down after stepping into the room in front of Eli.

Carlos was on the floor, curled up and pressed against the wall closest to the door, rocking slightly. His hoodie sleeve was smoldering and Eli suspected there was burned flesh peeking through the gaping holes. Carlos stared directly ahead, blinking rapidly and muttering something. Eli couldn't make out whatever he was saying over the screams of agony from the Echoes around them.

Gathering his courage, Eli finally turned and faced the flames—the flames that were very real, very hot, and very large, though still contained to just one area. As he was about to rush in, he saw Ash. The sight froze him in his spot. His blood ran cold, so much so that he forgot about the heat overwhelming him, as he watched in horror and fear.

Ash stood a few feet away from Carlos, towards the collapsed wall that had once separated the two rooms with her arms spread out at her sides. Like most of the rooms, the walls had collapsed at some point, as had the ceiling. The fire was actually coming from the room next to them, past the collapsed wall, and as much as it was trying to spread, it somehow *couldn't*. Perhaps it was because Ash was keeping it at bay. Perhaps it was because the fire was unnatural and thus did not move like fire was expected to.

Eli did not know it was possible, but to his horror, the fire actually had a *shape*.

Humanoid. That was the word that popped into Eli's mind. What else to call something that was human-shaped, but so very obviously not human? Its form towered over them, though hunched over to fit in the room, ignoring the fact that there was no ceiling to hold it down.

Deittman looked torn as he glanced between Carlos, Ash, and the fiery beast that should have logically been overtaking the building. Eli could practically see the thoughts running through the man's mind—this was the opportunity of a *lifetime*. He wanted to document the occurrence.

"An elemental..." Deittman breathed, his eyes darting around.

Carlos's camera was on the ground a few feet away. Though it didn't *look* damaged, Eli couldn't imagine that it would hold long against such heat. Regardless, Deittman grabbed the camera and hurried to position it on Ash and the fiery figure before helping to hoist Carlos up from the ground.

Carlos's leg was also burned, and his front was covered in dirt and soot. His hoodie was snagged and torn, so much so that Eli spied dark, bloody flesh from the glow of the flickering flames. By the way the front was covered in plaster residue and grey dust, it almost looked as though Carlos had been dragged along the ground.

After some balancing, Deittman started to move, helping Carlos limp out of the doorway and then down the hallway, back toward the Doctor's Quarters and the sole, safe stairwell on that side of the building.

"Ash!" Eli coughed, "Deittman and Carlos are gone! We need to get out of here!"

Ash didn't respond or give any indication that she had heard him. All of her focus was on the figure made of fire. Against his better judgment, Eli stepped forward and grabbed her arm, pulling her a few steps back.

Her body was stiff and before he managed to drag her anywhere, she yanked herself away from him. Eli turned back to shout at her, but his words caught in his throat.

Ash's head was cocked to the side, tilted at a near-unnatural angle. She seemed to regard him with interest, almost as if she had never seen him before.

It took Eli a moment to realize that her eyes, her dark brown eyes, had become yellow.

At first, he thought it may have been a trick of the light or the glow of the fire, but she was facing *away* from the flames. In fact, because of the darkness of the room and the light of the fire, her entire silhouette was dark *except* for her eyes.

They were sharp, fiery--predatory.

Eli swallowed hard and took a slow step back. The hair on the back of his neck stood on end as a sense of danger overwhelmed him. He felt like he was being watched by a wild animal, one ready to pounce. He glanced down when he noticed her finger start to twitch—or, spasm really. For a brief moment, he thought that Ash, or *whatever* she was right now, was ready to turn on him.

Maybe she was.

However, before she had the chance, the fiery creature let out a roar coming from everywhere and nowhere at once, and lurched forward at the pair of them.

Ash snapped back around, her arms wide and legs splayed in a defensive stance. The beast could do nothing but lean forward until its face-like area was a mere foot away from Ash's own. Eli stumbled backward, the sudden proximity of the fire scorching his skin.

The beast bellowed once more, but its roar was choked out. The flames of its body began to fold in on themselves until the beast was nothing more than a small campfire burning merrily in the corner of the room.

Ash thrusted her right hand upward and closed it into a fist, extinguishing the last of the flames.

There was only smoke left behind, but it was enough evidence to prove what Eli had seen was real.

The room was dark—pitch black. The windows, which Eli suspected had been replaced after the fire, were covered with so much soot that not even the moonlight shone through. Unfortunately, the tension in the air wasn't snuffed with the fire. Once the screaming around him faded, and the Echoes disappeared, Eli was left in silence, body frozen in fear.

He begged the floor to be silent under his weight, terrified that a single creak might set Ash upon him.

The heaviness in the atmosphere began to lighten until it remained hovering around only Ash, or where he supposed she was still standing since he couldn't see her, but he hadn't heard her move either. He took a careful step backward, his arm outstretched behind as he felt around for the doorframe. He found it but kicked something on the floor as he tried to creep toward it. It started to roll away, but he caught it with his foot before crouching down to grab it. To his relief, it was Carlos's flashlight.

Eli took a deep breath and stood again. He gathered his courage and clicked the light on, shining it on Ash.

She was still standing, facing the other room just as she had before it went dark. She was twitching—her fingers, her shoulders, her neck. Eli swallowed and stepped forward, this time choosing not to touch her. He stepped around until he was in front of her. Her eyes were still yellow, but she didn't seem to notice him as they darted around the room.

"...Ash?"

At the sound of her name, she stopped twitching and stared at him, yellow eyes unnaturally sharp. Eli's breath caught in his throat.

He shouldn't have done that.

He shouldn't have said anything. He should have left when he had the chance.

Eli scrambled backward only to find the floor was weak. His foot went straight through the burned area. Eli yelped as he fell, now stuck in the floor, the flashlight falling from his grip. It rolled away from him, shining on Ash as she took a slow step toward him.

And another.

And then another.

Before she closed in on him, there was a worrisome creaking, and the rest of the floor around Eli began to crumble as his other leg went through the floor. Eli barely managed to catch himself on an iron rod from the foundation as his lower half dropped into the room below him.

To his surprise, he felt arms on his legs. Immediately, he started kicking out of panic.

"Eli!" shouted an angry voice below him. It was Stevens. "Stop! I'm going to put your legs around my head—you're a tall guy, and I'm a tall guy. If you have the strength to lower yourself down about a foot, I can get you down onto my shoulders. Like a game of Chicken."

Great. Putting his life on the line with a game of *Chicken*. But Eli couldn't have responded if he wanted to. His eyes were still on Ash. She had frozen and stopped approaching him—either because of Stevens's voice below or because of the creaking that had resumed on the floor.

Eli took a deep breath and did his best to use his arms to cling to the crumbling floor and lower his chest through the hole. Just as he thought he was going to slip, he felt Stevens's shoulders beneath his thighs. As awkward as it may have been, the fear of the yellow-eyed Ash and the crumbling floor superseded anything else. Once Stevens had a hold on him, he let himself slide through the opening and rest on the other man. Eli gingerly felt around and used the bits of broken ceiling to steady himself as Stevens started to kneel, lowering him to the ground.

His dismount was far from graceful. Eli stumbled away from Stevens and fell on the floor, his bad leg giving way under their combined weight. Rubble from above covered the old tiles, some of it still hot to the touch. He had a few cuts and bruises, but otherwise, he was fine.

"We need to go!" Eli managed to say once he stood up again. He heard the creaking above them. Ash was moving and the ceiling was threatening to cave in further.

"Ash is still—"

Eli shook his head vigorously. "She's the *problem*! I'll explain outside—we gotta go!"

Stevens looked up at the hole and then back at Eli. He nodded reluctantly and picked his flashlight up from the floor. "Come on, then. I got the door open after we couldn't get in upstairs."

They ran down the length of the hallway and straight to the open door. Eli feared that it might slam shut on them just before they reached it, but it did not. They made it outside but did not so much as pause.

"What happened up there?" Stevens asked as they ran across the lawn to meet up with the rest of the group. There was a cool breeze fluttering through the air, for which Eli was thankful. It was a blessing after the overwhelming heat and smoky air in the asylum.

"I don't know..." Eli said, stopping to hunch over, trying to catch his breath. His saliva tasted like the smoke that still burned in his lungs. "There was something in there, and Ash held it back. But something *happened* to her—"

"Where is Ash? Is she hurt?" Deittman asked, immediately stepping away from Carlos, who was being attended to by Isabella.

Eli shook his head and then shrugged. "I don't know. Her—her eyes—they weren't *normal*. She didn't say a word. She just..." He couldn't describe it. He didn't know how to describe it. As he searched his mind for an explanation, Ash's words from a few days earlier came back to him.

Some people would call me a pyrokinetic, I guess.

Some people had called her that, she'd said.

But she had never called herself one.

There was something more to it—something that she deliberately didn't tell him. Did she tell Deittman? Based on the doctor's confused, concerned look, Eli would venture to guess *no*.

"Well, I certainly hope she's okay now," Markus said, nonchalantly. He pointed in the direction Eli and Stevens had come from. "Because she's coming this way."

Eli whirled around in terror to find that Ash was about a hundred feet from them. She was standing and staring with her arms tense at her side.

Even from that distance, Eli could feel something was wrong. And this time he wasn't the only one.

"Isabella?" Markus said, causing Eli to glance behind him. Isabella was slowly moving backward, shaking her head, and putting her hands in front of her defensively. Isabella felt it as well.

"What do we *do?*" Garrett asked from behind Carlos. "We can't very well hurt her, can we? Or, I mean, even if we *would*, could we?"

"I can knock her out," Stevens replied instantly. "If I can get close enough to her. Can't do that though if she's going to start throwing fireballs at me."

"I don't think she can. She's a hell of a lot stronger than I gave her credit for, but I don't think she can do anything without having a flame or spark. I figure that's why she's always smoking," Eli said, shrugging helplessly, not entirely convinced of his own words. "As long as she doesn't light up, she's just fucking scary."

Together, the group—except for Isabella and Carlos—fanned out and marched towards Ash. She froze, watching them. Eli realized that though her hands twitched, she did not go for her lighter. Maybe she couldn't? Maybe she didn't know how to use it anymore in this strange, primal state.

As soon as she paused, the group rushed forward, almost as one. Markus reached her first, tackling her to the ground. Ash forced her knees between them, using them as leverage to shove Markus off her, trying to scramble back onto her feet. By that point, Eli and Stevens had also reached her. Eli dove and grabbed her legs to keep her from kicking any of them, throwing his weight on them to hold her down. Stevens got around to her back and locked her head into his arms in a chokehold, one arm around her neck and braced by his other arm.

"You'll kill her!" Garrett shouted.

"Hold her arms! I can knock her out," Stevens said through gritted teeth.

Eli watched Ash's eyes returned to normal after several agonizingly long seconds before they rolled back into her head. Her body went limp and they slowly backed away from her, letting her lay peacefully on the ground.

"She's still breathing," Markus confirmed.

"This isn't my first rodeo," Stevens said, quite seriously. Perhaps he was annoyed.

Eli ran his hands through his hair and shook his head. This was too much for him; it was all too weird. If he had been scared *before* because of the Echoes, he was downright terrified *now*.

"Deittman, did she say anything during your interviews? Seems she left some things out," Garrett asked frantically, staring down at Ash.

The older man looked completely bewildered. "What? No! She didn't mention anything about…" He waved at Ash's unconscious body. "*That!*"

"What do we do?" Markus asked after a few moments. His voice was measured and calm, and it helped to bring everyone's tension levels down. "Do we lock her up? Tie her up? Will she be fine when she wakes up?"

Eli hardly found the idea right—they had already practically assaulted her, and now they wanted to lock her up? Restrain her? He had images of Ash strung up in one of the patient rooms, her arms and legs pulled away from her by chains, just like Markus had said was done to patients in the asylum at one point in time. They couldn't honestly be thinking of doing that, could they?

But what choice did they have? Eli was afraid. It was a true, deep terror. He had been as afraid of Ash as he had been of the fiery beast—perhaps even *more* so. He recalled his initial internal warning of her when they had met and the way his skin crawled when he held her gaze. It was as if his senses had been trying to warn him of her other nature.

And he had taken her home on a whim.

He wondered if he was lucky to be alive.

CHAPTER 19

"Where are Marina and Jackson?" Deittman asked once most of them had gathered back in the base.

That was the million-dollar question, wasn't it? The pair had been on their own for the better part of almost thirty-six hours. They were conveniently *missing* when something truly horrible happened to one of the most vulnerable team members—the young, naive intern.

"We haven't seen them," Markus replied, glancing around to find no one else was going to answer Deittman. "We shouted down the basement stairs, but they may not have heard us. We haven't seen them on the basement camera feed either. As far as we can tell, they haven't neared the stairs. No one has had a chance to go look for them because, well…" He glanced down at the unconscious young woman lying next to him.

Markus and Isabella were sitting and watching Ash. They moved a cot from their living quarters and put it into one of the patient rooms. Stevens had zip-tied Ash's arms to the edge of the cot to keep her from moving around once she woke, though she showed no signs of stirring. No one was comfortable with fully restraining her, but neither did they want to let Ash out of their sight. At least, not until they had a chance to talk to her and figure out what was going on.

The most they had been able to do was to double-check that the fire was out in the asylum. The only evidence there had ever been any danger was a smoldering mattress and the massive amounts of smoke slowly wafting through broken windows and holes in the asylum roof. Had the building not been so well constructed, with brick and mortar supports, the outcome might have been far, far worse.

Garrett and Stevens quickly quieted their hushed but heated conversation. Garrett looked down, avoiding eye contact with Deittman, while Stevens turned and frowned deeply.

"We have a problem," Stevens said sternly. Deittman raised his brow and tilted his chin, indicating that Stevens should continue. "We need to take Carlos to the hospital for his burns. However, we're missing two missing bags. One is ours with our cell phones and other personal effects. The other is your bag of custom equipment."

Deittman's expression was wiped away, leaving an eerie calm in its wake. "I see."

Eli understood the implication immediately. As far as he knew, the missing bag also had Deittman's cell phone, which he brought for emergencies.

They were now completely cut off—isolated from the town and any potential help if things worsened further.

Eli found Jackson and Marina's absence to be more conspicuous than ever Was it possible they had done something to draw everyone away from the base in order to gain access to the only cellphones on the property? Marina didn't seem the type, not after Eli's conversation with her, but Jackson...

Jackson had intentionally isolated himself from the group, set on capturing some sort of *interesting* footage to secure his television show... Surely, he wouldn't go so far as to try to hurt someone, right?

That's what Eli wanted to think.

Though even if he *would*, Eli couldn't forget the image of the fiery monster he had stared down only an hour or so ago. No matter what Jackson's intentions may have been, there was no way Eli believed a person could have created that *thing*. No one had that sort of ability. Except... well...

Eli glanced over at Ash and he shook his head. A pit started to form in his stomach and ultimately, he had to take a seat and let it all sink in.

"How is Mr. Torres?" Deittman asked, ignoring the situation at hand.

Deittman asked Stevens as if Carlos wasn't there, and, for the most part, Carlos *wasn't* there—at least, not mentally. He had sat down in the corner with his arms wrapped around himself despite his injuries, refusing to speak to anyone. He was in shock.

"He's hurting—" Stevens started.

"—and scared," Garrett interrupted, finally turning to face Deittman. "This is *not* what we signed on for! We've had two instances of actual, physical danger. Carlos needs medical attention, and even then, he'll be left with scars that may never go away. We are *scientists*! We don't deal with... with demons!"

Deittman shrugged and put his hands in front of him, almost as if he were conceding. "You are welcome to leave. Everyone is welcome to leave, and whenever they want, at that. You are merely responsible for finding your own transportation. And, of course, you will lose the money you agreed upon. You signed the contract as the others did, need I remind you?"

Garrett took an aggressive step forward—ready, it seemed, to give Deittman a piece of his mind. However, he didn't have the chance.

Stevens stepped in front of him, blocking Garrett from getting to Deittman. "We understand. Therefore, I will leave to take Carlos to the hospital. Garrett can stay and he will still be eligible for payment. Is that correct?"

Deittman nodded. "Indeed."

"Then it's settled. Carlos, I'll help you to the van. We'll call your gram from the hospital."

Stevens went to Carlos's side and put his arm under the boy's shoulders, helping him to stand. Carlos winced and hissed as weight was put onto his injured leg. Stevens shifted to take on more of Carlos's weight to try and help ease the pain. Garrett jogged over to their sleeping quarters, presumably to get Carlos's bag.

Eli followed after the pair, wondering if he should take the chance to leave as well. He held his flashlight so they had enough light to guide them and keep them from tripping over any of the rubble in the hallway. As they reached the front door, Garret was already behind them with Carlos's belongings.

Stevens's van wasn't far from the entrance, but it was still an annoying trek in the dark. He unlocked the vehicle with his fob so its lights flared to life, illuminating the surrounding area. When he reached it, he maneuvered around to the side to load Carlos into the passenger seat.

"I'll come back after I get Carlos checked in," Stevens said, rounding back to the driver's side. "I'm going to grab a pay-as-you-go phone. I know you wanted us off the grid for this, Deittman, but this is too dangerous. We need to be able to call for help."

Deittman had followed them but stopped at the entrance to the building. Deittman wisely chose not to say anything.

Eli made his decision. He wouldn't go with Stevens at that moment, but perhaps when he returned. Maybe then they could *all* decide to just leave if things continued to escalate. Though, he wondered, could things really get any worse when some sort of *fire demon* had already appeared?

Regardless, Eli wouldn't feel right leaving. Not when Ash was asleep and zip-tied to a cot while he rode back to civilization.

Stevens started the van. Eli raised his brow at the grinding sound it made, but kept his mouth shut. He didn't know much about cars since he had lived so long in the city without one. Garrett took a step forward though, brows furrowed.

"That didn't sound good," he muttered.

Stevens backed out of his makeshift space and started down the worn and overgrown driveway. He barely made it to the tree line before the van stopped and shut off, the engine dying with a whine. He tried to turn it back on as the group started to walk down towards him before he got out of the van and popped open the hood.

He pulled a flashlight from one of his pockets and disappeared from sight, under the hood. He remained in his spot as Eli and Garrett caught up to him.

"What's wrong?" Garrett asked.

"No idea. It just stopped. Want to take a look?"

Garrett obliged and took Stevens's flashlight to inspect the vehicle. He reached forward and checked a few things before shaking his head. "Nothing that I can see, but it's so dark it's hard to tell. The usual suspects seem to be in place."

"Spirits have been known to drain batteries," Deittman said, almost gleefully. Garrett and Stevens shared a look—Stevens actually pinched the bridge of his nose.

"We'll have to wait until morning," Garrett said and sighed. Carlos put his head into his hands, clearly distraught. "Maybe I can find what's wrong once we have more light. Come on, let's go back inside."

Garrett and Stevens grabbed Carlos and his things, and everyone trudged back up the hill. Eli's legs felt heavy as they approached the dark building once more. He had a horrible feeling in the pit of his stomach.

They needed to find Jackson and Marina.

CHAPTER 20

Ash woke with a groan more than an hour after Stevens had knocked her out. Eli watched as she tried to move, and then quickly started to panic. She had been restrained. Stevens was the first one to his feet, moving over to tower over her in intimidation. Eli noticed from the corner of his eye that both Markus and Isabella had discreetly opened their water bottles, perhaps preparing for Ash to go haywire again.

"You've got to be fucking kidding me," she groaned out, thumping her head against her thin pillow. "Seriously, guys? Is this really necessary?"

"Yes!" came a chorus of responses, though Eli was not one of them.

"Yes," Stevens repeated. "Yes, it is necessary. You're apparently a greater threat than you let on. We expect an explanation."

Ash rolled her eyes. "Can you at least let me sit up? This is crazy."

Stevens opened his mouth to retort, and probably not in a particularly kind way, when Eli interjected.

"Take her lighter," he said, "just take her lighter. We know she can't make fire on her own. She's harmless without it."

Ash frowned, almost in a pouting sort of way. "I'm not harmless!"

Eli glared at her, and she huffed.

"Alright, fine. I have a mean right hook, but I can't go throwing fireballs if there's no fire if that's what you wanna hear."

Still, Stevens appeared disinclined to release her from her binds.

"She did save me," Carlos muttered from the corner of the room. Once they'd helped him sit, he refused to move. They turned to stare at him. He buried his face into his uninjured knee and shrugged. "She wasn't the one who hurt me is all I mean."

Markus and Isabella shared a look and then turned to Deittman, who sighed.

"Release her," he demanded.

Stevens whirled around. "She is a threat to *all of us*, and we cannot have someone like her loose—"

"I said, release her!" Deittman boomed, jumping up. It was the first time the man had shown any sort of emotion beyond academic interest. Stevens glared at him and shook his head.

"Any further damage is on your hands," he said, tossing up his arms in frustration. He pulled a utility knife from his pocket and leaned over, cutting Ash free. She waited until he was no longer towering over her with a weapon before sitting up. She moved slowly, perhaps trying not to spook anyone, and rubbed at her red wrists.

"I'd just...I'd really like to take a shower, okay? I smell like smoke and I'm covered in ash. Even I have my limits," she said.

Eli wondered if Stevens was really going to allow Ash to disappear on her own before giving them any sort of explanation— he hadn't been eager to free her. Stevens took a step forward to speak, but Deittman held up a hand.

"You shouldn't go alone," Deittman said, quite seriously. "No one should be alone here."

Ash glared up at him coolly. "I'll be fine."

"We don't we will," Garrett muttered.

Deittman's mouth twitched as if he had something more to say on the subject. He chose to remain silent.

"He's right," Markus replied, somewhat uneasily. "Perhaps.... Perhaps Isabella should go with you."

Ash's expression changed to almost a snarl, causing nearly everyone in the room to take an involuntary step backward. "Do you think I'm fucking stupid? Do you think I can't tell you're all terrified of me? You think I haven't seen it before? I didn't *want* to do it, you know. I keep it in check. But if I hadn't, that fool—" She threw her hand in Carlos's direction "—would be dead! Burned to a crisp!"

A heavy silence fell over the room for a moment before Isabella uncapped her marker and scribbled on her notepad.

I'm not afraid. I'll go with you.

Ash's eyes flicked over the notebook and she closed her eyes, sighing. "Well, that's great and all, but if something *did* happen, you can't exactly call for help, can you?"

Markus was quick to leap, literally, to his sister's defense. "That is uncalled for! She is simply trying to be nice, though you are hardly deserving!"

Ash was on her feet as well now, standing only an inch below Markus, meeting him eye to eye. "And putting myself in danger *twice* now for you morons is nothing, then?"

For the second time since meeting him, Eli saw Markus's expression change at the drop of a dime. His sharp features contorted, and it seemed as if he were ready to say something particularly cruel. He didn't have the chance, however, because Stevens bellowed over the group, "Stand down!"

Neither of the two in question did so, but they did keep their words to themselves.

Deittman stepped aside to let Stevens back into the room before he spoke. "Now, everyone needs to calm down. We are all going to be stuck here with each other until our ride comes, so I *suggest* everyone take a breath and recalibrate. So long as Ash can assure us that she isn't going to hurt us, we need to listen and work as a team. If we are divided now, it will only complicate matters, understood?"

There were a few nods around.

"Good," Deittman replied, "everyone should take some time and cool down."

"So, can you assure us you're safe?" Stevens asked, not letting the matter go quite yet.

Ash looked over at him and shrugged. "For the most part. I mean, if I get angry, sometimes it rears its head—usually only for a moment, and usually only to scare people off. I only have to worry about losing control if I have to *really* let loose... So, as long as there aren't any fiery beasts or raging infernos for me to deal with... yeah, I'm fine. Been dealing with this for almost a decade now. Haven't had any...Well, not too many issues."

Stevens nodded. "I won't pretend to understand what you can do. I'm not an expert. You *did* save my intern though, and I'll respect that. Now, this all started because you wanted a shower, right? If not Isabella, and Marina is nowhere to be found again, then maybe Garrett."

Garrett's brows shot up, mortified by the request, but stiffly nodded nevertheless. "I suppose that makes sense... I certainly promise not to look."

Ash looked at him and rolled her eyes. "Yeah... Thanks for the offer, but I'm fine—"

"This is *not* a request," Stevens said immediately, shutting down the rest of her sentence. "No one goes anywhere alone. We should send a team to find Jackson and Mariana. We have to assume they've taken our equipment and we don't know to what extent they will go to in order to film their documentary or whatever it is they're doing. We take no risks. So, Garrett goes with you."

"No," Ash replied sharply. Stevens opened his mouth to insist, but she held up her hand. "Not Garrett. Eli. He's at least seen it all before, even if he was too wasted to remember most of it."

Eli felt his neck and cheeks flush in embarrassment as the eyes in the room turned upon him. He wasn't one to kiss and tell, and he certainly wasn't one to—well, *that*. And, out of all of them, he was the only one to experience her power firsthand. It terrified him more than any of the others could know. What if she was just looking to lure him away to get rid of witnesses or something?

He felt everyone's eyes on him, waiting for a response. He swallowed and quickly nodded, wanting the moment to end. "Yeah, fine. I'll do it."

Eli followed Ash into the living quarters where she retrieved her bag. She grabbed it and walked by him again, almost ignoring him entirely. She practically shut the bathroom door in his face when he wasn't moving fast enough.

"It's fucking cold in here," he muttered, sitting down on a dusty stool set below a mirror that had been roughly wiped clean. It was streaked and barely reflected anything in the poor light. All they had was one of the larger lanterns to generate any light in the room. "You couldn't pay me to take a shower now."

"I run hot," Ash replied, almost snapping. As Vincent had explained, the shower had no curtain and was almost centered in the middle of the room, serving once as an emergency biohazard wash. She cranked the faucet entirely to the hot setting despite the fact it wouldn't help. Once the shower was running and not obviously showing signs of brown water pouring out, Ash didn't hesitate to pull off her shirt.

Though he tried to quickly advert his eyes and give her some privacy, Eli still caught a glimpse of a sprawling tattoo on her back. After trying to suppress the urge for a moment longer, he tried to discreetly turn his gaze toward her. It was hard to see, as she hunched over while she pulled off her pants, but once she stood straight again, he saw it was a bird. It was mostly red, orange, and yellow, with a bit of black mixed in. It covered almost her entire back, though it looked like it wasn't finished. An entire wing had feathers that weren't yet filled.

"You stared at it the other night, too," she said, not sparing him a single glimpse over her shoulder. She knew he was looking. He hurried and turned away again. "I figured you didn't remember."

"Sorry," he muttered.

"I'm not modest," she said with a snort.

"Then why did it matter if I came and not Garrett?" Eli asked, keeping his face looking directly at the door.

"Because," she replied with a sigh, "Garrett is a *scientist*. Garrett is the sort of person who would love to put me, and probably you too, under a microscope. I've had people see what I can do before and decide they *want* that kind of power. It doesn't end well. That's why I typically lay low."

"Deittman said you didn't tell him about... well, about whatever that was."

"I didn't. It's hard to discuss and have people take you seriously. Even Deittman has his limits. He's opened-minded to things he thinks he can explain or eventually explain with his gadgets and data. There are other things in this world that will never be explainable by science." She had stepped into the shower and the water was spattering on the ground. She sighed loudly--contently--at the freezing water.

Eli thought about it for a moment, wondering what exactly Ash could mean. "You don't mean... like, magic, do you?"

"I guess I do."

It was Eli's turn to snort as he gave a wry smile and shook his head. "Yeah, I can see why you would say people won't listen to that."

"Yup," she replied, unamused. "I'm not talking 'Boy-Who-Lived-Wand-Waving' sort of magic. I'm talking Old Magic. Like druidic rituals and shit. It's fucked up, believe me."

"And you're saying you have this magic?"

There was a pause and Eli could hear a bottle pop open. "No, that's not what I'm saying. I'm saying that it *exists*, and I'm a victim of it. I wasn't born with these abilities. They were a 'gift' bestowed upon me when I was a stupid, sixteen-year-old girl who needed to feel important."

Eli knew a thing or two about unwanted abilities, and though she didn't come out and say it, he could tell it was what she was getting at. She was cursed, just like him.

"Can you get rid of them?"

"Yeah," Ash said with a sigh. It sounded like she had stopped moving in the shower, though she was still under the water.

"So why don't you, if they're such a problem?"

"I'd have to pass them on to someone else. They don't just go away."

"So? I'm sure there are plenty of people who would be willing to control fire like you do. It's an active ability, like you said," Eli said.

"There's more to it than that," she muttered and moved to shut off the water. Eli waited, back toward her, as she dried off. It wasn't much longer before he could hear her pulling her pants back on. "It's not the *abilities* that are passed on. You have to learn how to use them. It's the *Thing Inside* that gives you the abilities. It's... it's like another being. A Fire Spirit, I guess—that's what I call it. The longer you have it inside of you, the more damage it does. My body is slowly deteriorating. I don't have another decade. If I give it to someone else, it will do the same thing to them. And if they don't figure it out as fast as I did, it'll burn through them before they know it. I've only managed to last this long because I hardly use my abilities, and if I do, it's in small amounts."

189

Eli remained quiet. He didn't know what to say. What could he say that would comfort her? She didn't sound sad or angry. She sounded as though she had accepted her doomed fate, like someone suffering from terminal illness.

He jumped when she put a hand on his shoulder. "I'm ready. Do me a favor, and don't tell the others. I don't go around advertising my weaknesses."

"Then why tell me at all? You didn't have to. I didn't ask."

Ash shook her head and gave him a bitter smile. "In case I don't make it out of here, I just wanted you to know I'm not a total monster. Don't get me wrong—I'm a bit of a monster. But not because of the *Thing Inside*."

When Eli and Ash returned to the base, it was something of a madhouse. No one bothered to give them anything more than a glance. Garrett had his hand in his hair as he paced around the room and Stevens was continuously clicking the walkie-talkie, asking for someone to come in.

Eli looked about the room and saw almost everyone crammed into the space—everyone except for Jackson and Marina.

"What's going on?" Eli asked Markus quietly. Markus's eyes flickered over him, then over Ash. He hummed and gave the woman a cool look. Apparently, he had yet to forgive her for her sleight against Isabella.

"We can't find Jackson or Marina," he replied, returning his gaze to the monitors. "And the basement camera is dark."

Eli frowned. Dark? What did he mean by *dark*?

"So, someone messed with the camera," Ash said.

"Someone or something," Markus answered simply.

"We've looked everywhere," Carlos croaked from his seat against the wall. He stared off at nothing in particular, his eyes glazed. Eli had to wonder what the early signs of PTSD or shock were, and if it was possible for Carlos to have been suffering from them already. If Eli had been lured into an asylum, dragged down a hall, and put face-to-face with a fire demon, he might have been just as fucked up. "We did a playback on the recording and found them in the basement. They ran over towards the asylum side of the basement, and then the cameras cut out. We don't have any other cameras down there, so we can't see anything else."

"Did you guys have a look at the cameras? Are they damaged?" Eli asked.

"They're missing," Deittman replied, his hands balled into fists. "It's as if they have simply... vanished."

Ash hummed and crossed her arms, a brow raised. She almost looked skeptical.

"Do you doubt that they're gone? Do you think I am spinning a tale?" Deittman practically snapped. His sudden harshness didn't perturb her at all.

"No," she said and shrugged, "no, I totally believe they're gone. What I don't believe is that Jackson and Marina have nothing to do with it. I mean, c'mon, they've been in the basement, like, this entire time. They were trying to figure out how to fabricate evidence for them to record and go viral. Seems pretty convenient they're the ones who have 'mysteriously' vanished."

"You yourself have experienced two separate instances of paranormal activity, and yet you are doubtful?" Markus asked, his face practically curled in disgust.

Ash rolled her eyes. "I'm not saying there isn't something paranormal going on—hell, I know better than anyone. I'm just saying that, besides Eli's experiences with something in the basement, nothing strange has happened there. *Nothing*. If they disappeared in the Doctor's Quarters, maybe I wouldn't be as skeptical."

"She has a point," Stevens said with a sigh. "It's possible they staged this, using the chaos as an opportunity to pull a stunt. They might reappear with some farfetched story."

"Or maybe they're the ones who grabbed Carlos and dragged him down the dark hallway," Eli muttered, though he received no responses beyond a few weary glances. For some reason, it seemed some of his teammates found it easier to believe in the paranormal activity rather than the possibility that Jackson had hurt Carlos, not that Carlos had been able to see anything in the darkness.

After taking some moments to regroup, the team split into three smaller groups—Ash, Isabella, and Carlos watching the monitors, Deittman and Markus searching the upper floors, and Stevens, Garrett, and Eli doing another lap in the basement. Surely between all of them looking, they would be able to find the missing pair, right?

Jackson and Marina never revealed themselves.

The teams searched until the early hours of the morning, with nothing to show for their efforts beyond exhausted bodies and minds.

Half of the group remained huddled up in the base for the rest of the night, but Ash, along with Eli, Carlos, and Deittman did not. They returned to the living quarters to try to sleep. Since her own cot had been moved into the room they had restrained her in, Ash took over Jackson's cot. Despite her claim of being a night owl, she practically passed out the moment her head hit the pillow. Eli had to cover her up because she hadn't bothered with a blanket.

Carlos could be heard sniffling from his cot next to Ash. Eli didn't blame the kid for crying in the dark. He was probably terrified after nearly being burned to a crisp only a few hours earlier. And now he was stuck here. He couldn't even get any medical attention for his burns.

Eli had a hard time falling asleep himself. He lay on his cot, trying not to shift too much lest the squeaky springs disturb Deittman two cots over from him. For whatever reason, he felt like he was missing something. It was as if his mind was trying to connect the pieces to a puzzle, but things weren't quite fitting.

Eventually, he did manage to slip into dark dreams, the fiery beast haunting his nightmares.

When he awoke in the morning, it was to shouting.

CHAPTER 21

"Carlos!"

Garrett was shouting down the hallway. Eli bolted upright and slid his shoes on, the grogginess of half-sleep shaking away instantly. He'd chosen not to change before bed in case he had to jump into action. He was glad he hadn't, given he was now running through the hallways to find the rest of the group—who had apparently left him *alone* in their living quarters.

"What's going on?" he demanded when he managed to find Markus. The poor guy probably hadn't slept at all during the night based on the rings forming under his eyes.

"When Garrett went in to grab his things and change, he realized Carlos wasn't on his cot. No one's seen him all morning. We don't know when he managed to slip off or where he could have gone."

It briefly crossed Eli's mind that Carlos may have been willing to try to walk back to the town. It was an extremely stupid idea but when people were scared, they did stupid things.

Ash ran into the room a few moments later, her approach signaled by the sound of her boots squealing as she moved.

"It's starting to rain," she said with a frown. She shook herself like a wet dog, her mess of hair whipping about. As if on cue, a gust of wind swept through the building, whistling and moaning through the halls.

Stevens pinched the bridge of his nose. "If I leave now, I can probably make it to town before it's dark. I can alert the authorities and come back here with help."

"You won't make it far," Garrett snapped at him. Eli stiffened, a moment of panic coursing through him. Garrett's words sounded as ominous as they came. "I'm sure your leg is already killing you. If you go trying to do a fifteen-mile hike through the hills, you'll probably collapse along the way."

"What choice do we have? Our equipment is failing, we're down to one generator, and it may not make it another twelve hours! *And* we're missing three people!"

Garrett threw his hands up in the air. "I don't know! But we can't go splitting up—especially not like that! Help will be here in twenty-six hours. Maybe we should just wait."

Stevens seemed to concede as he collapsed into a chair and stretched out his right leg with a groan. Eli hadn't noticed before, but now that Garrett pointed it out, Eli saw the edge of Stevens's black pants lift just enough to reveal the bottom of a prosthetic leg.

"We must keep two people here at all times," Deittman said with a sense of finality. "The rest of us will break up into groups and canvas the area for any signs of our missing group members. I am inclined to believe that this is not a stunt by Jackson for his videos. We must now take this matter seriously and comb the building. Outside as well if we can."

Ash groaned. Some of the group cast annoyed glares at her lack of worry but if they bothered her, she didn't show it.

"I would like to remain here with my sister," Markus said. Eli had practically forgotten about Isabella, who sat quietly in the corner of the room. She was more doll-like than ever—sitting perfectly still and gazing off absently at the floor with her hands in her lap. It was only when she blinked that it seemed she was alive. "I am sorry, but I must insist. If something were to happen and we were to be separated…"

"Of course," Garrett said with a nod. "That makes total sense. I will go with Deittman. You two stay here with Stevens—make sure he sits for a while. Ash, Eli—are you two fine together?"

Eli flicked his eyes over to Ash, who looked back at him with a raised brow. He nodded. "Yeah, we're fine."

"Good," Deittman replied. "You two start in the asylum since one of you is already wet."

Ash muttered something under her breath, but Eli couldn't tell what it was. He sighed and nodded, wishing he at least had a hood.

Eli was soaked by the time they made it into the asylum. The door had remained unlocked all night, which was hardly a comforting thought. Who knew what might be lurking in the darkness of the deteriorating patient rooms, waiting for them to wander in? Or what could have wandered out?

It couldn't be much worse than a fire demon though, right? Eli hoped not.

In some ways, he was hoping the fire demon would make an appearance again, as awful a hope as it was, if only to warm him up and dry him off. The wet cold was chilling him to his bones. He knew it was a stupid thought, especially considering what it took to snuff the creature out. He didn't want to deal with a crazed, possessed Ash, or *whatever* she was.

They had made it down most of the hallway when he heard sobbing coming from somewhere ahead of them—male sobbing.

"*Shhh!*" he hissed despite Ash's silence. She stopped moving and looked over at him. When she started to open her mouth, he held his hand up and shook his head.

The sound was coming from the second floor, echoing down from the stairwell. "Do you hear that?"

"...No?"

Eli let out a breath and nodded. "Okay, alright. It's an Echo then. I thought it might've been Carlos or Jackson."

"You're getting pretty good at handling this stuff. You know--hearing and seeing those things," Ash commented. "You practically jumped at the first one."

"Well, yeah, that one was falling at me from the balcony," he grumbled. Then he stopped and sighed. "I guess you're right, though. I've never dealt with so many in such a short time frame. I feel like I'm becoming numb to them. Besides, they're nothing compared to the fire demon."

Ash shook her head. "Not a demon."

"Well... how do you know? It was all fiery and roaring. Seemed like a demon."

"I just do," she said with a shrug. "The Thing Inside of Me can pick up on certain energies—the good, the bad, and the in-between. That was an in-between, like my fire spirit. If I were to guess, though I'm not an expert, that thing had probably been lingering here for a while. Then we showed up and it fed on our psychic energy, causing it to manifest again. I would say someone with some loose knowledge of a summoning ritual brought it here in the seventies. They couldn't control it and it went berserk, causing the fire. Those things don't do well being summoned without a purpose. They just consume."

"Sounds like expert talk to me," Eli muttered.

"Definitely not an expert, but I know more than you," Ash snorted. "I'm serious, though. I knew you were the real deal too as soon as I met you. I could feel it."

She had told him she thought they would be working together. Maybe she wasn't making it up. Shit, he had no reason to think she *was* after what he experienced.

Eli didn't respond as they resumed their scan of the area, turning their flashlights into the dark rooms. It was only about ten in the morning, but everything was quickly growing dark again with the storm picking up outside. When they reached the stairwell, Eli looked up with a frown. He wasn't eager to go back up after the fire demon (he was sticking with the term 'demon') and the continuous sobbing wasn't any more encouraging.

"You still hear it?"

Eli nodded. "Yeah. It's okay. I'm good. Let's go. I'd like to get out of here as fast as possible anyhow."

The two slowly started to scale the steps, careful to avoid some of the damaged areas and fallen plaster. Ash went first, but Eli grabbed her before she walked into the hallway.

"What?" she asked sharply.

Eli nodded to a spot a little bit ahead of them. "It's the Echo."

But it wasn't just *an* Echo. It was the doctor—Dr. Pollock.

Eli only recognized him because Ash had shown him the old staff photo, but now that he saw such a realistic representation of the man, he realized how rough and grainy the old photo had been.

The Echo was sobbing on the ground, rocking back and forth. If Eli were to guess, perhaps the doctor had been cradling his dead wife. Nothing was there—at least nothing that Eli could see. It was possible this was an Echo of the worst moment in the doctor's life and not the woman's death. Dr. Pollock might have been so incredibly distraught that he permanently left behind a piece of himself in that moment, doomed to repeat itself over and over, for only someone like Eli to witness.

Eli slowly released the breath he had been holding and cautiously stepped to the side for a better view of the Echo. Though he didn't typically *try* to get a good look at the Echoes around him, Eli felt like something was important about this one. He crouched down to eye level with the Doctor. After a few moments, the Echo looked up and made eye contact with Eli.

Eli fell backward out of shock. Upon further inspection, the Echo wasn't looking at him, but at the room behind him. The man was furious—or, perhaps, *crazed* was the better word.

He furrowed his brows and cocked his head to the side. Something was familiar about the man, but he couldn't quite put his finger on it. As much as he wanted to try to keep studying the Echo, he ran out of time. The Echo disappeared, and the sobbing with him.

"Is it gone?" Ash asked, pulling Eli from his thoughts. He nodded.

"Yeah, sorry. There was just something... Never mind. Let's keep looking and head back. Do you think they want us to check out the Doctor's Quarters?" He nodded towards the door a few yards away from them.

Ash shrugged. "Either that or we go back in the rain."

"Rain," Eli replied instantly. "I'd definitely prefer the rain."

Down they went on the debris-covered stairs as the crumbling asylum side creaked around them. It would have been so much easier to go through the Doctor's Quarters, but Eli was terrified they would be locked in and forced to come face to face with whomever—or *whatever*—might have taken their missing teammates.

"Do you think we should just do a walk-through around back?" Eli asked as they stood in the doorway to leave the asylum again.

"I mean... probably? I don't really want to, but I guess we're already wet." Ash frowned and zipped up her coat again in an attempt to protect her mostly dry shirt. "I don't care what they say. I'm starting a damned fire in one of those empty rooms. Let them try to stop me."

Eli was inclined to let her even if he didn't think it was the best idea. He was freezing his ass off too.

"Sounds good," he muttered. He stepped out into the pouring rain, shoving his cold hands into his pockets. He didn't know what they expected to find outside but he figured they needed to at least *look*. They walked around slowly, careful not to slip in the mud, looking all around them for any signs of their missing teammates. Part of him was afraid they *would* find something—a pool of blood or something. But as they rounded halfway around the building there was nothing.

Something caught his attention from the corner of his eye, drawing his gaze to the sealed building behind the facility.

"Do you see something?" Ash asked him, wiping water from her face. He shrugged.

"I don't know. I know the building is sealed up, but... should we look?"

Ash sighed loudly. "Yeah, I *guess*..."

The two of them trekked over to the unusual building. Eli's skin crawled with alarm as they approached it. He hadn't actually checked it out since arriving, and at that moment, he was glad he hadn't.

If he thought the medical facility was bad, the sealed building felt positively *evil*.

"I don't like this," Eli said flatly. "I don't know *what* it is, but I don't like it."

Ash shook her head. "Neither do I. There's a lot of energy here. Feels almost like it was sealed inside—all pent-up or something. Maybe that was intentional." She reached out and touched the door—or what had *been* a door. There was no knob or anything to try to open. Her fingers barely grazed the door before she pulled away, shaking her head violently. "Nope. Nope. Not even trying. If Carlos is in there, he's *fucked*."

Eli didn't see *how* someone would have gotten in unless they just ... materialized on the other side of the door or something. That couldn't actually happen, could it?

"Let's go. We did our part," Ash said. She turned on her heel, putting as much distance between herself and the building as possible with each step she took. Eli wasn't far behind.

The atmosphere was dismal as most of the group huddled around the small fire Ash had been allowed to build in the stairwell. Stevens had only permitted her after hearing Eli's teeth start to chatter in the cold. There was enough ventilation over the four stories to let the smoke rise and not bother them. Both Ash and Eli changed out of their drenched clothes and hung them over the railings near the fire in hopes of getting them to dry faster. Garrett and Isabella both lent each of them jackets or sweaters to help warm the wet duo and then joined them by the fire.

"We really need the police out here," Garrett said quietly. "I can't believe this is happening. Carlos was a good kid. I'm never going to forgive myself if something happened to him."

Eli kept his mouth shut as he stared at the dancing flames. He figured that Carlos's family wasn't likely to forgive Garrett or Stevens either if that were the case.

As thoughts of family floated through his mind, images of Sarah and Sophia flashed before his eyes. Was he overreacting in thinking that he may never see them again? Surely this was all a misunderstanding and Jackson and Marina were going to show up with some sort of staged footage to post online. And Carlos was going to send word back that he had got a ride to the hospital or something.

The pit in Eli's stomach told him otherwise.

He brought his knees to his chest and crossed his arms over them to bury his head away, much like Ash was doing—only her eyes were visible as they stared at the red and yellow flames before her.

Eli clenched his jaw and closed his eyes.

He should never have come here.

CHAPTER 22

Eli tightened his jacket around himself as a shiver went down his spine. The storm had finally reached them, bringing strong winds and cold temperatures. The group hoped that it would leave as quickly as it came on, but with their luck this weekend, Eli had doubts.

"Any luck?" Markus asked as Stevens and Garrett walked back into their headquarters. It had been their turn to search the basement for any sign of their missing teammates. Every area had been combed three times or more. The building might have been massive, but most of it was empty enough that pairs could swap out and quickly canvas whenever a sound or movements on camera caught their attention--though it did mean leaving their little base unattended from time to time.

Based on Stevens's and Garrett's expressions, however, they hadn't found anything particularly useful in the basement either.

Stevens shook his head and hoisted an old, worn workman's bag onto the equipment table. Garrett gave a *tsk* and hurried to move his own gadgets out of the way.

"No, but we did find some miscellaneous tools in the boiler room. If we come across any other doors we can't open, we can force our way in."

"That," Garrett added, "and they make for some decent weapons."

As a clap of thunder echoed through the air, a terrible foreboding feeling settling across the room.

Stevens glanced out the window and then gave a nod and a shrug in agreement with Garrett.

"I don't think a wrench will help us fight off spirits," Deittman huffed, frowning as Stevens started to lay out some of the tools he had found.

Isabella scribbled something and turned her notebook around. It read, *Unless they're iron.*

Deittman hummed thoughtfully. "Oh yes, actually. In that case, they may be useful. Any way for us to determine which of those items might be made of iron?"

Stevens and Garrett shared a look from the corner of their eyes as Stevens's jaw clenched tightly. Neither answered the doctor and if the way Garrett chewed his lip while decidedly keeping his back to Deittman was any indication, he was not amused by Deittman's question. Ghosts or no ghosts--the two men were readying for a fight.

Apparently, the two investigation teams had different views on what they were up against—if they were up against anything at all. There was still a chance that Jackson, Marina, and Carlos had simply caught a ride into town and didn't have a chance to tell them. Eli hoped beyond hope that they were all safe and that was the case.

The others... Eli could see that they were all starting to close ranks--afraid that something worse had happened. Eli glanced at Ash who was sitting in the hallway, her bottle of whiskey next to her. She hadn't been joking when she said she had a bottle with her. While both teams might have wanted her to join them, or, more likely, did not want her as opposition, she chose neither. Instead, she sat, smoking a cigarette and listening to the others plot and plan.

Eli wondered if there would be a moment where he was forced to side with one group or the other, and if so, who would he choose?

A violent gust of wind swept through the building, causing the decaying structure to shudder with a moan. A window in their base shattered as a fallen tree branch was sent careening into the pane. It was a mad scramble to try to block the wind and rain from coming in through the broken window to Eli's left. They used whatever they could find—first a blanket, then a chair, but none of it seemed to work.

From above them came another set of bangs and crashes. The existing cracked walls and damaged windows created a vortex of wind, causing doors to bang and hospital bed curtains to whip about. A glance at the monitors showed that numerous cameras had gone dark and several audio devices had cut out, possibly knocked from their stands in the chaos.

"Check the other floors!" Deittman shouted over the thunder and the whistling of the air leaking in through the broken panes. "Our equipment will be irreparably damaged if caught in the rain!"

Garrett was already out the door, and then Markus, Isabella, Ash, and Stevens were out after him, all running off into different areas with flashlights in hand. The afternoon storm had darkened the sky, casting the hospital into a premature nighttime.

Eli remained behind with Deittman, trying to hold the now-soaking blanket in place while Deittman hurried to move cords and monitors from the nearby table. Garrett reappeared a moment later, a cardboard box in hand. He flipped it open and used a pen to break the packaging tape on the backside, folding the box in half right away.

"Here, I just found this. This may hold for the time being," he said. Eli removed the drenched blanket and Garrett slid the broken-down box against the broken window. It was large enough to cover the damaged area, though it would probably be soaked through within an hour if the rain continued its torrential downpour. Still, it was their best option to protect their electronics.

Eli searched out a roll of duct tape from one of the equipment cases. Between Garrett, himself, and half the roll of duct tape, they were able to seal the cardboard in place. They kept the chair in front of it for support, just in case.

"That was alarming," Eli muttered, wiping his wet hands on the back of his jacket. Part of his front was wet, but he figured if he could sit in front of one of Ash's fires, he would dry up. He helped Garrett kick away some of the glass then dropped the soaked blanket on top of the pile to cover it. "Thought you ran off to look for the other equipment."

"I was going to but found the box. Figured I should save the bulk of the equipment here first," Garrett replied with a chuckle. "I'm sure the others can reestablish connection as needed. Or bring down whatever I have to fix…"

"Markus and Isabella are quite capable," Deittman said as he finished rearranging the monitors. Garrett turned to help him reconnect a few cords.

"And Stevens knows what to do," Garrett added.

"Ash…" Eli started but trailed off. They stopped and looked at one another.

"Well, she can help carry things," Garrett said with a sigh.

Eli smiled in agreement. "Ten bucks says she breaks something and blames it on the storm."

As the rush of adrenaline faded, so did Eli's small smile. He glanced around the disheveled headquarters and felt his shoulders slump. It had already been cluttered, but now… well, now it was a disaster It reminded him that Carlos, who had been put in charge of keeping their little base tidy, was gone.

While Garrett fiddled with some cords, Deittman took the opportunity to sit down on a dry chair and wait for the others to return. Eli didn't feel like sitting; it would only make him worry that someone wasn't going to return from the equipment check—that someone else was going to disappear into the darkness.

As he set about straightening up their area, he had a sinking feeling that he was right to worry.

Markus and Isabella returned with a camera and a recording device in hand.

"Where are Stevens and Ash?" Garrett asked.

The twins looked at one another and shrugged. "We were just upstairs on the second floor. Ash and Stevens went up," Markus replied, pointing upwards. As Garrett opened his mouth to ask something, however, they heard soft footsteps coming from the atrium.

Eli peered out one of the headquarters' doorways and saw a small red glow that he recognized as one of Ash's cigarettes. She took her time wandering over, an audio recorder in her hand, which she casually tapped against her thigh.

"Battery's dead, but I think it's fine. One broken window on the third floor, but I'm pretty sure it was already like that when we got here," she said, walking into their base and setting the device down. "Stevens isn't back yet?"

"He's not with you?" Garrett asked. Eli watched the other man's shoulders grow tense as he took a step forward.

Ash looked around at everyone and shook her head slowly. "No... I went to the third floor and came back down. He went up to the fourth."

"You let him go alone?" Garrett shouted, taking another two steps towards the woman. Ash's face grew sharp, her eyes narrowing. She stood straighter and held her cigarette to the side as if daring Garrett to make a move against her.

"Yeah, I did. He told me to go on without him since I can protect myself. Figured he knew what he was doing. Maybe he's still getting equipment," she replied tersely. She and Garrett stared each other down, though there wasn't much the man could do against her, especially while she had a lit cigarette in her hand. He eyed it, perhaps wondering if he could try to put it out. As if reading his mind, Ash reached into her pocket and pulled out her lighter.

Garrett opened his mouth to speak but closed it as a roar of thunder crashed overhead—it sounded like it was right above them, or even within the building.

"We'll give him five minutes," Deittman said, standing and placing a hand on Garrett's shoulder. "We'll replace our torch batteries and go as two groups to the fourth floor—one up the main staircase and one up the side, yes?"

Garrett finally took his eyes off of Ash and nodded, swallowing hard. They started to sort through the battery packs for their flashlights.

Five minutes passed with no Stevens and they split off into two groups—Deittman, Garrett, and Isabella in one, and Markus, Eli, and Ash in the other, in an effort to keep conflicts to a minimum. They met back up on the fourth floor as planned, only to find it was empty.

Down they went, checking each floor, but Stevens was nowhere to be found.

They all dragged their feet as they met back up in the base, a feeling of defeat sweeping the air.

"What the hell is happening in this place?" Eli snapped, pounding a fist against the wall, causing some loose plaster to crumble to the ground. "Marina and Jackson are one thing—though Marina made it clear to me she was freaked out. Carlos? He could hardly move. It makes no sense for him to go wandering off by himself. But Stevens? C'mon. He would have *known* better than to just up and disappear on us, especially after we've spent all this time looking for the others."

Garrett nodded along. "Yes, I agree wholeheartedly. Stevens wouldn't leave without telling us. Something is wrong, and I don't know how to find him."

Markus and Isabella shared a look.

"What is it?" Eli asked, causing the two to jump. They were clearly reluctant to share whatever it was they were thinking—and thinking they were. Based on their expressions, it was almost as if they had an entire conversation without anyone else hearing.

Markus rubbed the back of his head and shrugged. "We have an idea of how to find them, but... it would only work if something had happened to them—something bad."

Deittman hummed curiously as if he already knew where Markus was going with his words.

"But we could at least *try*. Isabella is willing."

The older gentleman clapped his hands together. "Fantastic, this will be an excellent chance to make some research notes. She does tend to stir up some activity when she writes."

"Yeah, because more activity is just what we need," Ash muttered from her spot in the hallway. Everyone ignored her.

"We will need a few personal belongings to make the attempt. We'll set up in the entryway. It's spacious and if something goes awry with the candles there isn't much to catch on fire. Give us a few minutes." Markus and Isabella headed off down the hallway to the sleeping quarters, which still held some of their belongings.

Eli slumped against the wall, his head hanging. He supposed it would be interesting to see Isabella use her supposed *automatic writing* ability, but he was also a bit terrified—if it worked, it meant that some (or *all*) of their teammates were dead.

CHAPTER 23

Markus folded a blanket and set it down so Isabella had a cushion to sit on rather than the dirty floor. She knelt and set her notebook in front of her, tearing off a handful of pages from the top so she could easily move onto a new page as needed. Her brother set half-burned, white pillar candles in a circle around her.

"Alright, so, our process may not be what you've seen before. We've experimented with a few different methods of summoning a specific spirit. In a place such as this, where many spirits may reside, Isabella must narrow her focus, or else *anyone* might come through. Though that can be interesting and provide good results, it isn't what we want right now. We are going to try to use the belongings of our missing teammates to see if we can find one of them."

Ash let out a puff from her cigarette. "If you do though… doesn't that mean someone's dead?"

Eli had been thinking the same thing, but he didn't want to say it. He hated to think that something bad had happened to anyone on their team.

It didn't bode well for the rest of them.

"Unfortunately, yes," Markus sighed, "But as we have no other leads, it seems the best option."

"This is all I could find," Garrett said, walking into the atrium. In his hands were a hairbrush, a toothbrush, a baseball cap, and a watch. "You said something with DNA would be best if I didn't know of an item of importance. These are from Marina and Jackson's bags, and these are from Carlos's and Stevens's."

Markus nodded and evaluated the items. "These were important to them?"

"Yes, I'm certain. Carlos wore the hat all the time. I think his mother gave it to him before she died. Stevens said this watch was invincible—he and his military buddies got matching ones."

Isabella gestured to an embroidered cloth she had unfolded ahead of her notebook. Garrett gently laid each item out, spacing them an equal distance from one another. After one last adjustment, he stepped outside the circle of candles.

"Alright, I'm going to light the candles—"

"I got it," Ash said and clicked her lighter. She swept her hand, the one holding the lighter away from her, and the flame jumped from her lighter to the candle in front of her. She waved her hand four more times, each time sending the little flame from one wick to the other.

Markus's mouth twitched upward in almost a smug smile before it disappeared and his usual passive expression returned. "Thank you. Now, we may ask questions and Isabella will do her best to transcribe responses from the spirits. That is, of course, *if* she is able to make contact. I will stand behind her and read whatever she writes aloud for everyone."

Deittman entered the room, dragging a chair behind him. He didn't look particularly impressed by the twins' setup, but Eli suspected he had seen it many times before. Deittman picked a spot to the left of Isabella and sat down, opening a notebook and flipping through a few pages. He gave the young woman a nod, which she returned. Right as she adjusted her makeshift cushion, ready to begin, a cold breeze rushed through the entryway, threatening to put out the flames if Ash wasn't diligent.

Garrett stood from his spot on the ground and went to the large, heavy front doors. He did his best to move the one that had been stuck open since they arrived but it barely budged. Eli decided to give him a hand. He didn't want to sit in the freezing entryway either.

The hinges had rusted out years ago, keeping the door permanently ajar. Together, the two men were able to loosen it. Once they did, the door practically shut on its own. No, in fact, Eli was *sure* it was shutting on its own. He had stopped pushing after their initial heave. Garrett seemed to notice it too and let go of the door.

It didn't exactly slam shut but Eli swore it was as if the building had closed them in on purpose. Eli shuddered as he squeezed his eyes shut—for the third time during their stay, his vision had started to tunnel as other *things* began to creep in from the corners of his eyes. When the echoing of the door closing had stopped, he opened his eyes and found he felt fine again.

Still, the chill down his back lingered, despite cutting off the freezing wind from outside.

Eli and Garrett turned from the door and reclaimed their seats, both eager to watch Isabella, though neither showed it.

Isabella placed her marker on the paper and closed her eyes. She started off by making loops on the pages in a straight and even line. It was likely that she had done this many, many times as she knew exactly when to slide down to the next row as she reached the end of the paper, even with her eyes shut.

She went through a full two sheets without anything happening. Eli was starting to think it might be a bust (and that his behind was getting numb from sitting on the cold, marble tile of the entryway) when Isabella's eyes shot open. The candles flickered and their flames grew, causing Ash to sit at attention, up from her lounging position on an old, wicker chair.

Isabella tensed and her slow loops turned into twitchy writing. Markus leaned over her to watch what she wrote, though Eli noticed his attention jumping between Isabella's paper and her body. His mouth was pressed into a thin line and despite his attempts to come off as relaxed with his hands in his pockets, Markus was on guard.

"*Elevator*," he said, "*elevator, elevator, elevator.*"

One page went by, and then another, and another.

Markus shrugged. "It... it reads *elevator* over and over again. Who is this? Who is contacting us?"

Isabella's writing changed again.

"*CS. CS, CS...* I suppose Stevens? *Yes, yes, yes, yes.*"

Eli's stomach clenched. If it were true, if it were Stevens, that meant he was dead and not missing. He felt himself shake at the thought. Of course, the fear had been there since Jackson and Marina had vanished, but they had hoped they were just missing— or holed up somewhere faking evidence for their YouTube channel and book. But getting confirmation that Stevens was dead...

"This is a load of shit," Garrett snapped. He jumped up, kicking a piece of equipment he had brought with him hard, sending it careening down the hallway toward their base. It skidded and bounced off the wall. "I am a *scientist*. For all I know, you're just making this up to play on our fears, to perpetuate some sort of desire for evidence. Stevens isn't dead—he just—he *can't* be—"

Garrett put his hands on his head, pressing his dark blonde hair against his forehead. He paced around for a few moments before stopping to pull off his glasses and wipe his hand down his face.

While everyone's attention was on Garrett, Eli noticed Isabella had stopped writing. She was looking upwards, but her body was tense—jerky.

"Um, is she supposed to—"

Isabella's hand shot out, back to the paper and resumed writing, this time in a different script. She was scribbling at a furious pace to the point where Markus didn't have a chance to read what she was writing before she was onto a new page. He picked up the first discarded paper, his brows furrowed.

"It says... well, it's hard to read. I think it says, *no, no, not the darkness again, don't take me into the dark—*" Markus picked up the next sheet. "*Please, no. No more water, no more water.*"

Markus was about to reach down to pick up the last sheet, but Isabella went rigid and then started to fall forward. Eli, who was sitting a few feet in front of her, lurched forward. He threw his arms out and caught her before she fell face-first onto the cloth holding their teammates' belongings. Markus crouched down and put his arm around Isabella's waist, shifting her weight so she would lean on him, then maneuvered her to get his hands under her knees.

Eli was a bit surprised at how easily Markus lifted her—he was much stronger than his slight, cardigan-wearing form led Eli to believe.

"She needs to rest. Channeling takes a lot of energy, especially if a spirit is strong."

"You believe it was a strong one?" Deittman asked, speaking for the first time. He had been rather intent on being only an observer, taking notes throughout the ordeal.

Markus shrugged and started to head towards the hallway door. "Strong enough to bypass our calls to Stevens and the others, unless something truly terrible happened to one of our teammates. The purified candles, blessed cloth, and use of personal items is supposed to keep that from happening. Ash, the candles, if you don't mind?"

Ash hummed in confirmation and swept her hand to the side, snuffing out the small flames.

Eli waited until the candles were out before stepping into the circle and grabbing the last piece of Isabella's paper.

"What does it say?" Deittman asked, clicking his pen and standing as well.

Eli swallowed hard.

"It says, *Doctor, you're killing me.*"

"We should go check the elevator," Garrett said, standing in the entryway of their little sleeping area. "If you really *did* contact a spirit, then maybe it's a clue."

Markus shrugged and nodded. He sat at Isabella's side as she lay on his cot. Eli couldn't help but notice how peaceful she looked. Once again, he was reminded of a porcelain doll. He doubted he looked so carefree when *he* slept.

"I agree," Markus said. "You should go check the elevator."

"You should come too since you're the one who read the pages. In fact, all of us should go. We should stay together." Garrett said, shifting his weight back and forth. Eli had the distinct impression he had more he wanted to say but chose to hold his tongue.

Markus waved his hand at his sister's sleeping form, furrowing his brows. "I can't go. I can't leave Isabella."

"I should like to see the elevator," Deittman said, placing his notebook on one of the tables and turning to face Garrett. "Clear up this little mystery and all."

Garrett pursed his lips and looked at Markus, then Deittman, then back at Markus. His eyes were hard and his hands balled into fists. "If you don't come, Markus, I'm going to think that you had something to do with whatever we find."

Eli took a step backward, bumping into Ash behind him. Markus's expression went from concerned to confused to vicious in the blink of an eye. His teeth bared in a snarl, and his stature no longer seemed so slight. Something about him, call it a vibe or whatever, worried Eli.

"You think *I* had something to do with Stevens's disappearance—with *anyone's* disappearance? I have been nothing but kind and accommodating to you—all of you! Keep in mind that the three of us have worked together for *years*. We know each other and we look out for each other. All of *you*, however, are new. We have no reason to trust *any* of you, yet you don't see any of us accusing *you* of being killers. We have just as much to lose in his hellish place as *you*."

Markus took a step forward, and Eli wanted to move back another step, but he couldn't with Ash behind him. She placed a hand on his shoulder and turned, starting to slide through the space next to him.

"Well if you *notice*," Garrett snapped, taking a step forward towards Markus. "If you *notice*, all three of your team are *fine*. No one missing, no one hurt during this whole time. Also, aren't these two," he jabbed his fingers towards Ash and Eli, "supposed to be part of your team too? Convenient for you to leave them out. Maybe they'll end up *disappearing* too."

Deittman began to approach Markus as well, though slowly as if he didn't want to get involved.

Markus's fists clenched at his sides. "That sounds an awful lot like a threat. Do you expect me to just stand here and—"

As Markus took two quick steps towards Garrett, Ash side-stepped to block him, causing him to stop in surprise—as if he were surprised anyone would stand against him.

"Chill," she said, her voice laced with warning. She had a growing ball of fire in her left hand. "I'll stay with Isabella. She was nice enough to offer to go with me when I wanted to shower, and you were all afraid. I promise she's in no safer hands."

Markus stared at her for a moment, his jaw clenching and unclenching. Eli could practically see the thoughts running through his head: Ash was dangerous, but also a great ally. It was crucial that she was on the 'side' of Deittman's team if it came down to some sort of supernatural showdown. His shoulders started to relax, though the tension didn't fade away entirely. He nodded.

"You'll keep the last radio on you?"

Ash nodded. "Of course. I want to hear what you guys find anyway."

The electric atmosphere died down almost immediately as Markus relaxed. Eli was more than a little impressed. For someone so fiery, Ash had de-escalated the situation like a pro. Stevens probably would have even been proud... if he had been around to see it.

Deittman picked up a flashlight. "Well, with all of that is settled... shall we?"

In an uncomfortable silence, the four remaining men went off to the fourth floor to the open elevator doors, some of them more begrudgingly than others.

CHAPTER 24

They didn't speak as they ascended the stairs. Deittman tried his best not to show his struggle by the time they reached the fourth floor. Eli was also drained—having had little to eat over the past few days with poor sleep had left him fatigued. Deittman insisted the building was feeding off Eli's *psychic ability* but Eli ignored the man. He was growing tired of Deittman's prioritization of his research over the group's safety.

As they reached the top of the stairs and turned left to head towards the elevator, all of them began to hesitate. It was almost as if none of them really wanted to see what the elevator held for them. Maybe there would be nothing. Or maybe it was the wrong elevator. There was an older lift in the Doctor's Quarters, after all.

Before Eli could suggest it, Garrett was standing in front of the doors which were permanently stuck open.

"I feel like if this were a movie, the doors would shut on me as soon as I stuck my head in to look," Garrett said flatly. Eli grimaced and rubbed the back of his head. Yeah, that seemed about right. "Can someone just keep a hold of me? Not much here to grab, and I don't want to fall in."

"I've got you," Eli said quickly, figuring Garrett wasn't particularly keen on either Markus or Deittman standing behind him after his accusations. Eli grabbed onto the back of Garrett's jacket with one hand and planted his other on the wall for added support. With a deep breath, Garrett clicked on his flashlight and leaned forward, craning his neck to peer down the shaft.

"Oh God!" Garrett lurched backward, dropping his flashlight as he scrambled to the opposite wall, almost hugging it. The flashlight bounced off the ground and then tumbled down the shaft, clinking off bits of metal.

"What? What is it?" Eli asked, though he suspected he already knew.

Garrett slid down to his knees, his forehead *thunking* against the wall. He whispered, "It's Stevens."

Markus and Deittman looked at one another. Deittman raised a brow as if to say, *I'm not going to do it.* Reluctantly, Markus stepped forward, bracing himself against the other wall and peeking down the shaft. He also quickly pulled back, nodding.

Eli knew he would regret it, but he took Garrett's place.

At the bottom of the shaft—well, atop the elevator that must have been stuck on the basement floor—was Stevens's broken body. Garrett's flashlight had landed on the elevator top and was pointed in a way that illuminated Stevens's bloody, blank face and his twisted arm.

How had this happened? How had no one noticed him? Where was everyone else that they didn't see or hear him when he fell—or was pushed?

"This can't have been an accident," Garrett said, still sitting in his crouched position. "Stevens wasn't careless. He would never have fallen in. Someone had to have pushed him."

"Or... some*thing*," Markus added, exchanging glances with Deittman.

Garrett sat up with a jolt, a sneer on his face. "Don't even try to tell me that *ghosts* did this."

Deittman shrugged, stepping in front of Markus as a precaution. "We've seen strange things here. Quite a bit more activity than normal—objects moving and such. You cannot discount the creature in the fire that Carlos, Ash, Eli, and myself saw. This place is active."

"It's *dangerous*," Eli muttered. Deittman narrowed his eyes and frowned but nodded.

"You all knew the risks before coming. You signed a waiver. You all felt the money was worth it."

"It isn't worth our lives!" Eli snapped. Finally, the dam of emotions he had been holding back for all weekend—or possibly longer—burst. "None of this is worth our lives! You knowingly took all of us into a horrible, risky place, and for what? Some video footage? And how is *that* going?" He snarled at the doctor, anger in his eyes. "Your generator is *gone*, half of the team is *gone*, and we don't even know if we're going to make it another twenty-four hours without *disappearing*! You seemed too good to be true when I first heard you talk at that lecture—I guess *I was right*. You're a scientist and we're all lab rats. What do you *care* what happens to us, so long as you have your research?"

Eli stormed around in a fury, before turning to say something else to Deittman, but the older gentleman had such a nasty glint in his eye that Eli couldn't take it. Eli threw his hands up and turned to head for the stairs. "Fuck it. I'm *done* with all of this. I'm going to sit in one spot and not move until tomorrow."

Without anyone stopping him, Eli walked off, leaving the other three behind.

By the time he reached the bottom floor, Eli realized what a bad idea it was to go wandering on his own. He exited the stairwell and headed straight for the sleeping room—only to find the door was shut and locked.

"Ash?" he asked, fear creeping up his neck.

"Yeah, we're in here still. Door shut on us. It's jammed or something. Isabella is still asleep. I'm just sitting here. Can't open from this side," replied Ash's muffled voice. She sounded vaguely irritated, but fine nonetheless.

Eli tried the door, putting his weight into it, but to no avail. "I can't get it. I'll go grab the others. Do you have the radio?"

"Yeah, but it died a little bit after you guys left. Ghosts or something, I dunno. Wait, are you alone? Don't go alone! Wait for them to come down!"

"I'll be fine," Eli said, though he was sure his voice wasn't convincing. "That's what you'd say, right? They found Stevens. I think I should just go get them."

She went on a tirade about why he shouldn't go alone, but that didn't stop him. He promptly turned around and started to head back up to the fourth floor. He may be angry with Deittman, but he couldn't leave Ash and Isabella locked up. What if it was some sort of ploy to leave them vulnerable?

He had started to pass the doorway to the second-floor hallway when something caught his eye—the door to the Doctor's Quarters was open again. He heard a male voice as well shouting, *no, please, no!*

"Oh, c'mon, not *now*..." he muttered and squeezed his eyes shut. He couldn't be sure it was an Echo, but it didn't sound like any of his teammates. Surely it *had* to be an Echo... Eli felt a sort of tugging in the direction of the Doctor's Quarters, almost as if something wanted him to witness what was going on inside.

"*Fuck,*" he hissed, burying his hands into his hair and then exhaling loudly. Had adrenaline not been pumping through him, Eli never would have even considered investigating. So filled with anger and irritation at Deittman, however, any good decision-making skills were pushed to the back of his head.

Eli stepped onto the second floor, cautiously moving down the hallway, trying to make sure nothing would jump him from one of the patient rooms.

As he got to the base of the small set of stairs that lead up to the Doctor's Quarters, the Echo ended. He had missed it. Well, maybe it was for the better. Maybe he didn't need to—

"No, please, no!"

Eli turned. The Echo was repeating already. That wasn't normal. In fact, he couldn't think of another time when he had ever had an Echo repeat almost instantly. He hadn't been serious when he thought something wanted him to see that scene... but maybe something did. That thought terrified him, but he slowly walked up the stairs anyhow.

It was, indeed, an Echo. It was slightly transparent and paid no notice to him as he approached. Eli wanted to stay outside of the area if possible, but if he wanted to see the whole image, he would have to step inside. Shaking his head and muttering what a bad idea it was, Eli stepped onto the platform leading inside the Doctor's Quarters.

It was a man. He seemed like he was close to Eli's age, but more importantly, he was dressed... well, he was dressed *modern*. Unlike all of the other Echoes Eli had seen in Maple Hill, this one was different. He wore nice, pre-faded jeans, a sweater with a button-down beneath it, and a fairly fashionable canvas jacket. Eli stared at the Echo in confusion.

They hadn't heard any stories about someone dying at the hospital in recent years beyond the little girl in the basement.

Eli turned away as something was used to bash the man's head in. The cracking was sickening. What was worse was the man's labored breathing as he died, which took several seconds.

There was a sort of dragging sound. It was the same sound he had heard from the other side of the door when he investigated the asylum with Deittman, Markus, and Isabella. Eli looked back at the man to find that he was—

"What's going on?"

Eli jumped and, to his mortification, yelped a bit.

Deittman and Markus were standing behind him. He hadn't even noticed. That didn't bode well for him if he was trying to jumpstart his survival instincts. The two men stared at him curiously.

Eli exhaled and shook his head. The Echo had disappeared and—no, it started again. He waved at the area ahead of him.

"Echo," he said. "It's… it's a strange one."

"Oh?" Deittman asked, hurrying to pat his breast pocket. He frowned when he didn't find his little notebook. "Why is it strange?"

Eli shrugged. "This guy looks, like, recent. Like he's dressed like us, and kind of nicely. But we weren't told any stories of anyone dying here recently unless it was unreported or something."

Markus shook his head. "Nothing like that, as far as we are aware."

"Yeah, I don't know, it just…" Eli grimaced as he watched the Echo finish playing out. As the man died, it seemed he was dragged out of the room. "Wait."

"What is it?" Deittman asked.

Eli backed up and glanced around. "Wait, look. See--it's our footprints in the dust. You can tell that people hadn't been here for a while, right? But, look here." He pointed to where the Echo replayed and then pointed to the door. "A trail. We didn't notice it the last two times we were in here because of the door scare, and then because we were chasing Carlos. There's a trail where there's no dust. Like something was dragged out of here? Possibly… a rug?"

Both Markus and Deittman took a step back and inspected the area, nodding in agreement. Eli continued to scan the room and then stopped as his eyes fell on a cast iron container next to the fireplace near the back of the room. It held a few pokers that, theoretically, hadn't been touched in decades. His eyes dropped a little bit further and saw a small pool of dark liquid beneath it.

Eli walked over and slowly withdrew it from the container, holding it up to show the others. Markus approached and appraised it before kneeling down and putting a finger in the liquid.

"Blood," he said, "mostly dry. But... I can't imagine this is more than a few days old. If you're saying someone was attacked here, it must have been recent."

"Is there anything else you can get from the Echo, Eli?" Deittman asked, a hint of excitement in his voice. It made Eli want to gag. "Could you imagine if we were able to solve a crime using psychic powers? It would be great exposure—like when Ms. Gray was in the news..."

"Or the police will think we did it, like they'll think we killed Stevens and everyone else who is missing," Eli said dryly. Deittman scoffed.

"Is there anything else though?" Markus asked, raising a brow. "If this all ties together, it would be best we know as soon as possible."

Eli sighed and turned back to where the Echo was replaying yet again. He swore, as he watched the man's head get bashed in, the poker in his hand started to burn. "No, I don't think... Wait, maybe... He's got a keyring in his hand and—no, now it's gone. Like, uh, well, things only vanish when they aren't holding them or connected to them... it isn't an exact science but—"

"A key ring?" Deittman inquired.

The Echo had ended again. "Yeah, a key ring. It, well, it sort of looked like the one Vincent used to let us in. Remember the one he gave you with all of the asylum keys too?"

Markus brought a hand to his chin and hummed. "That is very interesting. We should ask Garrett about the people who brought the equipment onsite." At that, Markus stood straight and whirled around. "Where is Garrett? He was trailing behind us when we started down from the top floor."

Eli's heart sank. Another one of them had disappeared.

CHAPTER 25

The early afternoon storm had almost entirely passed them by the time the group, which had shrunk dramatically since the start of the weekend, reconvened in their headquarters. It was still sprinkling outside and the clouds in the distance warned of another wave of thunder and lightning approaching by nightfall. For the time being, they sought relief in the slivers of sunlight that peeked through every now and again.

"Maybe we can walk to town," Eli said, breaking the silence that had befallen the room. He had gone with Deittman and Markus to do a quick canvas for Garrett, but they found nothing. Just like Jackson, Marina, and Carlos, he had vanished.

With heavy hearts and a feeling of helplessness, they returned to Ash and Isabella. Their door had been locked and Deittman's keyring hadn't had a corresponding key. Fortunately, Stevens had found those workman's tools.

It had taken them over a half hour to get the old door off its hinges, but they succeeded in the end. Without the ability to shut and barricade the door, no one felt safe enough sleeping in the room. Rather than be so far away from their headquarters, the group of four--with Markus speaking on behalf of the sleeping Isabella--agreed to relocate to their base. They would stay together and hope that with eyes on one another, there would be no further disappearances.

Ash had no idea how the door had become locked. When Deittman had the nerve to suggest *she* had locked it by accident-- well, *carelessly* was his word--she looked ready to throw a punch.

"It's about..." Markus gazed up at the ceiling, running numbers through his head. "It's about a fifteen-mile or so walk to town. I could be wrong; I'm used to dealing with kilometers. Still, it is quite a trek."

Eli sighed and put his head back, staring at a piece of plaster that threatened to come down on them from the second floor at any moment. "A car might pass us and give us a ride into town. You never know. We need to get the police here. We have one body and four missing people. Each minute we waste here could be a minute we spend going to town."

Markus and Deittman looked at one another and Eli couldn't help but feel it was condescending.

"My boy, if *you* would like to attempt the journey, no one is stopping you. I know *I* certainly do not have the stamina and I think we are all already sleep deprived. On our way here, we didn't pass a single auto. You could be putting yourself in quite a bit of danger," Deittman said, folding his arms across his chest.

"We're already in danger," Ash replied flatly from her spot on one of the cots in the room. She had an arm thrown over her eyes as she tried to nap. "No matter what we do, we're in danger. Heading to town at least gives us a fighting chance."

Deittman sighed in annoyance, almost as if he were dealing with small children. "I certainly cannot stop you. Given the circumstances, I won't even count it as leaving the investigation early if you do attempt to seek out help."

Ash shot up from her spot and Eli twisted around. Both of them had mirrored expressions of anger.

"Wow, *so* gracious of you," Ash snapped.

"How can you be so... so *nonchalant* about this?" Eli asked, his voice rising louder than normal. Typically, he had a fairly cool composure--to the point where Sophia often chided him for his inability to express his emotions. But it was starting to crack. *He* was starting to crack. "Besides the fact that we absolutely *earned* that money for coming to this danger pit, that's really what you're thinking about right now? Why aren't you freaking out like the rest of us?"

Deittman pursed his lips and raised a condescending brow. "Freaking out like *you,* you mean."

"What?"

"Look at us—Isabella is sleeping quite soundly. Markus is evaluating our remaining generator power and rationing our batteries. I am documenting the events. It is *you two* who are 'freaking out.'"

Eli closed his eyes and exhaled. He was just so... tired. Tired and appalled. "We're really experiments, aren't we? You honestly don't care what happens to anyone, so long as you get your data. C'mon Ash. Let's do *something.*"

She needed no further prompting. She stood, zipped up her jacket, and stuffed her last remaining packs of cigarettes into her pocket. "Gladly."

It may have been damp and chilly, and they may have a five or six-hour walk ahead of them... But surely anything was better than spending one more second in the Hellhole that was Maple Hill.

As they headed down the road, Eli quickly realized that he wasn't going to be able to make the entire trek to town. He was too weak— and though Ash didn't want to admit it, he knew she was too. He was starting to believe that Deittman had been serious when he said psychics could help 'jumpstart' a building's paranormal activity. It was as if his energy had been leached from him and it would take days for him to recover… *if* he had the luxury of days to recover, that was.

"Maybe we should turn back," Eli finally said, his shoulders slumping. It was going to be dark before they managed to reach the town, just like Deittman had told them. They risked being hit on the road at this rate. If a car passed them at all.

He thought for a moment Ash would argue with him, saying that they were already soaked from the non-stop rain and that it would all be for nothing, but she was quiet as they slowed to a halt. "I think so. I'm… running on fumes. More than I thought. Maybe it was adrenaline keeping me going back there."

It was then that he noticed Ash's disheveled appearance. It wasn't her cool, casual, unkempt style that she wore when they met. She had dark circles forming under her eyes that she hadn't bothered to cover up with makeup. Her usual passive expression, which always seemed to have a hint of a smirk lurking beneath it, was an apathetic frown. She looked just as tired as he felt.

Maple Hill was hitting them hard—harder than the others, he ventured to guess. He wondered if Isabella was feeling the same way. They had left her sleeping the afternoon away.

They had only managed to make it two miles or so, though it was hard to reliably say since there were no mile markers on the old country road to follow, and they had no concept of how long they had been gone. With a heavy sigh, Eli settled and turned around. With a sense of miserable acceptance, they started to retrace their steps.

After perhaps ten minutes—or maybe only five, or twenty, who could say in their tired state?—Eli stopped and stared into a patch of trees off to their left.

"Do you see that?"

Ash stopped and stood next to him. She looked around but haphazardly shook her head. "What am I supposed to see?

Eli moved forward, motioning to a section of trees and pointing at the muddy ground. "There's like a dirt path, like an old, unpaved sideroad."

"Okay, and?"

Eli shrugged, waving his hand about for emphasis. "Follow the tire tracks. I think I see the top of a car."

Ash furrowed her brows then cocked her head to the side. "Oh, hey, yeah. Wanna look?"

Of course, he wanted to look. If there was a chance someone was out here who could help them out, he would take it. Sure, it could be a backwoods murderer, but was that really *worse* than what they were already dealing with at Maple Hill?

Eli didn't hesitate and all but had a skip in his step as a wave of rejuvenation surged within him. Well, as much of a skip as he could manage while trudging through the muddy pathway. After a few steps, he chose to walk off to the side, on top of piles of wet leaves instead.

His jolt of excitement and energy, however, was quick to pass. Though the car seemed drivable, it was abandoned. There were no keys and no signs of anyone around. Based on the leaves and twigs and acorns littering its roof and hood, it had been sitting for a few days. Eli wondered if the car had hit something and pulled off to sit off the road since it reeked of roadkill.

Ash stood a few steps back as Eli checked the doors—not that Eli knew what he would do if they were unlocked. He didn't know how to hotwire a car. Maybe Garrett would... if they ever found him.

"What's wrong?" Eli asked, walking to the passenger side and trying the next set of doors. He pulled his shirt up to cover his mouth and nose to try to protect himself from the roadkill odor. Ash put her hand up to her face as well.

"It's a red Nissan," she said.

"Yeah, it's a nice car."

"Eli, Vincent left in a red Nissan."

Eli stopped and stepped back, looking at the car. Now that she mentioned it, he did remember Vincent leaving in a red vehicle like the one in front of him. He hadn't paid too much attention to it at the time, though. "Do you think this is his car?"

Ash took a slow step forward and peered in the window of the hatchback. The shadows cast by the tall trees and dense shrubbery made it difficult to see through the tinted windows without a light, but she craned her neck and squinted in regardless. With a suspicious hum, Ash took a step back and picked up a baseball-sized rock.

"What are you doing?" Eli asked, walking around to meet her. He tried to take the rock from her, but she moved away from him.

"Something's in there."

Eli looked at her, then to the car, then back at her. Deep down, he already knew what she was saying, but he just didn't want to admit it. He wanted to find the keys, or hot wire the car, and escape this horrible place...

Ash threw the rock into the driver's side window, the glass shattering from the hit. Eli expected the alarm to go off, but it didn't. He hadn't known alarms not to go off unless they had been disabled.

A horrible, vomit-inducing stench escaped the car and a cluster of insects flew out of the now-broken window. Eli turned away and retched. Ash followed as well, gagging and vomiting on the other side of the car. After losing whatever was in her stomach, Ash covered her mouth and went to the car. Eli didn't even want to open his mouth to ask what she was doing.

She unlocked the front door and carefully reached in, avoiding the shattered glass, and popped the trunk.

As soon as it was unlatched and started to rise, a mass tumbled out of the SUV's trunk, causing Eli to jump.

It was the man he had seen in the Doctor's Quarters—the one who had been bashed in the head with a fire poker. He was wrapped in an old rug and covered with a moth-eaten blanket, or at least he *had* been until he rolled out of the trunk. Now, he lay splayed out on the ground, slowly sinking into the puddle of mud behind the red vehicle. Flies and maggots and other insects had already gotten to him over the course of a few days, his body bloated and his skin blotchy and discolored from laying in one position. It was so much worse than what he had seen with Stevens's broken corpse.

Ash immediately backed away from the car, shaking her head.

"We need to go," she said, her voice muffled by her shirt. Eli didn't need any further prompting. With one last look at the decaying face, he hurried back to the road, his heart racing.

CHAPTER 26

"Deittman!" Eli shouted as he and Ash stormed back into Maple Hill. They were wet, they were cold, and they were *angry*.

They marched down the hallways, leaving the front door thrown open despite the cold.

"Deittman!"

The older man looked over from the supply table, his jaw clenched, and brows furrowed in obvious signs of irritation. The bag of dead or broken equipment was twice the size as it was when Eli left. They would be lucky if they had enough batteries to power their flashlights through the night.

"I have a question," Eli snapped, slamming his hands down on the table, causing some of the devices to shuffle.

"What is it?" Deittman replied gruffly.

Eli took a moment to pause and think about his question again. In that time, Deittman glanced over at him twice more, waiting for Eli to speak.

"How well do you know Vincent?"

Deittman sighed loudly and tossed another useless lantern onto the table. Those took the most power out of all of their supplies. "I don't."

"What?"

"I don't," Deittman clarified, and turned to face Eli fully. "We had only ever communicated through email. We didn't actually speak until we were here."

Eli frowned. "So, you brought us here, to an old, dangerous, decrepit building, without ever actually talking to the owner?"

Deittman practically snarled at him. "I don't appreciate your implication, boy. Because of our time differences, it is quite common for me to work strictly via web communication. It's simply the nature of the business. I've hardly had problems in the past."

"Hardly?" Eli said immediately.

Deittman's mouth shut with an audible *click* and he pursed his lips, feigning nonchalance. He shrugged and nodded. "There's always a risk involved, though typically such risk means I lose money, not people."

Eli gave the man a long, hard stare. It shouldn't have surprised him after everything that had happened, and yet he could hardly believe the man. Just how far was Deittman willing to go in the pursuit of the paranormal? Was he truly so selfish as to put his team in possible danger? Then again, the man made a living off of his research. What was a little bit of danger when there were book deals and talk shows to be had? Sighing, Eli walked over to the pile of books and records Ash had been sifting through the day before. He found the one she dog-eared.

"Take a look at this," he said and flipped it open. Deittman glanced down at it.

"It's a staff photo. There are many around here, if I'm not mistaken."

"Yeah, I know that," Eli replied dryly. "But take a closer look. This is the doctor—Dr. Pollock. The one who lost his license."

"And?"

"And this here is the woman Vincent claimed was his grandmother. However, he didn't know she was already married and pregnant at the time she worked here. By my math, she'd probably be his great-grandmother. Don't you find it weird that he knew so much about the doctor and his activities, but when it came to his own grandmother, he knew *nothing* about her?"

Deittman opened his mouth, perhaps to rationalize the discrepancy, but closed it again. He stared at the picture, lifting the book to eye level and wiping away some of the dust. "Perhaps... perhaps there is a bit of resemblance. However, now I cannot be sure if it was the power of suggestion which led me to see such—"

Eli held his hand up. "I saw the doctor's Echo in the asylum with Ash. The man looked familiar, but I couldn't figure out why. Vincent. He looked like Vincent."

Deittman fell silent and gazed off into the darkness to his right. "Even so... what do you suggest? He happens to resemble the doctor. Are you suggesting... he is a reincarnation? Perhaps that the doctor has possessed him?"

Eli raised his brow and slowly shook his head. "No? I *suggest*, maybe, that the guy is actually related to the doctor and he's a nutcase? *Maybe* he didn't leave the property? We found the car he drove off in—there was a body in the trunk. The man I saw as an Echo in the Doctor's Quarters. I think... I think Vincent might've killed him. Our 'Vincent' may not be the *real* Vincent at all."

Eli had been expecting a bigger reaction from Deittman. He figured the man would be shocked and appalled, but in typical Deittman form, he instead merely made notes, as if finding a corpse in the trunk of a car was *research*. Eli was starting to wonder if *Doctor Deittman* was in need of a psychological evaluation himself. He was far too calm, and level-headed, considering the fact that six people now were either *dead* or *missing*.

"Oh," Deittman replied with a hum. "Well, I suppose that would be a more plausible conclusion, wouldn't it? Do you discount the paranormal activity we've all witnessed here then, too? Do you write it off as human interference?"

Good question. Eli couldn't deny that the door in the Doctor's Quarters closed on Ash or the fire demon in the asylum. He had seen plenty of Echoes as well, but those were a different sort of activity in his opinion.

"No, I don't," Eli replied with a sense of finality. "But I also don't think the paranormal had anything to do with our teammates disappearing one by one. Do we have enough battery power for me to review footage on some of the cameras?"

Deittman stared back at the sole generator still running. "It's about dead, I'm afraid. We planned the trip for three generators, not two."

"Which, if I'm not mistaken, could have actually been loaded in. We have three cases and two generators. Vincent was the first one here to let the load in guys into the building, right? Maybe he swiped one before Garrett and Stevens arrived," Eli pointed out.

"It would have been difficult for one person, but not impossible if they were particularly *crafty,*" Deittman replied, stroking his beard in contemplation. "Alright, if you think you may find something, you can redirect the power to the cameras and monitors. I suggest you move quickly, however, as even then, you won't have much time."

Eli couldn't help but feel a sense of urgency and paranoia. He knew he was onto something, he could *feel* it—but that only heightened his awareness around him, as if he expected Vincent to pop out of the shadows. The more he thought about it, however, the more he was *sure* he was right.

"How's it going?" Ash asked, causing Eli to jump. He hadn't noticed her enter their headquarters because the glare of the monitors made it hard to see anything else in the dark. Not a reassuring sign. He might very well be attacked, and he wouldn't even have time to react because he was blind to the things around him.

Ash set down a little bowl of soup for him with one of the last water bottles and some nearly-stale bread. He didn't hesitate to start devouring it.

"So, you said you have some experience with *other* sorts of paranormal things, right? I was wondering..." He paused to dip his bread into the soup and shove it into his mouth. "So, yeah, that fire thing, the one in the asylum. In your opinion did it attack Carlos?"

Ash crossed her arms and casually leaned up against the wall. She hummed and tapped her index finger against her sleeve. "In my opinion... no."

"Why do you say that?"

She shrugged. "I was first on the scene, so to speak. That thing left Carlos alone for the most part. It looked like it had grabbed Carlos by the arm and the leg as it was forming and pulled him down the hall and into the room. Then it let him go. By the time I actually got into the room it had already retreated to where you saw it. If it had wanted to *really* hurt Carlos, it would have."

Eli nodded almost vigorously. "Okay, okay, I'm inclined to believe you. Check this out." He brushed his hands on his jeans and clicked around on the sole computer screen he could afford to have running. "You've got to watch closely though. This is the one basement camera."

"The quality sucks," Ash muttered as she leaned over Eli's shoulder to get a better look at the screen. "Looks like movement down there."

"Keep watching."

Despite the graininess of the feed, a black figure crept along the far edge of the frame. It ultimately hurried across the far back of the basement, up to the steps leading to the asylum. For a brief moment, it looked as though there was a flash of light—possibly from the door opening at the top of the stairs off-screen.

"Isn't that supposed to be sealed?" Ash asked, pointing up towards where the asylum door theoretically was.

"Theoretically. But who said it was sealed?"

"Vincent," she replied in a deadpanned tone.

"Exactly. Now, Garrett and Stevens checked that door when they were looking for Carlos. It was locked, but not necessarily sealed—not in the sense that the other building out back of here is *sealed*. I think Vincent lied so we wouldn't know the door was actually usable. If it is him, he comes back to the basement just after the fire starts. I'm going to switch to another camera."

Eli minimized the feed and pulled up a new window. This time it was of the hallway leading from the Doctor's Quarters. They didn't have many cameras throughout that section of the building because they didn't have the generator power to keep them running, so there was only that one and the one by the main door into the asylum.

Again, it appeared as if the cloaked figure made it a point to stick to the outer edges of the camera's line of sight, if in sight at all. A brief scurry of movement flashed on the bottom edge of the camera--possibly as someone approached the door of the Doctor's Quarters. Eli had timed it up with the camera Carlos had gone to check on and found that it was just about a minute before Carlos walked into the room. Carlos then found the open door and approached it.

Smoke started somewhere down the hall at just about the same moment. The bit of the cloaked figure that had been visible backed away, perhaps back into the stairwell. Carlos entered the hallway, staring at the camera in his hands. The edge of the cloak appeared again, and—

And Carlos fell to the ground. He started sliding further down the hallway, but the camera's feed became too fuzzy to see anything afterward. Eli figured that the 'figure' could have attacked Carlos and dragged him towards the fire— the attack hadn't been supernatural at all. Maybe Vincent encountered the fire demon and ran, abandoning whatever his plan was for Carlos.

Eli paused the video and pulled the basement feed up once more. It was only a few moments later when the door opened again, and a barely visible black mass crossed the edge of the line of sight before disappearing into the darkness.

"Because there are so many camera feeds, it's hard to watch them all in real-time—Garrett said they spend *weeks* reviewing everything after they're done. Once Garrett went running from leave the room, everyone rushed away from the monitors, no one was watching anything at that point."

Ash stood and nodded, "yeah, okay, I buy it. I figured it was unlikely that some *spirits* stole Deittman's equipment bag."

"We were all gone for enough time for someone to run up from the basement, take our stuff, and go back. The cameras in the basement cut at about the same time too. If he realized no one was watching the monitors, it gave him enough time to go and shut them off without anyone coming to investigate," Eli replied.

"What about Jackson and Marina? What happened to them? There's no way everyone would have missed them if they left the basement."

Eli's shoulders slumped. "Yeah. I agree. That's... about where my theory falls apart. Unless they're in that sealed building, which is, you know, *sealed.*"

"That's still a pretty good theory—you've got some evidence to back it up too."

"I guess..." he said with a sigh, "honestly, you were the one who got me thinking once you showed me that picture."

"Happy to help. Now, if you don't mind, I need a cigarette." She clapped him on the shoulder and didn't give him a chance to object before she lit up.

CHAPTER 27

Their generators sputtered out as sunset faded away. Eli was still wet and cold from his trek down the road with Ash, and his mood had soured. He swore that after he got his money for this job, he would never see Deittman again. No amount of money would ever be worth his horrific experiences at the hellhole that was Maple Hill.

Ash was fidgety and irritated as well. She didn't like sitting still, especially not with the tension radiating through the air. She took to wandering around the floor outside headquarters, where the five of them had camped out for the past few hours except when leaving to go to the bathroom in pairs.

"You shouldn't go too far," Markus advised as she passed by the doorway once more, cigarette in hand.

"I can't sit here and just *wait* to get picked off. We should be doing something."

"Vincent, or whoever he is, has proven to be much more resourceful than we could have expected. We are at a disadvantage," Markus said, standing up and placing his hands in the pockets of his slacks. "Don't let him get to you."

"He better get to me next," Ash muttered, cigarette in her mouth. "If he's smart, at least. If he doesn't, I swear to God I'm going to shove a fireball down his throat."

"You shouldn't be trying to make yourself a target," Eli said with a frown, wrapping his blanket around him tighter.

Ash threw her hands up and then let them hit against her thighs with a *slap*. "I'm not a coward. I'll go find him *myself* if I have to. You all have fun hiding here until he comes for you. Your flashlights won't last all night, and then what? I'm not sitting around long enough to find out."

Eli sighed. She was right. Believing in safety in numbers was all well and good, but Jackson and Marina had disappeared at the same time. Stevens, who was the strongest, physically, out of all of them, had been caught off-guard and likely pushed down an elevator shaft. Garrett had been trailing behind Deittman and Markus and he had disappeared as well.

"I'll go with you," Eli conceded. "Where do you want to start?"

"I dunno," she sighed, letting out a puff of smoke. "I guess top floor down, where Garrett was last seen. Maybe there's, like, a secret passage or something we missed."

"It's unlikely a place like this would have a secret passage," Markus said, and Isabella nodded in agreement. She had woken up before sunset, looking a bit pale—paler than normal, at least. "Kirkbride buildings are fairly straightforward."

Ash rolled her eyes. "We have ghosts closing doors and starting fires. A psychotic killer on the loose. Seems like a secret passage isn't too insane."

Eli almost laughed. She had a point.

He wished she didn't.

Markus didn't try to stop them, but he did hand Eli one of their last flashlights as he left.

As Eli and Ash started to leave the area, Eli gave one last look back into the headquarters and watched as the Deittman trio clustered up against the wall, watching the two entrances, as if afraid of who might come in.

Eli's nerves were at their worst when he and Ash started up the dark stairwell to the fourth floor. He led the way since he had the flashlight, and to be honest, he preferred it that way. He figured he would have a better chance fighting something off if it came at him from the front rather than jumping him from behind. Though Ash appeared to be calm and relaxed, he heard her repeatedly clicking her lighter open and close.

"Do you really think we'll find anything?" Eli asked, trying to break the tension despite the wave in his voice that betrayed his nervousness.

"I don't know," she sighed. "Probably not. But at least I won't feel guilty for not trying."

"You didn't strike me as the guilty type," Eli said as they reached the top. He stepped out and flicked his flashlight around, scanning for any danger. They seemed to be alone.

Behind him, Ash was silent--she even stopped her nervous clicking. Eli turned, shining his light on her just to make sure she was still with him. She squinted and turned away, shrugging.

"There were a lot of times when I needed help and didn't get it," Ash said. "I wouldn't feel right knowing I didn't try when that's all I ever wanted from someone else."

Eli let the light drop away from her, its beam instead filling the stairwell. It was easy to look at her, with her unflappable confidence and rough demeanor, and think her cold or callous. All throughout the weekend, however, she had been nothing but a pillar of strength, stepping in to help, to reassure, to *protect*. And what had they given her?

Condescending attitudes and red welts from zip ties.

And yet here she was, looking for their missing teammates anyhow.

Eli could only sigh and wish for a fraction of her courage.

He did not like the fourth floor, and he did not like that they had to keep returning to it. As Isabella had pointed out, it had a bit of a fun house effect due to the spacing of the doors and the height of the ceiling. Add in the way the floorboards sent moaning and creaking bouncing off the wall... It felt like there was more than just the two of them in that damned hallway.

Ash ambled through, cigarette in hand, peeking into each room. "I guess there's nothing here but the elevator. The elevator and..."

"Yeah," Eli said. "Yeah, Stevens. I... wouldn't look, if I were you."

"I won't. Next floor?"

The third floor was no different. Eli was relieved to find nothing, as he didn't actually know what he would do if they *had* found any sign of Vincent. It only left the second floor, and then, he supposed, the asylum side and basement.

When they began down the hallway, they were greeted by the soft glow of Deittman's flashlights from their headquarters below the balcony. While it provided additional illumination, it did, however, mean that strange shapes and shadows formed against the nurses' station and side walls, setting Eli's teeth on edge.

There was nothing in the rooms except for old bedding and furniture—and, of course, papers all over the floor. They had been eerie enough at the start of the weekend, but now... Now, Eli saw everything as a threat. Each jagged edge and rusted piece of metal could be a weapon. Every shadow cast upon the wall could be an attacker. Despite the new sense of menace that had taken over the atmosphere, nothing was out of place.

Without finding anything of interest, the pair went to the Doctor's Quarters.

"Door's locked again," Ash said, shaking her head and turning around. "Thing's got a mind of its own."

"I guess we should try it from the asylum side. I mean, I don't really *want* to, and I don't think Garrett's inside the Doctor's Quarters since I was in it when he disappeared... but we had better check the asylum at least."

Ash nodded and started back down the stairs. Eli turned around and together they went to the side stairwell they had been using once more.

Eli put his hand out, blocking Ash's path.

"What is it?" She asked, following Eli's gaze.

He kept his hand out and watched as an elderly woman floated through the hallway. By the way she moved her hands, Eli figured she was in a wheelchair. Vincent, or not Vincent or whoever he was, did tell them of a report of a woman falling down a flight of stairs.

"Well, I guess she wasn't murdered," Eli muttered.

"What was that?"

Eli waved his arm at the stairwell, not that Ash saw the vision ahead of time. "Old woman in a wheelchair. She's just muttering to herself. She probably got confused and—" there was a crash at the foot of the stairs and then some brief gasping. "Yeah, she wheeled herself down the stairs all by herself. She wasn't pushed."

"Guess that's ... good to know. Safe now?"

Eli nodded and then started to lead the way, heading down the last flight of stairs once the Echo was gone.

"Anything?" Markus asked as they started to walk past the entrances of the headquarters.

"No, nothing," Eli said and shook his head.

"We're going to take a look in the asylum, and then we'll be back," Ash replied. Again, Markus advised them against wandering, but the pair ignored him. It would be cold and miserable, but honestly, Eli felt safer outside than he did within the building.

Eli should have asked what time it was. The hours had started to blend together since nightfall, and he felt like it should have been in the wee hours of the morning. He doubted he would be so lucky, though.

They had taken a few steps out the front door when Eli heard screaming. He closed his eyes and inwardly sighed. He was getting tired of seeing so many Echoes. He was certain that after his time at Maple Hill, he was going to be able to handle the normal ones around the city so much better.

"Wait," Eli sighed, "there's another—"

"*Shhh!*" Ash hissed, waving her hand around to silence him.

He stared at her in shock. She couldn't possibly—

"Do you hear that?"

Eli swallowed hard and turned to her in alarm. "The screaming?"

She returned his look of shock and nodded, her mouth slightly agape.

"Shit!" Eli shouted as the two of them took off running to the sound of the screaming. It led them to the entrance of the basement. "Shit, shit, *shit!* I assumed it was an Echo! I didn't think you could hear it too!"

Ash was the first one through the door, storming down the stairs, her hand fumbling in her pocket for her lighter. She stopped when she reached the bottom and looked around, taking a moment to adjust to the darkness.

Even once they were in the basement, it sounded as if the screaming—which very well could have belonged to Garrett—was far away. They were closer, that was for sure, but not close enough.

"Where the fuck is it coming from?" Ash hissed, looking around. Eli would have said it was from the asylum side, knowing now there was an accessible entrance from the basement, but that wasn't possible. They wouldn't have been able to hear through the thick metal door separating the floors.

Eli whirled around, his flashlight beam bouncing off of the useless *crap* littering the basement. He wanted nothing more than to just bring it all crashing down out of frustration, but that wouldn't do anything to save their teammates. The only thing that caught his eye was a mass of cobwebs that seemed to be moving on their own.

Well, not moving on their own, he realized. They moved as if caught in a breeze—and there was definitely *no* breeze in the stuffy basement.

"Ash, over here," he said and waved her towards the center of the area of the basement. He approached carefully, trying to scan the area for anything that might threaten to jump out at him. There was nothing—nothing besides the sounds of Garrett's screams that were getting slightly louder as he moved.

Once at the cobwebs, Eli slowly scanned his flashlight across the wall, looking for anything else unusual. He saw more moving cobwebs and a worn sheet that fluttered around the edge. It was behind a towering bookcase still housing a few medical books. Whatever the sheet was covering came out a few feet from the wall, but Eli couldn't get a good look at it because of the other furniture pieces in the way.

"Do you want me to do it?" Ash asked quietly.

Eli shook his head. "I got it. Get a fireball ready or something."

He was pleased to know she didn't even hesitate—he could hear the clicking of her lighter behind him.

He slipped through the gap between the bookcase and a desk with a few suitcases on top of it. Gathering up his courage, Eli reached out and grabbed the sheet, yanking it towards him and he stepped back into the little aisleway near Ash. She had a little flame in her hand, ready to throw it at an attacker, but nothing was there.

Well, that wasn't quite right. The sheet had certainly been hiding *something*: a door. A large, metal double door. Both doors were propped wide open. The huge sheet had been covering them, making it appear to be a rectangular, solid object behind the bookcase.

Garrett's shouts were coming from somewhere beyond the open doors—though they were growing quieter, with longer gaps in between.

"We need to go get Deittman," Eli said quietly, taking another step back, away from the door.

"You go get him," Ash said, "I'm going in. Garrett could be dying—he *sounds* like he is dying!" She pushed passed him and started to slip through the gap between the bookshelf and the desk.

Eli grabbed her, forcing her to stop. "You can't! What if it's a trap? What if Vincent is waiting for us—waiting to do whatever he did to the others."

"I can't stand here and listen to those screams. I *won't*. If I can help, I have to try."

Ash's face was a mix of fear and determination—and fear seemed to be winning out. Still, she raised her hand, holding her little *fireball* between her two palms. Eli knew he wasn't going to be able to convince her to turn back. He sighed and glanced around, spotting a broken wooden chair. He walked over and raised his foot, bringing it down on the already busted leg.

At least he had a weapon.

"Fine. But if it looks futile, we come right back."

Ash nodded and turned again, scooting between the bookcase and the door, disappearing through the opening.

Eli took a deep breath and followed after her.

It was a tunnel. It was dark, damp, and smelled horrible—like something had died in it. Ash led the way with the light of her little flame. Eli's flashlight caused her shadow to walk just ahead of her, which he found made him jumpy enough to hurry his pace to walk next to her.

The screaming had stopped. The sound of silence, beyond their own steps and nervous breathing, was deafening.

The tunnel itself was old—older than the rest of the Maple Hill building. The ground was an uneven concrete that had likely been poured by hand and seemingly repaired a few times over. It was in desperate need of repair again, Eli noted, as he stepped in a dip that had settled lower than the rest of the floor. The walls were stone blocks that allowed moisture to seep through the cracks. There were old wires hanging across the bricks and fixtures Eli supposed were for lights, but any bulbs had long since burned out or burst.

It occurred to him as they walked on toward another door, a door which was outlined by a faint glow, that they were walking to the area behind the main building.

They were walking straight to the smaller, boarded up house—the house that radiated pure malice.

When the pair approached the door, Eli reached a hand out, trying to steady his shaking, and touched the handle. It was metal and industrial, albeit old. Eli looked towards Ash and gave her a nod. She returned it and he inhaled deeply before slowly pulling it open.

The old hinges screeched loudly in such a high pitch that Eli winced. If Vincent hadn't heard them coming before, he had probably heard them now.

Shit.

Eli released the breath he was holding and shook his head. This was a bad idea. It was a terrible, horrible idea, and just as he was going to tell Ash that they should wait, she slid between the gap he had made.

Guess we're going in.

The door led to a small area that had probably been a basement at some point in time. There was a ramp with a small set of stairs filling most of the area straight ahead of them, leading to the first floor. The architecture of the building, from the little he saw in the low light, showed that the structure was much, much older than the main part of Maple Hill.

If he remembered correctly, Vincent had said the property had been a home for the destitute—a poor farm. This building hadn't been used since Maple Hill was built... But that was what *Vincent* had told them. They didn't have actual proof and judging by an old gurney sitting to the side of the ramp, Vincent hadn't been telling the whole truth.

Old medical coats and some sort of outdated scrubs were hung up along the walls. The floors were covered in a thick coat of dust, and there were papers scattered about one side—papers covered in dark blotches of mold and mildew. Eli reflexively covered his mouth and grimaced. If Vincent didn't kill them, then whatever spores they were breathing in very well might.

A cry rang out from somewhere above them, though it sounded lackluster compared to what they had heard before. A cruel laugh followed the cry.

Ash nodded her head towards the ramp and started to move forward.

Eli clicked off his flashlight. He feared it would be a literal spotlight—a beacon to show Vincent exactly where they were. There was enough light in the area to walk around, though they had to be careful not to step on anything. Vincent had, indeed, acquired the missing third generator that Carlos had mentioned and was using it to power a strip of LED lights. Combined with a few of Deittman's stolen lanterns, it was well-lit compared to what they had grown used to at night over the past seventy-two hours.

They tried to move slowly and carefully, keeping the creaking of the stairs to a minimum. The flooring on the first level was all wood but stable enough despite its age. At the top and to the left of the ramp-stair combo was a main staircase with carved wood banisters leading up to a second floor with something akin to a nurses' station.

There were a few rooms on the first floor, though they were too dark for either of them to see into. At one point in time, Eli guessed, they had been sitting rooms and parlors since they sat to the left and the right of the foyer they had entered from the basement ramp. Considering the basement level, he doubted they were still quaint sitting rooms. As they moved, Eli continuously scanned the area, waiting to see if something was going to ambush them—but there was nothing.

The only thing he noticed were the intense barricades placed on the front door and windows behind them. The structures were old, likely as old as the boards on the outside of the building. When this section of the asylum was shut down, it seemed someone wanted to keep it closed up for good.

One other thing caught Eli's eye—a familiar duffle bag sitting within the doorway to another room. It was Deittman's padded bag, the one containing some of his custom equipment.

Maybe Eli could grab it on his way out. Maybe they could find Deittman's cell phone.

They heard voices—well, Vincent's voice and some other grunting they hoped belonged to Garrett—up on the second floor. With only a brief pause, they went onwards, Ash leading the way.

CHAPTER 28

"Hey, at least it isn't the water, right?" Vincent said, amusement in his voice.

Eli and Ash crept up the stairs, trying to keep any extra sound to a minimum as they listened.

"I mean, that was pretty awful. But it was the only way to *shut him up*. Guy kept shouting about cameras, like he thought that it was going to be a prank show. I think he finally got it after the second time I held him under. He finally—"

The stairs creaked under Ash's foot and they both winced, freezing in place, not even daring to breathe. Vincent stopped speaking at the same time; he heard them. They paused, hoping, *praying* that he wouldn't come after them. They weren't ready—not that they would ever *be* ready.

There was suddenly screaming—a loud, high-pitched screaming that overtook the full atrium. Eli tensed and panicked, ready to whirl around to see where it was coming from. But Ash didn't move, and Vincent resumed speaking, and Eli knew.

It was an Echo. An Echo was starting. What horrendous timing. Eli squeezed his eyes shut and tried to block it out. Ash had started moving again and had to maintain his focus.

"Haven't used the electro-shock chamber yet. Needed to wait since I didn't want to alert the rest of your team... But now that half of you are gone, I think I can risk it soon. But not yet, not for you. Just wanna test out my hand and see how steady I can hold a scalpel—see if I inherited that from my grandfather."

The pair reached the top of the stairs and quietly rounded the banister to head into one of the medical rooms. It was very clearly once a bedroom with a doorway that was too narrow for a standard medical ward. They moved delicately, stopping once Ash was in the doorway, just a yard or so away from Vincent.

He wore a dark coat—one that he likely found on the premises. It didn't fit him very well, but it was long and likely helped make him remain unseen in the shadows of Maple Hill. Garrett was strapped into a bed, which was bolted to the floor. The mattress, though likely already dirty and ruined, was now littered with blotches that looked black in the poor lantern light Vincent had rigged up in the building. Garrett was bleeding—from his head, his arms, his legs... None of the cuts seemed particularly deep, but there were a *lot* of cuts.

"Vincent," Ash warned, holding her fireball in front of her. "Vincent, put the scalpel down and step away from Garrett."

Vincent whirled around, a lopsided smile on his face. "Damn! You scared me! Thought you were a ghost."

Eli looked between Ash and Vincent, occasionally glancing over at Garrett who had turned his head to gaze at Eli through squinted eyes. He wasn't wearing his glasses and probably couldn't see much anyhow.

Ash's nostrils flared, reminding him, not for the first time, of a wild animal. Eli briefly wondered if he would see a repeat of the other night—the possessed, uncontrollable Ash. Maybe they needed that if they were going to make it out alive... but Vincent was just a man. A human being. They should be able to handle him, right?

"I guess you guys really are psychic to have tracked me down all the way over here. Took you longer to find the tunnel than I thought it would. But then again, you didn't have a journal telling you where the entrance was... And I stayed pretty well hidden. None of you even noticed when I snuck into your base and stole half your equipment. Too preoccupied looking for *ghosts* to notice one of the living."

Eli hated the sheer *delight* that covered Vincent's face. It was as though he was *proud* of outsmarting them long enough to make a few of them disappear. It was sickening.

"Neat trick with the little fireball. I bet you impress all of the paranormal lovers with that. I don't buy it. Bet my grandfather would have *loved* to have gotten his hands on you. Cut you up like his other projects," Vincent said, fingering the scalpel in his right hand lovingly. Ash took a tentative step to her right, trying to maneuver behind him. He turned the blade downwards, facing it towards Garrett's chest. "I wouldn't do that if I were you."

Eli clenched his jaw and tried to think of something. How did he get here? How was he in the position that a man's life was hanging in his hands? He was an IT guy, for Christ's sake! He debugged programs! He didn't play the hero!

"Why are you doing this?" Eli asked, hoping to distract Vincent so Ash could do something. *Anything.* She was the one with the firepower—literally. "We found a staff picture and saw Doctor Pollock. He looked an awful lot like you."

Vincent's lopsided grin widened.

"A staff picture? You should have said it was your *psychic powers.* I might have even believed you," Vincent said with a laugh before his face contorted into a snarl. "But yeah—yeah. He was my grandfather. Sick old bastard. Remarried after his wife died. Had my mom. She and my grandmother were never as good as Dianna and baby Delia, and he made sure they knew it every day of their lives. I lived with him in his last few years. Heard his stories. The things he did. He was a fucked-up guy."

Eli nodded. "Uh huh... that, uh, says a lot from the guy who's torturing an innocent man."

Vincent frowned. "Yeah, well, I guess it runs in the family." He raised his scalpel threateningly as his face contorted, readying to put some force behind the blow.

Ash was faster, and she launched a fireball squarely at Vincent's chest.

Vincent cried out in shock as the fire hit him. His arms flailed about, desperate to snuff the flames starting to eat at his heavy black coat. He twisted and crashed into a tray of surgical instruments, sending them clanking across the wooden floor. Eli ran forward and quickly undid the leather straps that held Garrett in place, dropping his makeshift weapon at his feet.

Ash threw her hand outwards, aiming at Vincent and the now smoldering flames. A small lick of fire jumped off the jacket and toward her hand. She threw it to her other palm and then back, trying to get it to grow big enough to do more damage.

"You bitch!" Vincent charged at Ash, slamming into her and pushing her out of the room and into the wooden banister running along the balcony and down the stairs. Eli watched as Ash threw the modest fireball at Vincent, but it did little more than cause a fresh batch of smoldering. He grabbed her upper arms and shoved her again, the railing creaking against their combined weight. There was more creaking as some of the banister's spokes popped out of place.

Eli kept glancing over his shoulder as he undid the last straps. Garrett groaned and started trying to move but he was just too slow. Eli stumbled around the medical bed, jumping over the downed supplies cart and into the hallway. He grabbed Vincent by the collar and yanked him backward, giving Ash enough room to slip free.

Then, without any hesitation, Eli shoved Vincent forward into the broken banister. It splintered, sending Vincent onto the large staircase. He tumbled down with a *thud, thud, thudthudthud.*

Eli stood at the top of the wreckage and stared down. Vincent lay unmoving at the bottom atop a moth-eaten rug.

"Help me," Ash hissed from behind him.

She had Garrett and was helping him to limp out of the room. Blood poured from his temple and numerous cuts on his body. He was barely conscious. Vincent had done a number on him.

With Eli and Ash on either side of him, they carried Garrett down the stairs—luckily the man was fairly light.

Vincent groaned from the foot of the stairs, apparently not knocked out entirely.

They tried to scoot around him, but Vincent haphazardly flailed out as he regained consciousness, grabbing onto Eli's foot. Eli was able to kick him off rather easily, but he knew that Vincent would be up and moving before they made it to the tunnel entrance.

"We aren't going to make it," he muttered, trying to pick up the pace. Ash wasn't as strong as him, however, and wasn't able to move much faster with the burden of half of Garrett.

"Leave me..." Garrett said quietly, his voice weak.

"We came to get you," Ash said through her teeth, straining as she hoisted Garrett along. "We're not leaving you."

Garrett shook his head, though it was more like rolling side to side. "No, I'm going to pass out. I'll be deadweight. Get out of here."

Eli had all of about ten seconds to decide what to do. Sure, he and Ash might be able to take on Vincent on their own—he was only one man, after all. But they were tired. *So, so tired.* Maple Hill had depleted them. If they didn't tell someone where they were, they could both be stuck with Garrett. Deittman may never notice the tunnel and Vincent would be free to continue to pick off the rest of the team.

The thought of poor, innocent Isabella being grabbed in the dark because Eli hadn't made it back to warn the others was enough for Eli to decide.

"We can come back with Deittman and Markus," Eli said. "We can come back with them, get Garrett, and tie Vincent up until we can bring the police tomorrow."

"Shit," Ash hissed and then stopped moving. She let out a few phrases in a language that Eli didn't know. "Fine. Fuck, I don't like this. Fine. But let's at least hide Garrett."

"Good idea." Eli nudged them in Ash's direction, to their right, towards one of the dark 'parlor rooms' off of the foyer. Vincent had started to sit up, rubbing his head and shoulders. "We'll come back and get him. Maybe we can lure Vincent back to the main building and take him down with the others. Keep him away from Garrett."

Ash nodded and tried her best to hurry.

The dark room they entered, as it turned out, was a hydro-therapy room—just like the one Deittman had asked Vincent about on their first day. Not only had Vincent lied about finding the hydro-therapy room, but he also lied about the water situation. There was still water in the pipes, it seemed, though dirty.

A stench hit Eli, making him gag. Eli wondered how they hadn't noticed the odor when they first walked into the room. Perhaps it was the moldy smell of the building that had covered it, but now that he was near stagnant water, it just reeked... It reeked like a—

"Fuck, I'm going to be sick, sorry Garret!" Ash choked out, bending over and heaving, dropping her side of Garrett's now unconscious form to the ground. Eli followed suit, but only because he didn't have a chance to move Garrett. Eli turned around and saw...

—a body.

He knew what happened to Jackson. His body bobbed in the massive tub of disgusting water. His spiky hair was stuck to his face, which was blotchy and discolored. It was obvious he had been drowned. Eli gagged, but there wasn't anything left in his stomach to come up.

"We've got to go," Eli muttered, "Gotta get out of here..."

He backed out of the hydro-therapy room and Ash followed suit, covering her mouth and shaking her head as she looked into the tub as well.

They were about to turn away when Eli accidentally kicked Deittman's duffle in the hallway. He quickly crouched down and unzipped it, clicking on his flashlight.

"We have to go!" Ash said, watching as Vincent slowly regained his bearings down the hall. His momentary stunning hadn't even lasted a minute. If they had more time, if they had more resources, maybe they could have subdued him—but they didn't. The best they could do was run for help.

"Cell phone!" Eli replied and continued sorting through the bag. Deittman's stupid, high-pitch device was inside, but no cell phone. Vincent had likely taken it… destroyed it even.

"He's getting up!"

Eli swore and stood, leaving the cumbersome bag behind.

They scrambled across the foyer, trying not to trip over one another, and then dashed down the ramp toward the tunnel. Ash reached the door first and threw it open, running through. Eli was hot on her heels, with Vincent not far behind. They hadn't managed to slow him down for long, much to Eli's dismay, and he had clearly spent the past few days trekking the area in the dark. He knew the area much better than either Eli or Ash, which became obvious as both of them tripped on the area of the floor that dipped into the ground. Ash fell first, with Eli crashing into her.

"You think I'm going to let you escape?" Vincent asked with a laugh, grabbing Eli's jacket. "You think I'm going to let *any* of you escape? This hellhole is all my grandfather ever talked about. He never should have left here—no one should have ever left here—ugh!"

Eli kicked outwards and his sneakered foot landed squarely on Vincent's chest, throwing him off. Eli tried to regain his footing but before he could stand, he felt a hand on his calf—and then blinding pain.

Eli gasped, agony searing through his mind, so intense he was unable to make a sound. Something incredibly sharp had cut through his flesh and muscle. He had never felt so much pain in his life. After a few staggered breaths, his voice caught up to him and he screamed.

Ash dove at Vincent and held him down, struggling to keep him on the ground while Eli felt around his leg. There was a thin handle protruding from Eli's leg. Vincent had stabbed him with a scalpel or some other surgical instrument.

"Get up, Eli!" Ash shouted, "get up!!!"

Eli pulled the little instrument from his leg and forced himself to stand, choking out in pain with each step. He had to brace himself against the wall and limp towards the double doors leading to the Maple Hill building.

He heard thuds behind him and Ash's panicked grunts. Soon after, she sprint up behind him.

"Go, go!!"

Eli pushed through the door with Ash behind him, shoving him onwards. They navigated the dark labyrinth of the basement, knocking things down behind them to slow Vincent down.

"Fuck, he got me good!" Eli groaned as they neared the stairs leading to the first floor. They could hear Vincent charging through the rubble, shouting obscenities at them. Eli hobbled up the stairs as fast as possible on his injured leg, though he was sure his vision was starting to darken around the corners now that he had some light to look upon.

"Just go, run!" Ash cried. "Go find Deittman. I'll try to hold him off! I'll—"

She didn't finish whatever it was she was going to say.

He heard Ash let out a pain-filled shriek followed by a loud *slam!* Eli barely had time to glance over his shoulder to see that she had gone down, face first, onto the cement steps. Vincent's cloaked figure had grabbed her by the leg and dragged her into the darkness once more.

Eli froze at the top of the stairs, wondering for a moment if he should go back down after her.

But she told him to run, so run he did.

He needed to find Deittman and get help. If their monster was really just a person, then they could team up and fight that. It would be stupid for him to go alone—but he would go back. He wouldn't just hole up and wait for help, not when Ash still had a chance.

As he limped down the hallway, quickly scanning each room for a sign of the others, he couldn't help but realize that out of all of them, Ash was the only one who was willing to try to be a hero. He wasn't a hero, he knew that. He wouldn't have even gone to try to find Garrett if she hadn't been willing to go off on her own to at least attempt it. She had even been scared, but that hadn't stopped her. She refused to sit back and leave Garrett to die.

But would they be willing to do the same for her?

CHAPTER 29

"He's got Ash!" Eli breathed out as soon as he was finally let into the room where Deittman, Markus, and Isabella had barricaded themselves. They had used the cots and chairs to create a wall to keep anyone from sneaking in while their backs were turned. "And we found Garrett. He's still alive. We can get both of them."

Eli collapsed onto a chair, holding his leg. Markus was the first at his side after seeing his bleeding, and within moments Isabella was there too with Deittman's first aid kit in her hands. Markus wasted no time rolling up Eli's pant leg.

"What happened?"

"Vincent got the jump on us. While we were heading to the asylum, we heard screaming from the basement. It was faint, but enough that we followed. There's a tunnel leading to the boarded-up building out back. Hydro and electrotherapy I guess, or something. We figured we didn't have time to wait for you guys and went after, and—fuck!"

"Sorry, sorry," Markus said, apologetic. He had torn open a small packet of sanitized stitching thread and needle, and he wasted no time sewing Eli up.

"Does this—ah!—happen often?" Eli asked, squeezing his eyes shut. He rocked back and forth in pain while Isabella held his leg still for her brother to work.

Markus hummed, not breaking concentration. "Not often, but enough that we took a first aid course. You'll need to get to a hospital to get it cleaned. What did he stab you with?"

"How should I know?" Eli hissed, "it was dark, and we were running. Maybe a scalpel. Maybe something else pointy. I pulled it out and ran."

Markus finished up the stitching in a few quick minutes and then bandaged the wound. It still hurt like hell, but Eli felt like it would hold well enough for him to go and take down Vincent before he had a chance to finish whatever it was he was doing.

And they were going to take him down.

Weren't they?

"We've got to go back!" Eli said, gingerly rubbing his injured left leg. "We can still go get Ash and Garrett before it's too late."

There were looks shared between the others about the room. Neither Markus nor Deittman spoke up. Even Isabella looked away, avoiding his gaze.

"You've got to be kidding me!" Eli shouted at them, slamming his balled fist against the wall. "He's one guy! There's four of us! Unless he's, I don't know, a trained fighter or something, he can't take on four of us at once! We can take him!"

Markus's jaw clenched and he shook his head. "I—I'm sorry. I quite like Ash, I do. She's been more interesting to have on a case than almost anyone I've ever met... But I have my sister to worry about. I cannot leave her and risk her safety."

Isabella placed a hand on Markus's arm and gazed up at him with steepled brows. He looked down, truly looking remorseful, and shook his head.

Eli wiped his hand down his face and let out an angry snarl. "Deittman, you brought us here! You got us into this! You can't be willing to just sit here and let them possibly die! This isn't some supernatural force we're facing! It's *one man* who happened to know how to catch us when we weren't paying attention!"

Deittman said nothing. He stared at Eli for a moment before looking away to gaze out of the dirty window.

Once he realized he was on his own, his shoulders slumped. "Alright... fine. You can stay here, holed up until morning. I'm not. I'm going to at least try. I'm going to grab a weapon and do *something*."

The workman's tools were still cluttering up one of the equipment tables. Eli hobbled over and scanned over the items, settling on the heavy wrench Isabella had suggested could be used to 'fight spirits.' It was heavy, easy to carry, and could do damage with one well-placed hit.

Eli turned around, shoving the cot away from the entryway, and stepped out without so much as peeking his head out to make sure he wasn't going to get ambushed. He took a deep breath and held his head high as he stomped down the hallway to the stairwell once more.

Eli had no idea where any sort of bravery he had come from. Maybe it was the faint memories of his own failed suicide attempt, which had left him sure he would die but wishing that he wouldn't. Maybe it was his own trauma--which may have well left behind an Echo for some other poor, unfortunate soul to witness in the future--that made him want to try to save Ash and Garrett so badly. And he was absolutely sure they *would* die without his help. He may not have seen any signs of Carlos or Marina, but he had seen what had happened to Stevens and Jackson. He did not have hope that those two were the outliers.

Mouth set in a grim line, he headed for the basement door once more.

The door was still open. Personally, if Eli were a psychopathic kidnapper/killer hiding out in an asylum's basement, he would have shut the door so he had advanced warning if someone was coming after him. Since it wasn't, Eli had to wonder two things—had Vincent not had the chance to go back and shut it, or was he waiting just below for Eli to return? He was hoping for the former.

Eli rushed down the stairs and then put his back towards one of the towering piles of junk. He figured that if he moved quickly, it would give his attacker potentially less of an opportunity to strike out at him on his way down. Eli had seen far too many horror movies with scenes involving steps.

He had a flashlight on him but he didn't necessarily want to use it. If Vincent was somewhere in the room, Eli wanted to be able to use the shadows as his cover. So, he inched along the pathway, squeezing his eyes shut in short bouts, trying to force them to adjust to the darkness. Eli had only taken a few steps before his foot hit something small and sent it sliding across the floor. Though he hadn't planned to see what it was, his foot tapped it again as he moved on, so he reached down to feel around for the object.

When his hand touched cool metal, he knew it was Ash's lighter. His heart sank as he realized that even if she was alive and conscious, she couldn't pull off any of her tricks to defend herself.

Gotta keep moving, he told himself, his heart racing and his leg aching. His desire to turn back increased but he took another pained step forward anyhow.

Once Eli was fully immersed in the darkness, he held his breath and listened for any sounds of movement. There was nothing— nothing at all. He was sure he would have heard a mouse in the complete silence of the basement, but there wasn't even that. Eli was confident he was completely alone. Usually that sort of thought would have terrified him. Not now, however.

It was hard to navigate through the cluttered basement, even once his eyes had adjusted to the darkness. He desperately wanted to turn his flashlight on but knew it would, quite literally, be a death sentence.

By the time Eli reached the end of the tunnel again, he knew Vincent wasn't lying in wait for him. The door to the smaller building was tightly closed, but the latch moved under his hand. It was a different style than the door in the Maple Hill basement—older, rusty. He doubted Vincent ever actually had a key to it. It was just *stuck*.

Using his wrench, Eli slammed the metal instrument down on the handle, wincing as the metal-on-metal sound echoed through the hall. Vincent would hear him coming.

He'd just have to be prepared to go in swinging.

Finally, the handle broke off on his side of the door, and Eli used the head of the wrench to push the opposite side's handle through the exposed hole. He heard another piece of metal hit the floor, leading him to believe it had been barricaded, not locked.

Taking a deep breath, Eli tried to kick the door open with his good leg. He found he wasn't able to stand on his injured leg alone and quickly reconsidered. Using his shoulder, he pushed the door open and immediately started swinging his wrench wildly about him, in case Vincent was on the other side.

He was not.

Eli looked around, searching for some sort of trap or anything that might hurt him. He found nothing. Vincent must have been too preoccupied to take precautions. Eli figured he must have had his hands full with Ash.

Muffled screams echoed through the hallway, giving Eli hope—wherever she was, she was certainly still alive.

The lights were flickering, causing Eli's vision to distort. The LEDs Vincent had hooked up to the generators quickly dimmed then brightened again, causing the shadows on the wall to appear to move. Eli tried his best to remain calm, but on more than one occasion, he started wildly swinging his wrench again, thinking something was sneaking up on him.

As he carefully limped up the stairs next to the ramp, Eli realized it was possible Vincent hadn't heard his commotion at the doors at all. Not only were Ash's muffled screams still quite loud but the generator absolutely *roared* compared to either of the two Deittman had used all weekend.

That, and there was a violent crackling sound coming from Eli's right, in the room directly opposite of the hydro-therapy room.

Eli swallowed and steadied himself as he neared the final steps.

He moved up one more step and craned his neck to peek through the banister's spokes before going any further. Vincent was nowhere to be found, but Eli spotted Ash restrained in one of the bottom floor rooms. She was strapped down, just like Garrett had been on the second floor. Eli saw the lower half of her body--saw her convulse and scream every few seconds as the lights flickered.

Knowing it could be a trap, Eli hesitated.

Fuck! What was he doing!? Was he really going to run in there and try to save this woman he had only known for a few days? He had time--he could turn the fuck around right then and tell Deittman he couldn't get into the building. No one would know. He could sit and wait until their ride pulled up to take them home. His chances of surviving were *drastically* higher if he ran right now. He might live to go home and fix things with Sophia. He might live to go home and hug his daughter one more time.

But as Ash's screams echoed through the hall, he knew he couldn't live with himself if he didn't *try*.

For decades he had been forced to stand by and watch the final moments of tragic souls. How many times had he locked eyes with the Echoes of the past? How many times had he stepped into the role of a witness unwilling or unable to do anything more than watch as a life was snuffed out?

Too many.

He tightened his grip on his wrench and hurried up the stairs as fast as his limping leg would allow.

As he closed in on the room Eli saw the generator had been moved into Ash's room and was rigged up to some antique electrical device, which, in turn, was attached to Ash's head.

Eli barely took a step into the room when Vincent slammed into him from behind, sending him crashing to the ground. The wrench skidded somewhere beneath the medical device.

"Really didn't peg you for the hero type," Vincent said through gritted teeth, struggling to hold Eli down. He had some sort of cord in his hands that he was trying to get around Eli's neck.

Eli didn't respond as he shoved his hand between his neck and the cord, wiggling his forearm up so he had enough leverage to force the cord away from his body. The makeshift weapon started to slip from Vincent's grasp, and once it became obvious that Eli had the upper hand, Vincent let go. The sudden slack sent Eli's arm slamming forward, his palm landing directly on one of the bolts holding the medical bed into place.

As Eli cried out, his hand gushing blood, he felt Vincent's fingers in his hair as he tried to bash Eli's face into the ground. He succeeded on the first blow, breaking Eli's nose with a sickening crack, stars flashing and exploding behind his eye. Though disoriented, Eli managed to get his arm under his face so when Vincent tried again, his face didn't connect with the ground.

Unable to wrestle free, Eli stretched his left arm out, swiping up and down along the wood floor, looking for the wrench. Vincent stopped pulling his head to grab at his arm, but it was too late—Eli had found his weapon.

Ash screamed above him, and Eli could just barely smell the odor of burning hair and flesh through his broken, bloody nose. He flailed about, trying to hit Vincent with the wrench in hopes of getting the man off him.

Because he was being held to the ground, Eli wasn't able to do much with the wrench. He wasn't able to swing it back in such a way that hit Vincent very hard, which meant Vincent kept trying to take it from him. So, Eli did the only other thing he could think of in his dazed state—he started to hit the medical device in hopes it would stop shocking Ash.

"Fuck, give it up!" Vincent snapped, finally managing to catch Eli's arm. At that point, however, the damage was done. The aging and rusting device sparked, then fizzled, then smoked. The next thing Eli knew, a shower of sparks covered both him and Vincent. Vincent yelped and rolled away, shielding his head and abandoning Eli.

Eli struggled to stand, feeling around the medical bed for something to grab onto. He settled on the edges of the leather straps holding Ash in place and hoisted himself upwards.

"Ash, Ash!" He spat out a glob of blood that had poured from his nose into his mouth, his heart freezing as he leveraged himself up to see. Ash's eyes were closed, her body twitching. Eli fumbled with the straps, but his hands weren't cooperating, and his vision was still distorted from the blow to the head. He had barely managed to undo one of the clasps before he was pulled away.

Vincent had the cord again, and this time he managed to get it around Eli's throat. Eli struggled with him, lurching backward, trying to ram Vincent into the wall behind them. It proved useless, as Vincent clearly outmatched him... *he* wasn't suffering from a leg wound and head wound.

Eli let out a strangled croak as the cord started to cut off his air and blood flow. But just as he was starting to black out the old medical device caught fire.

Though the initial flame was small and confined to the contraption, it almost instantly tripled in size and quickly engulfed the generator, which still had some fuel left inside of it. Vincent seemed to come to the same realization at the same moment and loosened his grip. Eli used his momentary lapse to his advantage and threw himself backward with all of his weight. Vincent slammed against the door frame, his head thrown into the wooden paneling. Vincent hissed in pain and released him. Eli tumbled to the ground—at the same, exact moment generator exploded.

There wasn't so much fuel left that the explosion was particularly large, but it was enough to cause a few pieces of the generator to blow off as it lit up. Eli covered his head and groaned as a piece of something blunt hit his back and bounced off. He heard Vincent scream in agony above him.

Vincent slid to the floor next to him, and Eli looked over to see that he was holding his stomach. Something from the generator had blown off and hit him, causing him to clutch his abdomen. Eli didn't have much time to look at the details, however, as the room started to catch on fire.

Eli started to crawl out of the room, staying low to avoid the fuel-induced black smoke quickly consuming the air around him. Vincent, it seemed, had the same idea.

Eli grabbed his wrench on his way out and rolled onto his bruised back, ready to fight with the last bit of energy he had. It was hard to see in the atrium since the lights had now gone completely dark save for one battery-powered camp light somewhere on the second floor.

The only other light now came from the fire that was consuming the electro-shock room, and with each second that passed, it illuminated the atrium more and more.

Fighting was unnecessary, as it turned out. Vincent could barely drag himself out of the room, and as he did, he moaned in agony. He left a dark trail of liquid as he went—Eli realized that not only had the generator piece hit Vincent, it had *impaled* him. A jagged bit of shrapnel was sticking out from Vincent's gut, causing blood to pour out of his abdomen.

Vincent continued to crawl forward until he was at Eli's leg. He reached out one of his blood-stained hands, grabbing onto Eli's injured limb, causing him to wince.

"Can't—leave me here—"

Eli laughed. He laughed, and laughed, and laughed, tightening his grip on his wrench. "Fuck. You."

He whipped the tool against Vincent's head.

CHAPTER 30

Eli forced himself to stand. It took two attempts—the first sending him tumbling to the floor in dizziness from a combination of his head wound and the smoke inhalation. He steadied himself and tried again, covering his mouth with his shirt as he approached the burning electro-shock room.

"Ash?" he called out, "Ash!"

She was standing next to the ruined generator. The half-rotted straps that had held her in place smoldered into nothing more than embers. She was staring at the medical device that had been shocking her as if her gaze could cause it to crumble faster. Maybe it could, for all he knew.

Her clothes had started to burn in sections, but she didn't seem bothered. Her skin was unmarred besides some cuts and scrapes. Her light-colored, faded jeans were soaked with blood on the left leg, likely from Vincent wounding her while she was on the stairs. Beyond her awkward stance as she tried to keep weight off her injured leg, she hardly hurt despite what she had gone through only minutes before.

"We have to go—we have to get Garrett and get out of here!" Eli jumped through the flames and grabbed Ash's jacket to pull her away.

When he grabbed her arm and pulled her towards him, it took him a moment to realize just how *hot* she was. While she didn't burn him, he still jerked away as if she had. He looked up at her, pleading with his eyes to have her come with him. They could still run. They could escape before Vincent had a chance to gather himself and come after them. The flames were growing, but who cared? Let the place burn. Let all of the dark energy be cleansed by Ash's fire.

But she wasn't going to come with him. He saw it in her eyes as she turned to him, in the way she gazed at him—it was a mix of surprise and pity, but not fear.

She gave him a confused smile and said, "*run,*" as if it were the most obvious thing in the world.

And then the smile disappeared, and her eyes hardened as they started to change color, and Eli's blood froze.

Ash had lost control.

No matter how badly he wanted to drag her out of the damned building himself Eli knew he couldn't. The predatory eyes of the Thing Inside of Ash had locked onto him and her body twitched, perhaps thinking about striking out at him. Instead, she closed her eyes, almost reveling in the flames surrounding her.

Eli took that moment to back away from the room and turn towards the hydro-therapy room where they had hidden Garrett. Maybe Garrett had held on while they were fighting off Vincent. Maybe Eli could still save him.

As it turned out, he didn't have to—Deittman was already kneeling over Garrett, tying off the injured man's wounds. It seemed the rest of Eli's remaining teammates had snuck in while he was dealing with Vincent. Garrett was barely conscious, but he nodded in understanding at whatever it was Deittman said.

"Ash?" Eli heard Markus say from his right as Markus appeared from the hydro-therapy room, starting to come towards Eli and the electro-shock room.

Eli shook his head and looked away, blocking Markus's path. "She's up there but... She's gone. She's lost control again. I don't think we can stop her. She's lighting everything up."

Markus nodded in response but squeezed his eyes shut as he dropped his head. "I see... Yes, we had barely been able to put her down when she did not have any fire at her command. I imagine we won't be able to get near her if the house is ablaze."

Deittman was helping Garrett stand, though it seemed more like he was dragging the poor guy. Markus hurried over to help, hoisting half of Garrett's weight as they began to move towards the door. Eli watched for a moment before glancing up the stairs, which slowly filled with smoke even so far above the main fire.

Perhaps sensing his dilemma, Isabella pulled at Eli's sleeve. He almost jumped when she did. She furrowed her brows and shook her head.

"I know... I just...."

She tugged again, this time pulling a bit to direct him towards the entrance to the connecting tunnel. Reluctantly, Eli followed after her. Isabella kept her grasp on his jacket sleeve regardless, making sure he didn't decide to stay behind or go back for Ash.

As they neared the tunnel, Eli's stomach churned at the bloody mess that was Garrett. They had left Jackson's body behind. They hadn't found Marina or Carlos, though Eli guessed they were in the building somewhere. Would they ever be recovered? If the house collapsed, would they be trapped there, just like the many souls trapped in this purgatory?

Isabella made it a point to look straight ahead, ignoring the gore around them. Eli tried to do the same but it was difficult.

As they entered the tunnelway, Eli thought about the fact that Deittman had chosen to leave his stolen equipment behind. Part of him believed the man was callous enough to insist they take it over Garrett, but he was glad Deittman knew what to prioritize... even if it had been nearly too late.

Halfway through the tunnel, Eli stopped, a lightbulb practically appearing above his head.

"The equipment!" Eli said suddenly. He wasn't sure if anyone had even heard him since no one bothered to stop moving or look back. "I can stop Ash. I can do it"

Markus paused, forcing Deittman to come to a halt, unable to continue with Garrett. "Eli--you're bleeding and you can barely stand straight. You can't--"

"I've got to try!"

"Eli!" Deittman warned from a few steps in front of him, but it was too late. Eli had already yanked himself from Isabella's grip and began staggering back down toward the set of open doors.

Eli crossed through the doors and limped up the stairs, scanning the area for Deittman's duffle bag. Where had he found it, again? Everything had moved so fast that it was a blur—though that could have also been due to his head wound.

It had to be around somewhere... It only took a moment for Eli to rule out the foyer. It hadn't been in the electro-shock room where Ash had been. The only place left for him to look was the hydro-therapy room.

Swallowing down anything that threatened to come back up his throat at the thought of reentering, Eli clenched his jaw and went straight into the room. The room was dark despite the flames overtaking the opposite side of the building, but Eli had his little pen light on him, and it cast just enough light for him to scan the area. When he swept over the tub Eli tensed when he saw Jackson's dead eyes staring back at him.

It was a terrible thought, but Eli couldn't help but feel relieved it was only Jackson's body and not his Echo. If Jackson's Echo were to appear, probably flailing about in the tub as he drowned, Eli had no intention of sticking around to watch it.

He was about to leave when he saw the bag he was searching for tucked back in the corner of the room where he must have shoved it after looking for Deittman's cell phone. Eli rushed over, grabbed it, and fled into the foyer once more, swerving around Vincent's now unmoving body.

Eli set the bag down at the foot of the main staircase, glancing up to see the second floor nearly covered with smoke. Would he even be able to find Ash in such a thick blanket of black? She hadn't been on the first floor, in the electro-shock or hydro-shock rooms, and he hadn't seen her in the other exam rooms when he scanned them with his penlight. She had to be on the second floor, possibly where they had first found Garrett.

Would he die in the smoke before he could reach her?

No, he told himself, *no, I'll reach her.*

Whether it was true or not it was enough reassurance to cause him to rip open the bag and roughly dig around until he pulled out the roughly shoe-box-sized device from his interview. It looked easy enough to use—all he needed to do was flip a switch to turn it on and crank up the dial to increase its power. Eli didn't pretend to understand what the device emitted and how it affected psychics including himself, but none of that mattered. He just needed it to work.

Eli flipped it over and checked its batteries to see a set was still firmly in place.

"I hope this is enough..."

Eli slid the bag away from the steps so that if he had to run back down, he wouldn't trip over it. He pulled the neck of his shirt up over his nose, took a few deep breaths, and then ran up the stairs.

He found Ash in a room behind the nurse's station--one he hadn't investigated. Flames followed in her wake, drawn to the vortex that surrounded her. The fire licked at her exposed skin, eating away at the remnants of her leather jacket and bloodied jeans. She swayed to and fro, though her movements were not smooth— they were jerky, twitchy... like someone who wasn't used to using the body they were living in.

Eli inched into the room, hoping she wouldn't notice him. He tried not to take his eyes off her, but he kicked something soft that was set inside the doorway. He glanced down and then had to look again.

Marina and Carlos.

Stashed in a back room like objects.

Marina had been taken before Carlos. Her body was tossed aside, bloodied, bruised, and bloated. Her eyes were... Eli didn't know what they were. They were damaged. There was blood dried to her face and a long, pointy instrument protruding from her left tear duct, though it looked like it had been used on her right as well.

How long she had been missing before they had even noticed? How long had she been left *alive*? Who went first, Jackson or Marina? He imagined her restrained, forced to watch as Jackson-- the absolute *asshole* that had imposed isolation upon her when she was so very clearly terrified. She had *known*. She had *known* that something was wrong--that something had been in the basement with them, just waiting for when the pair was most vulnerable.

And Carlos... poor Carlos.

That boy didn't deserve anything that had come to him this weekend. He was partially covering Marina, thrown atop of her after the fact. He was wearing an old, stained straight jacket, and his face was discolored. Some sort of strap had been used around his neck, pulled tightly. His face was bloated, and his swollen tongue hung from his slack jaw. His eyes were bulging and staring at Eli. Eli stumbled backward and knocked over an old IV stand.

Ash faced him in an instant, stalking toward him like she was going to tear him to shreds.

Eli fumbled with Deittman's device but found he couldn't click it on with one hand. "C'mon, c'mon!" He felt around behind him, searching for the entrance without turning his gaze from Ash. He backed out and she followed, the flames behind her creating a menacing backdrop as she advanced.

Once in the hallway Eli stumbled into a wheelchair and fell backward. He gasped, inhaling a mouthful of smoke and coughing violently. As he struggled to regain his breath, Ash came to a halt over him, staring him down with a fireball growing in her hand. The flames behind her silhouetted her, casting her sharp face into shadows, leaving nothing but her bright, yellow eyes to draw him in.

As she leaned forward, perhaps thinking of shoving a fireball down his throat just as she had threatened to do to Vincent, Eli finally managed to get the device on with a *click*.

The effect was instantaneous.

Eli's head felt like it was going to burst open with pain and the creature that was Ash screamed. He cranked the little dial on top to the highest setting, and soon there was a high-pitched hum making his head throb. He squeezed one eye shut, dropping the device onto his chest and putting his hands to his ears to no avail. Ash mimicked the movement, the fireball disappearing, and backed away from him.

The scream that escaped her was inhuman. It was the roar of an inferno consuming everything in its path.

The device started to sputter and break up, as if the batteries were dying—though it could have been the heat of the growing fire that did it in. Eli was afraid it wouldn't be enough, but Ash fell to her knees, shaking her head vigorously. Then, she fell face forward onto the ground, unmoving.

Great, he thought numbly, *now what?*

There was too much smoke. He gasped and choked for air. The fire was coming closer, threatening to light him up along with the old medical equipment. The floor in the room with Marina and Carlos's bodies was already collapsing.

He turned onto his side, the device clinking off the ground, and tried to drag himself toward the stairs. No luck.

He couldn't breathe. His leg hurt. His head hurt. It was getting dark.

Maybe... maybe he would sleep. He deserved that, right? He'd done enough. Or he tried to, at least.

Well, at least Garrett had made it out.

"Ash?" came a male voice from nearby, "Eli?"

Just as Eli's vision began to fade, Isabella was next to him. Her white sweater was wet and pulled up over her mouth. Her slender hands worked their way under his arm and chest, and she heaved. She was too weak to force him up, but it was enough to rouse him into crawling once more. With her tugging, she managed to lead him to the stairs and to a patch of fresh air. After a few deep gasps, Eli felt something covering his own mouth. A wet scarf.

It wasn't perfect but it was enough to grant him a few filtered gulps of air. As he slid down a few of the stairs, he shifted to stand and she took on some of his weight, stabilizing him as he limped down the stairs.

Markus was rushing up behind him, Ash cradled in his arms. With a nod to his sister, Markus followed Eli and Isabella toward the exit.

Eli didn't remember much of the next few minutes, or of the next few hours, for that matter. Markus and Isabella had managed to pull down the boards on the front door of the building using the tools Ash had originally found in the basement. He tripped over one of them, but Isabella caught him and righted him before he could fall.

Deittman was outside waiting for them, a noticeably *safe* distance away from the burning building. Markus and Isabella did not stop until they joined the man in the wet grass. By the time they made it, Eli was collapsing.

"Vincent is dead," Markus said as their adrenaline levels all started to fall. "Ash is breathing. Eli, I must admit... you aren't what I expected when we met."

Isabella reached over and squeezed Eli's knee—on his uninjured leg, thankfully. He cracked an eye to look at her and she was giving him a sort of reassuring smile.

"You came for us..." Eli grunted.

"We couldn't let you have all of the heroics, after all," Markus replied with a low chuckle.

Heroics, huh? Eli thought, almost matching Markus's chuckle. Vincent had called him a hero, too. Eli had never been called a *hero* before. No, he had always been a coward who would rather self-medicate and drink himself into a stupor than accept who he was.

Maybe four days in this god forsaken place had been the medication he didn't know he'd needed.

Isabella released Eli and sat with her brother, who still held onto Ash, watching as the building burned. Eli wondered if the fire would somehow spread to the main building of Maple Hill. He hoped it would—both buildings deserved to crumble.

There were sirens in the distance, and Eli's eyes slipped closed.

EPILOGUE

Eli woke up in a hospital room.

The scent of cigarette smoke--something becoming a comfort to him--hung in the air. Ash had been by at some point, he was sure of it. He turned his bandaged head to his left with a groan and saw his daughter, Sarah, sitting in a chair in the corner, coloring in a book. She looked at him with a wide smile, throwing her crayons to the ground and jumping out of her chair. She practically leapt onto him, and though it hurt, he couldn't help but smile. He felt tears well up in his eyes, but he blinked them back rapidly and held onto her tightly.

He looked up when he heard footsteps come into the room. Sophia.

She looked tired—worried. She had a water bottle in her hand, but she quickly dropped it on the nearby rolling table and hurried to his other side, wrapping her arms around his neck and burying her head into his chest.

"I thought you weren't going to wake up! The doctor's said they didn't know what was wrong—they said your body was so weak that they were shocked you were still alive!"

Eli tried to push himself up on the bed so he didn't feel so smothered, but it was useless. The two ladies in his life had such a tight hold of him, they didn't seem to want to let go. He settled for putting his head back and reaching up to run his left hand through Sophia's hair to make sure she was real. "I'm fine. Really. Tired, but fine."

Honestly, he wasn't sure how he was alive. He had felt every bit of life drain out of him back in the asylum, and when his vision had started to fade, he thought that was it. He was done for. He would join the other spirits in that forsaken place. But assuming it wasn't all some sort of an illusion—which he didn't put past the spirits who had long since taunted him—then he was alive. Alive and safe, and with his family.

"What were you thinking?" his wife demanded as she pulled away from him and rubbed her eyes. They were already red and puffy, though Eli wasn't sure if they had been like that before. "The police said that place was practically falling apart. It should have been condemned! And you decided to spend a *weekend* there?"

Eli sighed and put a hand on his daughter's head, ruffling her hair. She finally released him and went back to her chair to sit quietly while her parents had another argument. Eli watched her with a falling heart. Maybe things weren't going to be much better after all.

"I just wanted to make some extra money," Eli said quietly. "I know Sarah's school payment is due soon, and I didn't want you to have to pull the money out of savings. The job offered more than a grand a day. How could I pass that up?"

His wife started to tear up again. She looked like she wanted to sob and hit him at the same time.

In fact, that's exactly what she did.

"Who cares about the money? You could have been killed! No amount of money would have been worth your life! I swear, if you ever do something like that again, I really will divorce you!"

Eli opened his mouth to object but then decided it was better to keep it shut. It seemed she was willing to make amends. "It... seemed like a good idea at the time."

"Well, it wasn't! It was stupid!"

Yes, it was had been stupid.

Very, *very* stupid.

Sophia lurched forward again, sniffling right into his chest. Eli wrapped his arms around her head and stroked her hair, noticing for the first time that his wedding band was back on his hand. He wasn't sure how it had made its way back, but he hoped it was a sign. He wanted nothing more than to try to have a normal life with the two women he loved most in the world.

Though, if he recalled, it had been in his suitcase with his personal belongings last he saw. He had never put it on himself.

Sophia pulled away and dug a crumpled tissue out of the pockets of her jeans. "The police--I did talk to them. They're going to want to talk to you. They said..." She looked over at Sarah, who was kicking her legs as she colored in her book. "Honey, do you have those quarters I gave you?"

The eight-year-old looked up and nodded. She grabbed the pencil case sitting on the chair next to her holding her crayons. Sarah opened it and pulled out a few quarters. "I can get a candy bar now?"

"Yes, honey, go get a candy bar."

Sarah smiled widely and hopped off her chair, disappearing from the room. Sophia sat down on the edge of Eli's bed, resting her hand on right leg. "Eli, the police said they found five bodies. Five! And you were nearly number six by the time the paramedics got to you!"

Eli didn't say anything. What could he say? She was right. She had no idea just how close he had come to dying. He looked away from her, which only caused her to let out sob. Sophia dabbed her eyes with the tissue then clutched it to her chest.

"And there was a body found down the road, too! They wouldn't tell me much, but they asked if I knew a man named Paul Richardson. They think he's responsible for the—for the—" Sophia choked on her words and shook her head. She took a few breaths and opened her mouth to speak again, but Sarah came back into the room. "Well, the police will want to talk to you."

Eli nodded and stared up at the ceiling. Paul Richardson. That was the name of the man who had terrorized them all weekend, not Vincent Colton. Paul Richardson, the grandson of the insane Dr. Pollock who had once used Maple Hill as his own medical playground over seventy years ago.

Sophia stood and adjusted Eli's blanket. She leaned over him and placed a kiss on his cheek, letting out a loud sigh.

"I'm going to go call your parents, okay? They were the ones who got the phone call saying you were in the hospital—why didn't you just put me down as your emergency contact? Did you think I wouldn't come? Jesus, Eli, I just wanted you to work things out, not…"

Sophia sighed and rubbed her forehead with the back of her hand. She shook her head and smiled wistfully. "Never mind. We'll talk about it later. Oh, by the way, there was a woman here. She was, I don't know. A biker looking chick, or something. She said she was 'with the team,' whatever that means. She dropped off your suitcase. I haven't looked inside of it yet, but I'll take it home and wash any of your clothes. I'm going to make that call. I'll be right back."

Eli gave her a nod and watched as Sophia left the room once more.

He gave one last look at Sarah as she hummed and colored in her book, oblivious to the concerns of the adults.

With a sigh, Eli put his head back and closed his eyes. Whatever the doctors had put him on had him feeling entirely too relaxed, which, honestly, was probably for the best while he was cooped up in the hospital. It was one of the last places he wanted to be while in a normal state.

"Daddy?" Sarah asked suddenly, staring at a section of wall at the foot of Eli's bed.

"Yes?"

"Who's that man in the corner and why is he bleeding?"

ABOUT THE AUTHOR

Alexandra is a globetrotting, ghost hunting enthusiast with an affinity for writing and a flair for creativity. After years of murder mystery party planning and paranormal investigating, she has put her killer experience to work in her new novel, Echoes and Ashes: A Paranormal Mystery. Alexandra has visited some of the (reputably) most haunted places in the world and she plans to continue to put pen to paper to bring her audience tales of spirits, psychics, and serial killers based on some of those mysterious locations!

Made in the USA
Middletown, DE
13 September 2024

60395972R00166